)

“Are you confuse

“Yes, no, I don’t know. Guess so.”

He sat very still – so still it alarmed me – just staring at me, his eyebrows squished together in confusion. Finally he jumped up, hurried into the bedroom, and came back with a small navy blue velvet box. Getting down on one knee, he opened it up and said, “Zoey, I love you with all my heart. Will you marry me?”

What?

There, on a tiny white satin pillow, sat the most gorgeous ring I’d ever seen – a shiny green emerald, surrounded by a wreath of rubies and diamonds. It was absolutely stunning.

I looked up at him.

“This is so beautiful,” I stammered out.

“It’s one of a kind. I designed it myself.”

“You did?”

“Yes. Picked a green emerald because I remembered you painted your office green, saying you found it calmed you down when you tackled paperwork late at night. Diamonds represent a touch of tradition and since your birthstone is a ruby, which I researched symbolizes happiness, love and passion, I added them as well. The wreath-effect represents our life together - a circle - continuous and never-ending. In short, forever.” He paused. “It’s how I feel about you.”

Damn. He’d done all this for me?

His face was earnest and his words soft and sincere. A part of me wanted to scream ‘yes’, slip the ring on and just forget about all my issues.

I can’t, Liam. I’m so sorry.”

What They Are Saying About Wings of the Past

In her new novel, *Wings of the Past*, Ms. Hurley delves deep into the heart of Zoey Avery, making her come alive with realistically written dialogue and emotions that every woman can relate to. I always feel that I know Ms. Hurley's heroines well, as she is a master at creating believable, sympathetic young women and telling their stories in an engrossing and heartwarming manner. In fact, all of her characters shine, including the requisite Hurley dog, Moxie.

On the surface, Zoey has a perfect life. She's a Vice-Principal at her school with a flair for helping young people with problems. She has friends, family, a social life, and a six-year relationship with her boyfriend, Liam. What's missing?

Nothing, or so it would seem, until one day Zoey starts thinking about marriage. She wants to get married. But should she consider marriage to Liam while another man, a love from her past, has begun to occupy her thoughts? That man from the past is Travis who broke her heart on the night of her prom.

Hoping to untangle her emotions, Zoey sets out for a solo vacation, even though this means a separation—perhaps permanent—from Liam. This sentimental journey takes her straight to Travis, now a successful bookseller.

Will she overcome the ghosts of the past in time to save her "happily ever after" future? Ms. Hurley provides the answers to these questions in a novel that will stay in your mind long after you read 'The End'.

Dorothy Bodoin www.dorothybodoin.com

Suzanne M. Hurley delves into the fragmented emotions of ***Ms. Zoey Avery,*** Vice Principal of Maitland High School, whose counseling skills aren't helping her solve her own muddled problems. Why are the men in her life no longer making sense? Love and Grief get scrambled in her mind and Zoey takes time for herself to straighten out her life's puzzle. This is definitely a worthwhile read of self-discovery.

JoEllen Conger www.congerbooks.com

Have you ever had to make a decision whether to sort out your past traumas or just leave them buried? Twenty-eight year old Zoey Avery reached that point in her life when events that rocked her as a teenager surfaced all over again, wreaking havoc and bringing confusion and uncertainty. Devastated, she runs away to a cottage to figure things out and with the help of good friends and a comical dog named Moxie, she finally discovers her heart's desire. Hurley's *Wings of the Past* is a great beach read that I highly recommend.

Peter Hurley – author of Beyond the Rain
http://peterhurley.weebly.com/

Other Works From The Pen Of

Suzanne M. Hurley

Chances – August 2009
FBI Agent Ryan Leam's son is missing. Psychologist Samantha Barclay risks her life to go undercover at Saced Heart Academy, seeking truth. The results are shocking and unbelievable.

Shades of Envy – November 2010
Dead bodies are stacking up! Teenagers want to be vampires! The sheriff is acting secretively! Psychologist Samantha Barclay sets out on a wild ride to uncover the truth. Her discoveries lead to confrontations of the deadly kind. Will she survive with her life, as well as her heart intact?

Nice Girls Can Win – April 2012
Lawyer Jessie White is fired, evicted and jilted, all on the same day. Hitting rock bottom, she moves back home and immediately ends up in a sparring match with 'Red', the hunky guy next door. She soon discovers that miracles really do happen and how love often finds you, just when you're not looking.

Who did it? November 2013
Who killed the beloved principal of St. Michael's High School? Newly minted FBI agent Samantha

Barclay's first case is to find the murderer. Only one problem. Everyone she meets has a reason to see him dead. Will she uncover who did it – before he or she strikes again?

To Kate,

Wings of the Past

by

Suzanne M. Hurley

A Wings ePress, Inc.

Women's Fiction

Wings ePress, Inc.

Edited by: Leslie Hodges
Copy Edited by: Rosalie Franklin
Senior Editor: Leslie Hodges
Executive Editor: Marilyn Kapp
Cover Artist:

Wings ePress Books
http://www.wings-press.com

ISBN 978-1-61309-811-0

Published In the United States Of America

June 2014

Wings ePress Inc.
403 Wallace Court
Richmond, KY 40475

Dedication

As always, I dedicate this book to Mike and Rico, with all my love, and to everyone who has faced pain in their lives and tried to run away from it. May you find solace in facing traumas and coming to peace with them, in order to live life to the fullest. May you also discover 'joy' every single day.

Although I spend many long hours alone writing my stories, they could not be created without the input, inspiration, feedback and laughter breaks from many people. I'd like to acknowledge and thank Marylou for listening intently to my plotlines and providing valuable insight, Lynda whose enthusiasm for writing inspires me, Dorothy and Teresa who encourage me in leaps and bounds, Sheila for her laughter which means a lot to me, my sister Maureen and my brother Brian and his wife Charlotte who promote my books tirelessly and my brother Peter, a fellow-author. Finally, I thank Trisha Fitzgerald for her thoughtful and delightful cover art. She is a joy to work with and her artistic skills, unsurpassed.

One

"Hey, Marta." I leaned closer. "How weird is this? Lately, I've been having all these wild, crazy thoughts about getting married."

There, I said it.

I'd finally voiced out loud what I'd been thinking about for the past three months, still not believing that I—Zoey Avery, dedicated work-a-holic extraordinaire—would suddenly find myself afloat, lost in imaginary worlds, daydreaming about tulle and veils and gowns. Marta had gotten engaged six months ago, so I figured she'd be the perfect one to talk to about this.

"What'd you say?" she yelled. "I can't hear you over the music."

Damn.

Karaoke was in full swing at the *Black Lagoon Bar* in downtown Burlington, Ontario, and a trio of businessmen slugging back beer, jackets off, ties askew, were singing and gyrating to *Gangnam Style.* We were at our usual table, way at the back where it was quieter, for our weekly martini and chat. Karaoke night was new and *Gangnam Style* was revving the crowd up more than usual. The bar was the rowdiest I'd ever seen, with most people trying to emulate Psy's moves. Go figure—it just happened to be tonight, when I had something serious to discuss.

"I want to get married," I yelled, just as the song ended. My words rang out, hovered, and I swear every person in the bar turned to look at me. It was one of those 'time stood still' kinda moments, only not in a good way.

"Hey, I'll marry you."

I looked over to see a jean-jacketed man straddling a stool, leering at me. He looked totally out of place with his wide-brimmed cowboy hat, scuffed boots and scruffy beard.

Oh no!

He clambered off and swaggered over to our table, slowly and dramatically, as everyone in the room began clapping and cheering him on.

I could feel my face redden.

Did they think this was planned? That it was a real proposal?

"Hello, gorgeous," he said, tipping his cowboy hat.

I watched in horror as he slid a cigar out of his shirt pocket, pulled the band off and got down on one knee. Holding up the paper ring, he placed his other hand against his heart, exclaiming, "Will you do me the honor of marrying me?"

Immediately, the crowd started chanting, "Say yes. Say yes."

"It's not real," I screamed out. "I don't even know this guy."

Frantic, I looked around for some help but my best

friend Marta, ignoring my dirty look, was laughing so hard, tears streamed down her face.

Oh hell, I knew it was in fun and in another place or time I might have found it hilarious, but not tonight. I was in somber mode.

"No, thank you," I said firmly, shrinking down on my chair, wishing I could disappear.

A groan echoed through the room. Someone led a chorus of boos, another hissed.

"Well, you're an old sourpuss," he said, looking indignant, as he stood up and swaggered on over to a young woman yelling, "Hey stud, I'll marry you."

Fortunately, another trio, this time women, jumped on stage and grabbed the microphone.

Good. Everyone would get off my case and focus on the new singers, but much to my horror they started singing Bruno Mars *Marry me*, urging on the new love match, all the while shooting daggers at me every five seconds. I sunk even lower in my seat, anymore and I'd be on the floor.

Marta, wiping away her tears, sputtered out, "I must be hearing things. Did you really say you want to get married?" She started to laugh even harder.

Glancing over at the singers to make sure they weren't going to stop any time soon, especially since I was about to answer Marta, I was happy to see they'd given up on me. Instead, everyone was now clapping for cowboy guy who had dragged his latest conquest onto the dance floor and was hamming it up, serenading her with exuberant gestures that went along with the music. Judging by her giggles, she seemed to be loving it. I decided I was in the clear.

"Just thinking about it," I answered.

Okay, to most people, the idea of getting married one day, or living with someone, or even looking for a relationship, was the norm. As evolved as us women were supposed to be, a lot of females I knew still dreamed of their wedding day and had been since they were tiny tots. Over the years, I'd been privy to many of their confidences at sleepovers, coffee dates, parties, or late night chats on cell phones. Dreams flew high as they conjured up long, flowing gowns, handsome grooms in tuxedoes and sentimental, teary-eyed vows in churches, barefoot on the beach, in the backyard, living room or any other favorite place of their choice. And of course, ear-splitting receptions that lasted all night and let's not forget—lavish honeymoons in exotic places, unless it was a destination wedding and they were already in paradise.

Oh sure, times had changed and lots of people lived together first, often for financial reasons, sometimes forever, but wedding days still seemed to worm their way to the forefront and multiple, endless plans were made. Especially, if they had children or were deciding to have them.

I was not among the norm.

I did have a boyfriend—Liam O'Reilly—even lived with him, but wedding plans did not exist in my take on life. I never thought of them—not even once. Nada. Never entered my mind. In fact, if even a whiff of a vow drifted up into my conscious level, it was crushed instantly in my quest to be the best ever vice principal to the teenagers at Maitland High, as well as a humanitarian to the many causes dear to my heart. Yup, I was one of those hard working, do-gooder types of people and proud of it. I was happy, content and thoroughly enjoying life.

So why, seemingly out of the blue, would marriage thoughts come crashing down, disturbing my sleep, my focus and turning me into a tired, confused, old hag? At least, that was how I felt lately—like tiny fissures were spreading throughout my perfect world, exhausting me and throwing me off kilter.

I just didn't get it.

So, for sure, marriage was a totally new topic of conversation initiated by me, for the very first time. I'd kept it tucked away until I finally felt I needed help figuring out what had propelled my hard-working approach to life off course into a fluffy cloud of daydreams—or nightmares in my case. I was hoping Marta could help me figure it all out. After all, that was the way we operated. We listened, helped and even guided each other through tough times and this was as tough a time as any for me. I was exhausted just trying to figure it all out.

I watched her closely, hoping to see enlightenment there, but her face changed from humor to surprise. She stared at me, eyebrows raised.

"Oh, c'mon. Married? You? You're kidding, right?"

Shaking my head, I said, "Nope. I'm serious."

Leaning over to feel my forehead, she said, "Are you ill? Coming down with something?"

"I'm fine." Annoyed, I brushed her hand away. "And what's wrong with my wanting to get married?"

Indignant, I put my empty martini glass down on the glass table with a bang, staring at her defiantly. This was not the reaction I'd expected. I thought she'd be happy to engage in a good old discussion of my feelings, helping me understand what was going on and giving me strategies on how to stop unwelcomed thoughts. Instead, she seemed to be treating my words as a joke, then insinuating I was sick.

"Well, for one, you've been living with Liam for years. Why change things now?" asked Marta, now looking taken aback as if I'd just announced I was planning on flying to the moon or something.

"Would you like another drink?" asked the perky waitress in a sing-songy voice, swooping in to clean up our empty glasses.

"Sure," I said.

Usually, one was my limit, but it wasn't every day you announced to your best friend your inner longing to get married. Judging by Marta's disapproving face, I wasn't sure why I'd even bothered. Just because Liam and I had been living together for a while, didn't mean it was always going to stay the same. Especially, the way I'd been feeling lately.

I stared at her as she ordered another drink. She looked like a supermodel with her short blonde hair shot through with blue streaks, black silk top, skinny jeans and stilettos that had to be at least three feet tall, no word of a lie. Always up on current fads, she was hip and together, taking seriously her job as a professor of fashion design at George Brown College in Toronto.

Suddenly self-conscious, I glanced down at my boring black pantsuit paired with a simple white blouse and low-heeled shoes, looking every inch the conservative, respectable high school vice principal I was. I only now noticed the ink stains that crisscrossed my white cuffs, left over from the workshop I gave to my staff. Guess I got more on me than the whiteboard I used to illustrate a few examples of new curriculum coming down the pike. A quick glance in my compact confirmed that I looked pale, frazzled and exhausted, with prominent bags under my eyes that I could pack a whole wardrobe in. Even my ponytail looked ragged and unkempt with strands escaping from the silver barrette I used to clip it back from my face. Damn wedding thoughts interfering in my sleep. It clearly showed on my face. No wonder Marta didn't believe me. Not only did I sound crazy, but I looked it as well—as if I weren't in my right mind or something.

Maybe I wasn't.

"I presume you mean that you want to marry Liam?" she asked, pulling her chair closer, still staring at me, wide-eyed and confused.

Liam's face rose before me—big blue eyes, soft chestnut hair, and a smile that made me want to curl up in his arms and never leave. He was the nicest boyfriend you could ever have. I had no complaints, whatsoever.

"Er… sure. Who else?" I hoped she hadn't noticed my too-long pause.

"Here you are," said our waitress, putting our drinks down on the table.

In unison, we both mumbled, "Thanks."

"Liam wants to get married, right?" Marta asked, her words a bit muffled as she chewed on the olive she snatched from her martini. "If I recall correctly, didn't he suggest it when you first moved in together?"

"Yes. But we vetoed it."

"Correction. It was you who didn't want to, right?"

"Not really. Liam didn't seem that keen on the idea, either."

I didn't want to talk about Liam.

Thinking of him upset me, for I wasn't sure how he factored into this new equation of mine. Yes, I didn't want to get married, but he'd seemed fine with that, relieved even, and we'd settled into what I thought was a happy, practical, living together relationship that worked for us. We were both so involved in our careers, it left little room for anything else. I didn't think he'd be too thrilled that I was thinking about changing the rules all these years later. So the less I discussed him, the better. I needed to focus on myself. My confusion was the main issue.

Sighing, I took another sip of my drink, then gulped the whole thing down. How ironic, that I was finally ready to talk about a problem of mine, just when Marta didn't seem too thrilled to discuss it. Did she think I was encroaching on her territory? After all, lately all our conversations revolved around her wedding plans.

Maybe I should have just kept my mouth shut.

But I was really disturbed by my thoughts.

At first I just started thinking of weddings in general, then it switched and I became the subject of my thoughts—contemplating the kind of dress I would like until it catapulted into opinions of wedding receptions and what band to hire.

Had I gone mad?

"Have you talked to Liam about your change of heart?"

"No. And I haven't changed my mind completely."

"What? You haven't talked to him yet?" exclaimed Marta.

I closed my eyes to blot out the sardonic look on her face.

"No."

"Well, don't you think you should?"

My eyes popped open. "Guess so."

"Still can't figure out why you'd want to get married anyway. I mean, look at Goldie Hawn and Kurt Russell. They've been happily together for over thirty years and they're not married. What's that saying? If it ain't broke, don't fix it? Why mess with a good thing? I mean, who needs a piece of paper after all these years?"

A good thing. Really? Was it? Because lately, I wasn't so sure. That was the whole problem. Maybe I finally wanted more. Maybe I wanted that piece of paper sealing the deal, making it forever in the eyes of the law. Maybe… oh crap, I had no idea why I was having these thoughts. That was the reason I'd wanted to talk about it in the first place—to get it out in the open and get help figuring it all out.

"I don't know why I'm thinking about it all the time.

Just that I am." Sighing, I regretted even saying a word. "Anyhow, forget about it. How are your wedding plans coming along? August twentieth is not that far away."

"Hey, I'm not done with you yet." She leaned forward. "You've got me curious, since you were adamant you didn't want to get married back when you first moved in with Liam. Pooh-poohed the whole idea." She paused as she sipped her drink, eyeing me the whole time. "You sure you're not coming down with something?"

"Well, maybe I am," I said, exasperated.

Instead of the sympathetic discussion I'd craved, this was turning into more of an interrogation.

"But, Marta, you're engaged," I added. "Surely *you* of all people can understand the possibility of my wanting to join in the whole wedding day thing?" She did look at least mildly interested, so I figured I'd give it one more shot before completely shutting down.

Would she be sympathetic? Or was it like I thought? Did she think I was messing with her special day, by drawing all the attention onto myself?

Was I?

Maybe that was what this was all about—attention-seeking behavior. After all, I'd been privy to every single detail of her plans for months. Maybe I was just tired of hearing about it, fed up and bored, but then again, when had I become so desperate that I wanted the spotlight on me? I was never like that, usually content to be the person in the background, spurring others onto success. I was Marta's sympathetic ear, the compassionate listener to calm her down and it was a role I excelled at.

"Well, it's just that you and Liam are like the perfect couple, without all the pomp and ceremony. I envy you. My wedding plans have been hell." Marta rolled her eyes. "Awful future mother-in-law arguing over every idea I have. Horrid seamstress messing up my measurements and making a dress that doesn't fit. Should have let my brother make it himself like he offered. But he's been so busy; I was trying to save him some work."

Marta's brother, Andrew, designed highly sought after haute couture dresses, so naturally he designed Marta's as well as my maid of honor get-up. I really did feel badly for her when it came to the dress for I knew it had created enormous trauma in her life. The fact that many of her students and colleagues would be attending the wedding, made it a real pressure point for her and she wanted it to be creative and well put together, in style and hip. I stayed quiet, not sure of what to say.

"I've been to so many stores looking for stuff," she continued, "I've gotten whiplash from walking in and out of them so quickly. Surely you don't want that kind of stress in your life?"

I picked out a few peanuts from the bowl on the table and crunched on them, wondering how to get on another topic.

"Yeah, yeah, you're right," I quickly said, forcing a grin. "Ha! Ha! You caught me. I'm kidding. Just trying to make you laugh." At this point I'd say anything to get her off the topic. "Figured you could do with a chuckle in the midst of all your planning and my getting married is a huge joke. It'll never happen."

"Aha. I thought you were kidding," she said, starting to smile. "You've always been anti-commitment. Couldn't see you going that route now. Not after all those years together."

"No way would I ever get married," I said emphatically. Hopefully, that would put an end to this conversation.

Sure wished she'd stop rhyming off about all the years Liam and I'd been together. So what? It really wasn't that long—just six short years that had galloped by at full speed. I sighed. My life seemed to resemble a pinwheel I'd once had as a kid. I used to take it outside when it was windy and hold it up against the sky watching its colors twirl round and round. That was how it was with me and Liam, for over the years we'd both been caught up in whirlwinds of schoolwork, term papers, exams, jobs and careers. Time had passed quickly. Besides, just because we'd been together for a while, did that mean I couldn't change my mind? I was only twenty-eight years old, Liam was thirty-two. Still lots of time to walk down the aisle. Most people were waiting until their thirties, even forties, if ever.

"Yeah, you fooled me for a bit," said Marta, fingering her huge yellow diamond engagement ring. "I've always envied your relationship. I couldn't handle the whole living together scene but it's cool that you can. Guess I'm just too old-fashioned."

"Hey, want to get up and sing?" I asked, noticing the last group were done.

"What?" asked Marta, eyes blinking in surprise. "You? But you never want to do karaoke. I've been trying to drag you to karaoke bars for years."

No, but I would tonight if it got me off the hook from talking about my stuff. Marta actually had a killer voice and loved nothing more than nights like these to showcase it. Singing would keep her busy and off my case.

"Well, there's always a first time." Anything to nip this conversion in the bud. It sure hadn't turned out the way I wanted.

"Well, I'm going to hold you to it before you back out. What song shall we pick?" asked Marty, looking excited.

"How about *Born to be Wild*. Kind of suits how I feel tonight." I was lying, but what the hell.

Sure it hurt that I'd shared my gut and Marta didn't want to talk about it, but on the other hand, usually she was really open to what I was going through. I mean, we'd been together since grade one, becoming fast friends when Freddy Marsden decided he'd pick on the two skinniest girls in his class, who happened to be us. He had teased us mercilessly until we came up with a plan. We put super glue on his seat and when he stood up to answer a question in class, his pants stuck to the chair and much to his embarrassment, we all saw his *SpongeBob Square Pants'* underpants. We sure fixed him. He never bothered us again. Marta and I had been a team, ever since.

Anyway, it was probably my fault. Maybe discussing my issues in a bar put a lighter spin on what I was saying and Marta wasn't sure I was serious or not. If I ever got up the nerve to talk about it again, I'd make sure I picked a better spot. Like when we were out for dinner or something.

"Yeah, Steppenwolf. An oldie but a goodie," screamed out Marta, jumping up, grabbing my hand and leading me to the stage.

Tentative at first, I then started singing my heart out leaving all my tormented wedding thoughts behind. It felt pretty darn great being able to let loose and I even managed to ignore cowboy guy who kept dancing in front of me, waving his arms, trying to get my attention. Guess he was trying to show off his new date. I was also glad this bar was in another city, where the chances of running into someone we knew was slim. Most of the time my vice principal role required that I acted in a dignified, conservative manner. Tonight, I was sure I looked ridiculous—ink-stained and rumpled, my hair flying around, having completely escaped my barrette, making me appear even more bedraggled. It felt good, though. Letting off steam was just what I needed, for I sure felt better after it was over and Marta looked on a high—flushed, excited and smiling nonstop.

The rest of the evening passed with lighter comments and the only marriage plans discussed were Marta's upcoming nuptials. Seating charts and place settings were the topic for the night—where to sit feuding relatives and what kind of table decorations were the classiest.

"Well, enough about me. Tell me about the trip you planned," said Marta, at the end of one of her rants about fresh as opposed to silk flowers. Silk won out, by the way.

"Trip?" My mind went blank.

"Yes, to Dubai. In September. Liam was talking to me

about it the last time I called. He has a conference there or something and you're going with him?"

"Oh, that trip." I'd completely forgotten about it. It was on the Labor Day weekend and I'd agreed to accompany him.

"Where are you staying?"

"At the Sheraton, in the downtown area."

"Oh, sounds great. Like the perfect honeymoon spot."

"Yeah, it'll be fun." I tried to inject the right amount of enthusiasm in my voice but my heart wasn't in it. It certainly didn't rate high on my list of honeymoon spots, the few times I'd actually thought about such things, which was never—until lately, of course. I was really not into swanky, expensive hotels and neither was Liam, but we figured we'd enjoy the experience. It would at least be a new one.

Camping was number one on my list of cool things to do. With real tents, too. None of this trailer stuff, for I liked roughing it in the bush. Liam and I had gone once and had a delightful time for it brought back warm memories of my dad, who used to take us all the time when I was a kid. It seemed like the perfect place to begin a marriage—sleeping under canvas that acted as a thin barrier between you and the stars, curled up in sleeping bags, sated after downing at least a dozen s'mores. It would be intimate and romantic and exactly my choice, that is—if I ever went on a honeymoon—which was not bloody likely.

"Sounds like more than fun, it's like a dream come true," said Marta. "We haven't figured out where we're going yet. Especially since all I can think about is hall décor and whether there should be bows on all the chairs, or not."

A headache that had been slowly making its presence, suddenly erupted, pounding away, signaling I'd had enough. I certainly didn't want to hear about any more wedding stuff for it was starting to really get to me. Marta was my friend, I wanted her happy and usually I had a great resource of compassion on tap, but tonight it was waning to zilch. Listening to her debate table favors was not something I was into at the moment. I'd reached my saturation point.

Glancing at my watch, I wondered if it was safe to leave without alarming her. Awww… hell. Figured, I'd just jump in and do it.

"Gotta go," I said, standing up. Yeah, I knew it was a bit abrupt but as my own wedding thoughts once again flooded me, I felt closed in, claustrophobic. I had to get out of there—*now.*

"So soon?" asked Marta.

"Yeah, Liam's off to California for a conference and I want to say goodbye. You know. Send your man off happy and all that stuff."

"See how lovey-dovey you guys are? You don't need a wedding certificate for that."

"You're right. You okay here by yourself?" I was sort of kidding. We'd been meeting here for over five years and knew all the regulars. Marta, who loved staying up late, since most of the classes she taught were in the afternoon or evening, often lagged behind, playing pool or just chatting up a storm. Now that they had karaoke, she'd be in her glory.

"Of course, I'm fine," said Marta. "See you next week."

As if I'd ever forget that. I looked forward to our get-togethers and even made sure I scheduled meetings on other dates so as not to miss them. They were top priority in my books. Maybe next week, we'd even be more in sync. Maybe I'd see if we could meet for supper first and I could bring the whole wedding thing up again in a more serious light.

"Oh, just one final question. I know you were only kidding, but it is Liam you want to marry, right?" asked Marta, as I got up from the table, slipping my purse strap over my arm.

Had she picked up on my earlier hesitation, after all?

Pretending not to hear, I walked away quickly, turned, waved, then ran out of the bar, flagging down a cab, well aware that my two drinks had done a number on my head. I didn't handle booze too well and I'd pick up my car tomorrow.

As I was spirited off to Hamilton and my apartment, I felt a tad guilty about lying to my best friend.

Three lies, as a matter of fact.

Lie number one. Liam had left this afternoon for the conference. I'd already said goodbye to him. I'd just used it as an excuse to get away.

Lie number two. I wasn't joking. I really did want to get married, or at least thought I did.

Lie number three. One of omission—did I want to marry Liam?

If so, then why, after all these years was I not only thinking of weddings… *but my first love, as well?*

But that was a secret.

No way would I ever confess that.

I could scarcely believe it myself.

Two

Travis Terrace. Sigh. My very first crush.

I closed my eyes and leaned back against the headrest, feeling fifteen again and madly in love. All those symptoms I'd read about in love stories, laughed at and even mocked, hit me hard back then. My heart pounded erratically every time Travis walked by, my face flushed red. I'd swooned and giggled and acted all kinds of weird, usually making a complete ass of myself. And do you think I could even string two words together to have a decent conversation? No way.

Sigh.

My love for him had been huge and overpowering. At times it was all I lived for. Definitely, all I'd thought about.

Travis Terrace.

I giggled, remembering the time he insisted he be called TT. He had a friend whose name was John Jackson and everyone called him JJ. Travis thought it was so cool to be known by just his initials—kind of mysterious-like.

"Well, my first name and last have the same initial too," he had said, with a grin. "Call me TT."

Of course, it was silly—just didn't sound right—but I went along with it, until Travis finally admitted it sounded stupid.

Sigh.

First love. Ahhhh… bliss. When everything was so simple and days were filled with laughter and fun and dreams of exciting tomorrows. The best ever.

I pictured his unruly black curls, green eyes, and long, lithe body and felt a swoon coming on. Then… total confusion.

Why in the world would I be thinking of him after all these years?

In fact, we'd left on pretty bad terms and I hadn't thought of him in just about forever, so why I couldn't get him out of my head lately was a mystery. An irritating, annoying mystery that buzzed around me, like a mosquito I couldn't swat or get rid of. The absolute truth was that it was more than just marriage that'd been on my mind, it'd been Travis, too. *Sigh.* The second crack in my ordered life. I just couldn't stop thinking of him, especially all the good times we had together.

"Hey, Lady, we're here. Four-twenty-five, Acorn Avenue, Hamilton."

Popping open my eyes, I saw the cab driver staring at me, an odd look on his face. *Was I drooling? I wiped my mouth. Snoring? Was mascara dripping down my face?* I considered pulling out my compact to sneak a look but nah—it'd be best just to get out of here. Pronto.

Quickly reaching into my purse, I grabbed my wallet and paid him, adding a hefty tip. As I stumbled out of the cab, I heard him yell out, "Sure hope that TT guy is deserving of you."

Oh crap, I'd muttered his name out loud?

So not only was I thinking about Travis, I was now babbling about him in front of total strangers. Worst of all, I didn't even realize it. Whatever I had, I had it bad and I sure wish I knew what was wrong with me and why I was doing this whole 'walk-down-memory-lane' thing. Along with dreams of white dresses and bouquets, it was driving me crazy to have an ex pop into my life taking over the starring role. That was thirteen years ago. Enough, already.

In a frantic attempt to run away from my thoughts, I rushed into the lobby and took the elevator up to our twelfth floor condo, stabbing the button repeatedly, as if that would make it go faster. I felt like a little kid, wanting to stick my fingers in my ears and chant, 'La, La, La'—anything to get my mind off raven hair and green eyes. It was as if a ghost from the past was haunting me and more than anything, I wanted to get away—run from that warm, gooey feeling I felt back then. It was in the past and I needed to leave it there. Liam was my present and hopefully, my future.

Get lost, Travis.

Hell, I didn't even know where he was these days. Had he moved far away? And what was he doing? Was he happy? Did he ever think of me?

Stop it! I was just a kid back then. *Stop being so childish.*

Letting myself in, I was immediately struck by how

quiet it was. Spookily so. The stillness hit me like a brick wall, stiff and unyielding.

I was used to hearing the TV when I got home around this time, because Liam worked long hard hours as a cardiologist at the Hamilton General Hospital and to unwind, watched TV in bed—dramas that engrossed him—to get his mind off his serious job. He usually fell asleep with the sound blaring and I always turned it off, making sure the covers were tucked up around his ears just the way he liked it. Now there was a horrid silence initiating a wave of claustrophobia that wrapped around me like a cocoon, smothering me, making me gasp for air.

Stopping in my tracks, I looked around the room as if seeing it for the first time. The beige couch, loveseat, rug and walls all blended together as one. I shook my head. Why was there no color in this room? Was I that boring? Bland? When did I become like this? When we first moved in, I was excited about decorating, with great plans to paint this room a warm, rich color and find fabulous art work for the walls. I just never got around to it, work always taking precedence. Liam and I were so darn busy that creating a cozy little nest at home was always pushed to the back of our minds, but I never realized before how dull everything looked.

Had life got so staid that my surroundings echoed its dullness?

Was that what was really bothering me? Was that why Travis was on my mind? I was in a rut and needed to add a bit of zest to my tedious days? So I remembered a time that was full of crazy fun and pure enjoyment? Had Liam and I gotten too serious about life? Had we forgotten what it was like to enjoy ourselves? Beyond our jobs?

Nah! That couldn't be it. I loved my work and was not bored in the least. So I needed to stop trying to make up useless, unrealistic reasons for my wretched thoughts. Obviously, I was trying to run from the truth, whatever that was.

Stop thinking about Travis.

It was stirring up things best left alone.

I ran over and turned on the TV and pushed up the volume button. I didn't care what was on, just wanted to crowd out my thoughts with something else—hopefully something light and nonsensical.

Throwing off my shoes and slipping into comfortable sweats, I popped some corn, poured on extra butter, added a dash of salt and curled up on the couch, snuggling under my favorite blanket, a crocheted quilt handmade by my mother. Sure it was well-worn after all these years, parts of it even thread-bare, but it was warm and soft and comfy and my go-to whenever I felt lonely or sad or in this case, confused as hell. Liam always kidded me about it, saying I was like a little kid, dragging it everywhere I went but it made me feel my mom was still around and I was shrouded in her warmth. I leaned my head against a pillow, which was another special keepsake. I still remembered Liam presenting it to me as a gift, right after we'd gone swimming with the dolphins in Florida, about five years ago.

"Just so you'll never forget that special day," he'd said, with his quirky lop-sided grin. "And the colors match your blankey."

I remembered opening up the bulky parcel and being thrilled with the velvety softness of the pillow patterned with large, gray dolphins that looked like they were smiling at me. I loved it and it did indeed go nicely with my afghan—creating a place of refuge on the couch when Liam worked long hours. He was like that, you know—sweet and thoughtful pretty much always. And reliable. I glanced at my watch just as the phone rang. Eleven o'clock as usual, right on time.

Leaning over, I grabbed our landline. "Hi," I said, knowing it was Liam checking in from his hotel.

"Hi Veep," he crooned. "How did your visit with Marta go?"

I smiled. Ever since I landed the vice principal job a year ago, he'd been calling me this in response to my promotion. I knew it was because he was proud of me, plus it elicited a giggle from me, every single time. Never one for the usual endearments such as honey, dear, or sweetie, Veep now beat out 'Aubie' which he used to call me due to my auburn hair. Not too original, but nevertheless, kind of cute.

"Fine, I guess." My giggling stopped in its tracks, as a rush of guilt flooded me, followed by a deluge of shame. I wondered how he'd feel if I told him the truth—that I was mooning over an old love—betrayal, for sure, and I wouldn't blame him one bit. *Don't think about that*. "Er, they have karaoke now. I even got up and sang," I quickly added.

"No way. You have to describe that for me. I need a good laugh."

That was Liam in a nutshell—always interested in everything I did, no matter how silly or trite. So much so, that sometimes he seemed too good to be true. Oh sure he had faults, for instance, he had this thing about bathrooms—they grossed him out. To date, he had never changed a toilet roll or cleaned the sink, toilet or tub—not even once. He snored like a banshee, and left trails of dirty dishes and clothes all over the condo. I was always following around behind him cleaning up until I eventually made a schedule so that we shared the housekeeping—no way could I do it all myself. In exchange for my keeping the bathroom clean, Liam tidied up the living room and kitchen. No problem—he kept up his share of the duties and even tried his hand at cooking several times a week, a chore I detested.

Damn.

He really was perfect.

"How are your workshops going?" I asked, after overly exaggerating my karaoke experience, making him laugh and trying to still the turmoil rocketing through my brain.

"Good. Definitely informative."

"Learning lots?"

"Certainly am."

"How about the one on heart arrhythmias?" Liam's best friend, Ted Meyers, suffered from one of the more deadly arrhythmias—ventricular tachycardia—and even had a defibrillator inserted. Liam was always studying various treatments, hoping to keep up with current methods that might help his friend.

"It went well. Met a Doctor Ingram who invited me to

observe him perform an electrical study of the heart on one of his patients, first thing tomorrow morning."

I could hear the excitement in his voice. Wouldn't surprise me if Liam studied to be a specialist in this area.

"That's fantastic."

"Can't wait." His voice bubbled with enthusiasm. "The procedure will be for an ablation where they are attempting to eradicate the patient's atrial fibrillation. If successful, the patient will never have to deal with that again."

"Truly miraculous," I crooned. By now, I felt I was almost an expert with arrhythmias along with Liam, for he loved to talk about his work and had educated me on the various heartbeats one could have. So I understood his conversations and was able to follow along when he discussed the various issues he encountered at work. I, too, found it fascinating and especially loved seeing the gleam in his eyes and hear the excitement in his voice. It echoed mine whenever I shared stories from school about students—especially those who succeeded when the odds were against them. We were both passionate about our jobs and loved to swap tales. That part, I loved about our relationship—the huge, interesting gab sessions where we were each other's sounding boards. How could I have even entertained for a moment that my life had grown dull? Boredom, was definitely not the impetus to what I was going through.

So what was it?

"I sure do miss you, though," he added, his voice low and husky.

"Miss you too." Unfortunately, my voice was too loud and high-pitched, not responding to his softer tone. Somehow, I couldn't.

But really, did I miss him?

Usually I told him everything. This was the first time I hadn't run to him to discuss what was bothering me. But how could I talk about something so personal as my constant wedding thoughts when I wasn't sure what they were all about? I also had no idea where he stood on the whole marriage thing, at this point in time. Would he run, thinking he'd escaped it the first time and might not the second? Not come home? Give me that sad old speech about how it wasn't me but him and suggest we part ways? Or would he embrace the idea and decide it'd be a good thing and then I'd have to tell him I wasn't sure if I wanted to marry him?

Another thing. How would he handle my telling him that my old boyfriend was on my mind all the time?

My troubled thoughts just weren't fair to him. He deserved the best, not an addled girlfriend adrift in memories of her fifteen-year-old crush along with planning imaginary weddings that didn't necessarily have him cast as the groom.

I was completely mixed up, so really, I didn't miss Liam. His physical presence set me off in more turmoil. Hell, my mind was constantly racing around like one of those demolition derby cars we went to see at the Rockland Fair last year—going round and round all over the place, avoiding others, just trying to survive. By day I was an organized, no nonsense vice principal, by night I turned into a whirling dervish caught in a maze. At least these last three months. Up until then, I'd been fine. Or at least I thought I was.

It all seemed to happen overnight.

One day, after enduring a particularly hard day at work, I'd been thoroughly enjoying a shoulder massage initiated by Liam who had sensed my stress level was higher than normal. I'd been thinking how lucky I was to have him in my life, then bang—the next thing I knew, I was daydreaming about weddings, which led to Travis.

What the hell?

You'd think that with all the training I had for my job, as well as dealing with every situation possible at school, I'd be a pro at figuring my own stuff out. Definitely not so in this case. Not when it came to me.

"You sound tired. I'd better let you get some sleep or you'll be no good at school tomorrow," said Liam, confusion evident in his louder voice. I didn't blame him, for usually, I'd respond more to his endearments and we'd keep this conversation going far longer, sometimes even hours.

"Yeah, you're right. I am pretty tired." *Lie number four tonight. But who was keeping score?*

I hung up the phone, knowing darn well sleep wasn't in the cards. My mind was set on slideshow mode, flashing alternating pictures of Travis and Liam and wedding gowns and flowers. Questions surfaced. Diversions I was sure, like what kind of dress would I wear? Would it have lace? What about a bouquet? How about invitations? Would I design them myself?

Travis' face held steady in my mind, like a slide in a carousel that'd gotten stuck and I couldn't help smiling when I thought about the time we had gone to an art gallery in Toronto and pretended we were human statues in one of the rooms. People strolling through didn't know whether we were part of the exhibit, real or fake. It was so much fun. That was what Travis was all about—fun and laughter and hilarious moments together.

I quickly squeezed that memory out of my system feeling disloyal to Liam, especially after just talking to him. Wasn't Travis what they called puppy love? Childish yearnings of youth? A first attempt at communicating with someone of the opposite sex in what we called 'going together'? He had been relegated to the past and should stay there.

I shook my head in frustration and clicked through the TV channels, once again searching for something to get my mind off it all. Oh crap! The movie *Bridesmaids* was playing. Entranced by Melissa McCarthy, I watched for a while, then turned it off. As if I needed a movie about weddings when I was trying to stop thinking of them. Deciding I needed a soda to wash down the mound of popcorn I'd eaten, I got up off the couch to head to the kitchen.

Ouch!

My foot hit the corner of something. Glancing down, I saw it was a magazine. Oh, right, my wedding magazine stash. Yep, I was that crazy—I'd been collecting wedding magazines, buying one or two a week and pouring over them.

I reached under the couch to pull out the stack I'd been hoarding and forgetting my soda for a while, I sat down, leafing through them, oohing and awing over the many styles and colors. Did I want to wear white? How about red? Orange? Blue? And what about shoes? And a handbag to match? Would I wear a veil or not? Pearls? A choker?

Really, I was going crazy. When did I ever care about stuff like that?

I slapped the magazines shut and stuffed them back in their hiding spot, safe from Liam finding them and declaring me certifiably insane.

Why now?

That question was like a drum roll that rang out every ten seconds, begging for answers. Unfortunately, I had none.

Upset, I grabbed my cell phone out of my purse and called my sister. If anyone could stop me thinking of marriage, she could, just by how hectic her life was.

"Hey Carm. How's it going?" I asked, knowing it was never too late to call her since it seemed like she only slept a couple of hours a night.

She let out a loud groan. "I'm sitting here with a tub of Hagen Daz. Finally got the kids to bed, my husband is out on the road and I'm plowing through a bunch of paperwork. Not doing so well."

"Dave gone again?"

"Sure is. He's in Chicago. I've been left alone to do my own work plus chauffeur the kids all over the place for their ballet and karate lessons. I'm worn out."

Waiting for the wave of peace to descend upon me whenever I talked to her, I never envied the fact that she had opened a travel agency, raised two children and had a husband who periodically traveled on business. I didn't know how she did it and always felt glad that my life was so much calmer. That was, until lately.

C'mon, peaceful feeling, show yourself.

Damn. Zilch.

My mind was still stuffed full of dresses and flowers which I really was sure, the more I thought about it, a distraction from thinking about Liam and Travis.

"Anything I can do? Do you want me to watch the kids some night?" I asked. That would be good, right about now. It would sure set straight the wedding thoughts I was having, for as much as I loved my niece and nephew, I was usually exhausted after watching them for a few hours. Marriage wouldn't look too appealing after that, especially if children were involved.

"Awwww… you're sweet. But that's okay. I'm sure you don't have much time to do that. Why don't you come over for dinner tomorrow night? Liam, too. I'd love the company."

"I can come. Liam's busy though. Off to a conference."

"He certainly goes to a lot of them."

"No, he's not having an affair," I protested, immediately. "Don't forget, your husband travels too."

My sister was a gossip hound, devouring People magazine and every tabloid she could get her hands on. If Lindsay Lohan skipped rehab or Suri Cruise got new shoes, she knew about it. How she found the time to squeeze in tabloid reading, I'd never know.

She'd often insinuated that Liam must be having an affair since he was away so much, not only at various conferences but working long hours. I didn't believe it one bit. Not my Liam. I trusted him one hundred percent. Another ripple of guilt winded its way through me. I used to be trustworthy too, until Travis' memory kept popping in my head. Was it cheating just thinking of another guy? *Stop it.*

"Hmmm…" she said. "Not as much as Liam. I'd worry if I were you. I'm worried myself about…"

She hesitated and I waited for her to continue. She didn't.

"What are you worried about?" I asked.

"Oh, nothing. Anyway, I'm making lasagna tomorrow. Why don't you stop by? We won't be eating until about seven o'clock. Does that work with your schedule? I'd like to talk to you about something."

"Can't we talk now?"

"Not over the phone. I want to make sure my kids aren't listening. When you get here, they'll be at karate with Dave."

I wondered what this was all about. *Was something wrong?* Nah, Carm was so logical and hard-working, nothing could be amiss in her world. Or at least, I sure hoped not. I quickly rifled through my blackberry to see what was on tomorrow—just a student council meeting after school. "Yes, I can make it."

This would be good for me, I thought, as we said our goodbyes. I would find out what she was worried about and I was sure after spending an evening with my sister and her family, marriage plans would shoot out the window for good. It'd be so hectic that I'd be left feeling happy with what I already had. Yes, going there would help a lot.

I finally got ready for bed, dragged my mother's quilt in and snuggled under it, hoping to get some sleep. The minute I closed my eyes, a wedding dress popped up in my mind—an unusual one—pale green with white lace around the collar and sleeves. In my mind's eye, I was smiling and happiness shone in my eyes, but to my horror, it was Travis not Liam who stood beside me.

My eyes flew open.

I was a mess.

Three

Somehow, not sure how, I'd managed to fall asleep last night—the deep sleep of the exhausted—and although I'd woken up still wiped out, the good news was that not one dream of weddings or Travis had wormed its way into my unconscious state. Hope skidded through me. Maybe talking about it last night, although not the discussion I'd hoped for, had done the trick.

"I think I'm healed," I said to Brownie, my old, worn teddy bear who sat on my bed table, privy to all my secrets. I picked her up and snuggled with her, like I'd always done as a kid and, I admit, sometimes as an adult. She gazed at me blankly, but I knew she had my back—she always did. Another memento, Liam teased me about. Just couldn't help myself—I had a strong attachment to any gift my parents had given me.

Glancing at the clock, I realized I needed to get ready for work, especially since I had to call a cab so that I could retrieve my car from the *Black Lagoon Bar's* parking lot. I placed my sweet teddy gently back on her perch, slowly eased out of bed, showered, got dressed, called a cab and managed to make it out the door and to

Burlington and back, without any disturbing thoughts. *Bonus.* Instead, my mind was filled with plans for the day and the work I needed to get done. I was also wondering if Janey Hill was doing okay with her parents' divorce and if Fred Saunders would be back after his father's funeral last week. I made a mental note to check in with both of them.

Feeling exhilarated and back to myself, I felt I was home-free. That was… until I walked in the door of Tim Horton's to get my morning coffee, stood at the back of the line and stared at a tall man at the counter, his back to me, black curls shining—lit up by a ray of sunshine peeking in through the windows.

Oh no!

My heart pounded.

Was that Travis?

Had all my thoughts over the past few months conspired to bring him here where we'd meet—at this particular moment? I stared, wondering whether to run or stay put, as the man picked up his coffee and turned around.

Whew.

It wasn't him.

But that was all it took for a rush of memories to flood my mind, swirl around and set me off.

Once again, I found myself thrust back into the days of high school—grade eleven Math class, to be exact. I could still see equations scrawled across the chalk board. Almost flunked out that year, as I'd spent the whole time staring at Travis.

He used to sit beside me and all through calculus we'd

stolen glances at each other, sharing secretive smiles and winks. Sometimes at lunch we'd head over to the park and have a picnic and I swear that never had peanut butter and jam tasted so good, then accompanied by one of Travis' tales. Totally enthralled with life, he had woven fascinating yarns that caught me up in his spell—like the time he went sailing with his uncle, the motor conked out and they were lost for days until the coast guard arrived. *Was it true?* I kind of doubted it—seemed pretty far-fetched to me—but I also knew that every Saturday he'd go to the library to load up on books which he read nonstop. It was probably a plot from one of them, but nonetheless it had been great fun hearing his colorful descriptions and the way he acted everything out. It was like watching an amusing sitcom on TV.

Cut it out!

I shook my head. I needed to quit it. *Now.* I was with Liam. He should be the only one I was thinking about, not some old boyfriend from my teens. Forget Travis. He was history.

But no matter how hard I tried, all I could picture was my old love's face and the same questions and thoughts rattled around and frankly, I was tired of them. I mean, come on! I wasn't really going to marry him back then—we were just kids. And anyway, wasn't marriage archaic these days? No longer the end all and be all of life? If I never wanted to get married before—never even thought about it—why would I care now? It had to be more than listening to Marta's plans. Something else was setting it all off. Only what?

Wait a second...

Every hair on my arms shot up as an old feeling churned inside me and slowly trickled out, as if dripping from a rusty old water crank that hadn't been used in well over a decade.

I was lying to myself.

I *had* thought about marriage before.

As a matter of fact, when I was with Travis, I thought about it all the time.

How could I have forgotten that?

I closed my eyes and summoned my Jungian *active imagination*—which my mom said I used way too much—and conjured up a box entitled *Old Buried Feelings* bursting forth from deep within my heart. The top was ripped opened, painful memories were spewing forth and I could remember, as clear as if it were yesterday, wanting to marry him, with a wreath of daisies atop my hair, a flowing white gown, barefoot on the beach. Travis would be in a white tuxedo, white shirt, and barefoot as well. Heart pounding, eyes wide open now, I recalled how back then, I used to daydream about weddings for days on end.

So I hadn't been truthful all these years.

Once upon a time, I, too, had planned my wedding, just like all my buddies had. I'd just forgotten, put it out of my mind, locked it away and piled heaps of other stuff on top of it—like homework, succeeding in school, in my job and endless responsibilities.

Damn. The truth shook me to the core.

"May I help you?"

Startled, I stared at the smiling Tim Hortons' worker. So lost in my past, I'd forgotten I was even here, standing in line, waiting my turn, as if by rote shuffling up a few steps at a time after each person was served.

I blinked, struggling to return to the present.

"Er, I'll have a decaf, please. One milk, one sweetener."

"Sure. Anything else?"

"Yes, a chocolate covered donut with sprinkles, please." I needed a sugar rush big-time. Or was I now trying to bury my emotions with food? Not sure what I was doing but all I knew was that chocolate would do me some good right about now.

"Coming right up."

After paying and picking up my coffee and donut, I took off out the door to my car and headed to work. In a desperate attempt to crowd out my muddled thoughts, I blared the radio and sang along to Beyoncé's song *Halo*. But when she burst into another one about single ladies and rings, I yanked at the knob and turned it off. Certainly didn't need that right about now or my mind would race off into the clouds again, day-dreaming about wedding cake or something. Or would cupcakes be a better choice? All different kinds with icing piled high, just the way I liked it. I shook my head—I needed to be focused, to get through the day.

Pulling into the parking lot, I grabbed my stuff and headed to my office, glad the halls were empty and I didn't have to talk to anyone. I always arrived early, to afford me a bit of peace before the craziness began. If there was one thing I'd learned about working in schools, was that you never knew what the day would bring, especially when there was one week of classes left and everyone was tired and grumpy, just wanting it all to end. Early mornings provided me with a time to plan my activities as much as I could, prepare for upcoming meetings and just ready myself for possible crises.

After all, summer holidays were fast approaching.

That was what most people were thinking about these days—warm weather, cottages, days by the beach and less stress. It wasn't just the students dreaming of no more schoolwork, it was staff, too. This week would see the last of classes before final exams began on Monday.

Holidays really didn't mean much to me since I was one of the minority who never thought of leisure or recreational activities. Often I'd be the only one at the school in July and August, slogging through mounds of paperwork. Both Marta and Carm thought I was crazy but to me, it was routine and I liked it this way. It definitely kept my mind occupied and busy with the work I thoroughly enjoyed. Liam totally understood, for he was just as committed to his job. Another plus—we definitely matched in this area.

"Hi, Zoey."

I turned to see Jim, the caretaker, coming out of the library, mop in hand. Although I treasured the solitude of early mornings at school, I never minded seeing Jim. He was a hard worker and always went the extra mile to make sure things ran smoothly. I truly admired him.

"Oh, hi there."

"I see you've got a full load. How about I hold onto your briefcase while you open the door?"

"Thank you."

I handed over the case and quickly unlocked the door. Jim leaned his mop against the wall and followed me in, putting the leather satchel down on the desk.

"How's your wife doing?" I asked, knowing she'd just had gall bladder surgery.

"Much better." He grinned. "Did as you said and bought her a silver bell to ring when she needs me and it's been going off every few seconds. I'm ready to throw it out the door."

I laughed. "Oops. Guess it wasn't such a great idea."

"Just kidding. She's looking so much better than before when she was in pain all the time. So that's a relief."

"Sure is. That's great news."

"Oh. Just to let you know. We've set up all the chairs in the gym. When classes end on Friday, we'll arrange the cafeteria as well."

"Thank you. I can always count on you." Since we were using the gym and cafeteria plus several classrooms for the writing of the exams, it took a while to get things sorted out. Glad to hear he was on top of it all. One less thing to worry about.

"Well, better get those doors unlocked by the gym. The cross country team is meeting there for a run." He grinned again and waved as he walked out the door, while I leaned over and flicked the switch to power up my computer.

Grabbing my coffee, I sat down and leaned back on my chair, watching my screensaver appear—a breathtaking sunset swathed in red, gold and orange hues. I'd gotten used to seeing it every day and didn't pay much attention, for my mind was usually racing with all the work I had to get done. Today, for some odd reason, I stared at it, enthralled by its loveliness which led to the memory of Liam and I camping, toasting the moment with wine. I'd jumped up and snapped a photo, wanting to remember forever how happy I felt back then—my boyfriend, s'mores, wine and now a gorgeous sunset. I remembered thinking that *life didn't get much better than that.*

Taking a sip of my coffee, I leaned closer to drink in the colors—they looked so peaceful and inviting—and within minutes I started to relax and something resonated inside me.

Maybe this was just what I needed.

To go away somewhere sunny and warm where I could calm down and do some thinking. To watch sunsets that would inspire me to get things sorted out. After all, I'd never been like this before. Usually at this time of the year I'd be pumped, going into cheerleader mode, supporting teachers to find the energy to get through these last couple of days and urging on students to do their best. Instead, for the first time in my life I was mooning around, lost in ancient memories that somehow seemed to think they were important enough to make their presence known, even when they weren't welcomed.

I took a bite of my donut, savoring its rich taste, while I swung into deeper reflection mode. For some reason, my dad's voice shouted out so loudly, I looked around. *Was he here?* Of course not, silly. I shook my head, trying to clear it, but once again I heard him. Damn that active imagination.

"Zoey, my dear. You gotta always listen to your heart. Your mind will try to reason things out but it is the heart that should make your final decisions, for the heart never lies."

And he should know. He was an artist who'd devoted his whole life to painting landscape after landscape of what he saw in his 'heart's mind'.

I heard him tell Mom one night, *"My goal is to have my watercolors hug everyone who views them."* And that was exactly what they did—their warm colors and gorgeous depictions made viewers feel happy and warm—exactly like being embraced. I had one in my office at home—a beautiful painting of trees, with a tiny fawn peeking out from behind one of them—which brought me instant joy whenever I took the time to drink it in. It definitely felt like a hug from my dad.

Sigh. I missed Dad so much. And Mom, too, of course. That was a whole other trauma in my life that had shaped me. But I didn't want to think about them right now or it'd send me off into a melancholic state. Something I didn't want to be in, especially at work. At least more than I already was.

I gazed back at my computer, once more eyeing the sunset. Maybe that really was what I needed to do. To get away! Listen to my heart. Find out what was bothering me.

But just how could I explain all that to Liam?

I stuffed the rest of the donut in my mouth and chewed slowly.

And also… *that I wanted to be by myself?*

I'd never done that before. Anywhere we went, we always went together—I even tried to attend as many of his conferences as I could. But if I was trying to figure out what all these wedding/Travis thoughts were all about, I didn't need Liam there as well. That would only mess with my head even more, not to mention my heart.

Nah, don't think about that. You don't need a vacation.

This marriage stuff would blow away, especially after visiting my sister. Yeah, that was the solution. I certainly didn't envy her life. It wasn't my dream world in the least and I was sure visions of black hair and green eyes would soon dissipate, leaving Travis where he belonged—securely locked back in that old box, the top nailed down and tucked away forever.

I didn't really need to get away. It could be classified as running and I wasn't into that.

Or was I?

Four

"Ahem."

Fighting through a fog of memories, I looked up to see my secretary standing there, staring at me. Bet she'd been there a while, if the strange look on her face meant anything. Sure hoped I hadn't been mumbling anything out loud like I had in that taxicab the other night.

"Are you free to see students now, Zoey?" she asked, when I continued to just sit there, looking at her, still lost in sweet daydreams of sunny beaches.

"Er, yes I am, Marilyn," I said quickly, managing to pull off a smile.

No wonder she looked surprised. First thing every morning, I dealt with students who were either truant the day before, legitimately away, or late today. They needed my okay before being sent back to class and usually by now, I'd be chomping at the bit to get started, not wanting anyone to miss valuable exam preparation time.

"Is something wrong?" she asked, looking alarmed.

"Nah, it's nothing. Just thinking."

"Well, the students who need to see you are all lined up. Are you ready to tackle them?"

"Send them in." Reluctantly, I took a final glance at the sunset, then flicked off my screensaver and opened up the student files. I sucked in a deep breath, and as I released it, I pictured tucking all my worries away on a shelf. I had work to do.

"Er, hi, Miss Avery."

I glanced up to see a tall, lanky guy with a bright thatch of red hair, standing at the door. John Newton. He had a ready smile and a gleam of mischief in his eyes that glowed like a lighthouse, big, bright and could be seen clear as anything. I couldn't help but smile back.

"Come on in, John." I beckoned him to a chair in front of my desk. When I talked to students, I liked to sit across from them without the hindrance of a piece of furniture between us, but since I constantly needed to write notes and update their charts on the computer, sitting at the desk made more sense. I leaned across.

"What's the excuse today, John?" I grinned. "New puppy? You got mugged? Your mom threw your essay away by mistake? Your locker got robbed?" All these he'd used in the past and it'd become a joke between us as to what outlandish story he'd come up with next. Eventually, after numerous questions, he usually admitted he'd had no reason—he'd just been tardy or hadn't done his homework in the first place.

"Nope. Just slept in." He grinned back.

"The truth, for a change?"

"Yup."

"Really?"

"Really. Guess all those talks of yours are finally sinking in."

"Great to hear."

John was a good student who'd unfortunately got into the habit of arriving late almost every day and couldn't manage to get his work in on time. I'd talked to his parents and discovered they left for work before he did for school. They'd get him up, his mom even prepared his breakfast but unknown to them, he'd just fall back to sleep. And as for his homework, he always told them he didn't have any. They were nice folks and unfortunately believed in their son way too much. He was quite the scammer, albeit a charming one.

"Guess what?"

"What?" I kept on smiling. He looked so excited about something.

"Next year I'm going to try even harder." His eyes lit up. "I found something I want to do. A goal." He pulled a crumpled brochure out of his back pocket and handed it to me.

Leafing through it, I said, "Animation at Sheridan College." I looked up at him. "This is perfect for you. I know how much you love to draw and do computer graphics." I pointed to the wall. "I still have that poster you did for me at the beginning of the year. The design is spectacular."

"Yup." He looked proud. "I have something now to work towards. Guess I'd better try harder to be on time, too. I'd really like to get involved in movies as part of their animation crew."

"Good for you and I know you can do it."

"Thanks, Miss. So what's my punishment today?"

"None. For being completely honest from the get go."

"Wow. That's cool. Guess honesty really does pay."

"That's what I've been trying to tell you."

I wrote out a slip for him to gain entry back to class. Handing it over, I said, "Keep dreaming those dreams, John. You've got the talent."

"Plan on doing that, Miss." He saluted, then left.

I had no doubt he could do anything he set his mind to, as long as he got his 'late' problem under control. Next year, I planned to work more on that with him and hopefully help prepare him for a successful future in animation.

This was one of my most favorite parts of my job—spurring on students to do their best and I'd worked hard to design strategies to guide them. I smiled as a scenario from my rookie days blasted forth. I once had a slew of male students who were always late for afternoon classes, claiming they'd taken their pregnant girlfriends to the doctor and got held up there. Concerned, I'd spent many long hours talking with them, listening and trying to guide them. There were just so many of them until it dawned on me that it was a scam. The apparent girlfriends didn't exist and the word was out that the new vice principal was sympathetic and never gave you a detention, if you used the pregnancy excuse. So I'd learned to navigate student's concerns and when to be discerning, firm, compassionate and wise. Hopefully, I was getting better at it.

Next, was Mary Simon. Cute, shy and nervous. I motioned for her to sit down and she crept forward and plunked down on the chair, looking tired and rumpled. Sadness oozed out of her.

"What's going on, Mary? Heard you missed Chemistry class yesterday."

Silence. I waited it out.

"I skipped," she whispered

She did? This was new behavior coming from her.

"Why?" I got up and sat beside her, figuring a gut-wrenching story was fast coming. It would surely take that for her to do such a thing. Not the norm, by far.

Mary put her head down and mumbled, "Got dumped by my boyfriend at prom, got back together and then he dumped me again. I couldn't handle him in class yesterday. It hurts way too much." She burst into tears.

Pain sliced through me, as an image of painted castles, moats, princesses and princes flickered to life.

Prom night, thirteen years ago.

The theme was Enchanted Fairy-tale Endings and it was one of the worst nights of my life—far from being enchanted and definitely no 'happy ever after' finale. I was fifteen, at my first-ever prom, the setting for Travis' devastating news that changed my life forever. I could still see his earnest face and hear the words that ripped me apart.

Get it together, Zoey.

This was not about you, it was all about Mary.

Here this poor girl was crying right in front of me and all I could think about was Travis and some stale old memory that had reared its ugly head. Nothing like bringing my own life events into this situation. A huge no-no.

I shook my head, physically trying to shake out those old thoughts. They needed to be filed away quickly.

"I'm so sorry to hear that, Mary," I said, getting up to hand her a Kleenex from a box on the bookcase up against the wall. I sat back down beside her and let her cry in silence to get it all out. Words seemed trite at the moment.

"Thanks," she said as she finally wiped her eyes, then looked up at me. Now, she appeared horrified. "Am I going to get a detention? Are you going to call my parents?"

I'd already made my decision. I knew she was a straight A student, who I figured needed a break. So often we were lenient with chronically troubled students who coped with numerous problems at home, but with the good ones we came down hard on them, expecting way too much. No way was I doing that to Mary, especially since I also knew too well the pain of heartbreak when I was around her age.

"No, I'll let you off this time."

"Gee, thanks." She blew her nose as her eyes welled up again. "I still really love him, Ms. Avery."

Shockingly, I could feel my own tears start up as my heart went out to her. Another rarity, for I never cried—ever. Damn. I needed to get in control fast. Tears be gone—*now*.

I stared at her. She looked so sad, I wished I could fix it all and take her pain away. I certainly didn't want to throw out corny platitudes like a lot of adults did. Things like "You're too young to be serious, anyway," or "You shouldn't be thinking about love, you need to concentrate on your homework." Who needed that when your whole world had just exploded around you? I could certainly attest to that. Feelings were very intense at that age and it really felt like life was over.

"It sure hurts, huh?" I figured acknowledging her pain was the most important thing I could do, so that she knew I had really 'heard' her.

Her eyes brightened at my understanding.

"Sure does." She shrunk down further in the chair. "Life sucks."

"You're right. Sometimes it does."

A knock at the door and Marilyn stuck her head in.

"The line-up's doubling and don't forget the assembly at ten."

"Thanks, Marilyn. They can wait." I gestured towards Mary.

"Oh, sure, no problem." She knew by now that if a student needed me, I wasn't going to rush them through as if on an assembly line. Often I discovered problems that were buried deep, only coming out due to a student's strange behavior, or his or her 'acting out'. Tears were common in my office.

"I can go," said Mary, starting to stand.

"No, please, sit down. You're hurting a lot. So let's chat for a bit, if you don't mind."

I was touched by how grateful she looked.

"Thanks. I just feel so horrible."

"I know but unfortunately, sometimes these things just don't work out."

"Have you ever got dumped, Miss?"

"Er, yes. At prom too, as a matter of fact." Most of the time I didn't share much about my own life, but I decided to in this case. We had a lot in common.

"Really?"

"Really."

"How did you get over it?"

"I immersed myself in my schoolwork, did well and got accepted into the university I wanted. And I hope that you don't let this stop you from achieving your goals." No way was I telling her that thirteen years later, thoughts of him had come back to haunt me.

She sighed. "You know, we'd probably break up eventually anyway. He never really wanted to do much but sit around and play video games." She rolled her eyes. "It's just that he was my first boyfriend."

"I understand. First boyfriends are hard to get over." I smiled. "And feel free to come and talk to me about it anytime. I'm worried though, that summer holidays will be here soon and school will be closed. Do you want me to set you up with a counselor to chat with until you're back in September?"

"Nah. Guess I could talk to my mom. We're pretty close." She rolled her eyes for the second time. "Just wish she wouldn't go on and on about how guys are like buses—if you miss one, there'll be another around the corner."

I couldn't help but chuckle, for I'd met her mother at

several parent/teacher interviews and Mary did a good job of imitating her.

"She's probably trying to make you feel better, but it's wonderful that you can talk to her." I leaned closer. "You'll get through this, you know. Give yourself the chance to mourn for a bit, then get right back into life." I got up, went to my desk and pulled a card out of my drawer. "Here's my cellphone number. Please call if you ever need to talk."

Another thing I never did, but decided it was the right thing to do in this situation. I especially hoped she didn't end up like me—still trying to deal with my first love as an adult.

"Hey, thanks."

"No problem. By the way, where did you go when you skipped?"

"Oh, went to the park and hung out. Actually cried my eyes out and ate two bags of potato chips. The large size. Ugh, was I ever sick after."

"Well, school is out in a few days but next year, if you ever get the urge to skip again, I'd rather you stay here where it's safe. Just come and see me."

"Okay." She got up and slowly went to the door. "Thanks," she said, turning around with a hint of a smile. "You're kinda cool."

"Why, thank you." I smiled back. "Anytime."

As the door shut, I quickly grabbed a tissue and wiped my wet eyes before the next student came in. I could now add emotional wreck to my list of issues at the moment. Usually, I never let my own feelings interfere in talks with students—they were my sole focus once they entered my office. I sure hoped I got this all sorted out soon. *I hated not being able to trust my reactions.*

Fortunately, the rest of the situations were not too serious and slowly, I wound my way through the line-up. I was disappointed that Janey and Fred didn't make it to school, and phone calls home just led to voicemail. Hopefully, they'd call me back. Next, glancing at my watch, I realized it was time for the assembly.

The MADD group—Mothers against Drunk Drivers—were meeting with the graduates to talk about the dangers of drinking and driving. I had them in every year, just before their graduation dance, which was this Thursday. It was always a worrisome time, hoping everyone was safe, especially since they had a tradition of camping together that night at a local park and unfortunately drugs and alcohol always managed to make their appearance. I dreaded watching the late-night news on TV for fear that one of our students didn't make it.

I quickly walked over to the PA system in the main office to call the grade twelve classes down. When I finished, I headed to the auditorium.

"Hi, Miss."

"Hi, Julie."

"Hi Fred."

"Hi Miss."

I smiled as I greeted and was greeted by hundreds of students on their way. Grinning, happy faces excited about graduating and looking forward to celebrating. After they were all seated, I took a deep breath and walked up to the microphone to kick-off the assembly. I made the same speech every year, but for some reason I felt more emotional today, probably due to all the upheaval going on in my life and Mary Simon's revelation that brought up even more sad memories of my own. I just hoped I made it through without weeping. I groaned. *That'd be great,* I thought, sarcastically—breaking down in front of the students. *Not!*

"When I was fifteen years old, my parents were killed by a drunk driver."

To get across my point, I always started off dramatically. I mean, why beat around the bush with such a serious topic?

I took a deep breath and continued. "They were both in their fifties, healthy and very involved in life. My father was an artist, my mother, a teacher. They were coming home from an art gallery featuring my dad's paintings, when a car ran a red light, swerved and hit them head on. The driver who killed them was eighteen and had spent the day drinking with his buddies. He never even had a scratch on him." *Pause.* "How sad it was to attend the funeral of my parents..."

Without warning, Travis' face flew before me.

Startled, I grabbed hold of the podium as I began to sway, picturing how he'd stood across from me at the cemetery, his eyes rich with compassion, as they lowered my parents into the ground.

How could I have forgotten how comforting he was during that time?

He was the impetus that got me through it all.

"Ahem."

Jerked out of my reverie, I glanced over to see Principal Margaret Sheen, trying to get my attention. She twirled her index finger, signaling me to wrap it up. I looked out at the students who were quietly staring at me, looking surprised. Still feeling shaky, I realized I'd been staring off into space way too long and to my further shock, I felt a solitary tear drift down my cheek.

Wiping it away, I quickly said, "To lose both my parents at once, was difficult to deal with. I just want you to understand that *not* drinking and driving is a cause near and dear to my heart and I would now like to introduce Elizabeth Armstrong, the president of MADD."

I quickly took my seat in the front row, ignoring the concerned looks students were giving me. Guess I'd freaked them out for they were used to seeing their vice principal in control at all times, not stopping mid-sentence and gazing off into space. So I could now add memories of my parents' deaths as the third crack in my life. It'd been ages since I'd really thought about that whole tragedy in any depth. *Why was I upset now? Along with all the other stuff?*

Trying to void out Travis' face, my mind drifted again to escapism—blue skies, warm weather and twinkling lakes. The more I thought of it, the more the idea of going away continued to appear attractive. As a matter of fact, I couldn't get it off my mind. Maybe I really needed to do that. I closed my eyes for a moment, thinking of beaches and trees and fresh air. Awwww… heaven.

"Ms. Avery."

Someone elbowed me. Twice.

"Huh?" My eyes flew open.

"Sorry for nudging you, but you didn't respond when I called your name a few times. Aren't you going to dismiss us? The principal already left."

I stared at the concerned teen sitting beside me who'd obviously been trying to get my attention for a while. Guess I'd drifted off.

"Oh, right." I stood up, then said, "Sorry about that."

"No problem, Miss." But he still looked worried.

I quickly scuttled up the stairs to the stage to thank the speaker, reiterated the importance of her message and released the students back to class. With sun and beaches still on my mind, I hurried to the sanctity of my office where I finished up some paperwork, then began scouring the internet for possible places to go and cottages to rent. I was curious to see if any place jumped out at me, which could be a clear sign that I definitely needed to get away. Normally, I wouldn't use my work computer for personal use but today I just couldn't seem to follow the rules and I had only a short span of time before I had to attend a few more meetings. It'd be ages before I could get back home to surf the net.

As I stared at picture after picture of people frolicking in the water, having the time of their lives, a longing to join them exploded in my heart. The 'fun' part of my life had obviously been put on hold for a long time and I wasn't sure if I would ever find the guts to get away, but I was certainly entertaining serious thoughts about trying. Maybe by doing so, I'd find some answers to my nagging worries.

It just might be a good plan—the perfect one for me.

Five

Somehow, I dragged myself through the rest of the day, glad nothing too serious cropped up and my paperwork was at a minimum. Mostly, I just sat and stared at my screensaver, still daydreaming about the possibility of going away for the summer. Finally the bell rang, signaling the end of the day and next on the agenda was the Student Council Meeting.

As an administrator, I didn't have to be an advisor with this group and could have assigned the job to others, but I was a fervent council devotee, believing that peers could really make a difference to the well-being of a school by representing their needs and ministering to them. Empowering young people was a passion of mine, so I helped out and thoroughly enjoyed it. Watching them grow as leaders, discover their talents and get things done they'd only dreamed about, also empowered me as an administrator. It was a win-win situation.

Today's agenda was the final assembly of the year, which encompassed saying goodbye to several teachers who were retiring. I sat quietly in the background like I always did, listening to their plans, not wanting to impose my own opinions unless necessary. Scott Overly, the president, had things well in hand and I was glad, for I had to admit that my mind was still in a muddle, swimming in a lake somewhere, catching some rays.

"Okay," said Scott, sounding firm, yet encouraging. "We all decided that we'd call the teachers up on stage and take turns reading a sentimental good-bye poem that had a stanza designated for each one of them. Is it ready?"

"Yes," said Leslie, the vice president, as she handed out copies of the poem to everyone.

"Shall we have a trial run?" asked Scott.

"Sure."

With great expression and emotion, they read it, impressing me. It was powerful, touching and obvious that a great deal of research for each teacher had gone into it. I clapped my approval which had Scott grinning. He was definitely pleased.

"Ms. Avery, did you get hold of their families?" he asked.

"They're all coming." I smiled.

"And they'll keep it as a surprise?"

"They promised."

"Good." He then moved on to the next item.

The meeting flew by, since all the work had already been done and it was just to make sure everything was ready. It was, thank goodness. So within forty-five minutes, I was headed to my sister's house, blaring the radio again—anything to block out the occasional thoughts of gowns and veils and Travis. Once again I consciously tried to immerse myself in thoughts of a real vacation, full of relaxation and fun, getting the feel for whether I could handle that, or not. The more I thought about it, the more it sounded like pure heaven to me—the perfect escape and possible road to recovery.

Arriving at my sister's house, I pulled into her driveway, my heart fluttering with excitement. *This for sure should help me*, I thought, as I took in the basketball, pitcher's glove and bat lying on the front grass along with a bike, skipping rope, doll's house, Barbies and several toy cars. It looked like a war zone, especially compared to my neat, orderly life. Already, I was relaxing and proud to be childless.

Eagerly, I tapped at the door, feeling good about my decision to be here, counting on it to straighten me out.

"Come on in," yelled out my sister. "I'm in the kitchen."

I hurried in to find Carm washing vegetables in the sink. I stood for a moment just watching her, a rush of gratitude racing through me. It was the same feeling I felt every time I saw her.

Carm was just twenty when our parents died and she agreed to take care of me since I was fifteen and still considered a minor, by law. Fortunately, I was able to stay with her and not be shipped off to some group home. She was part parent/part sister and I owed her a lot.

"Need some help?" I asked, when she looked up, brushing her blonde hair off her face, a confused expression in her eyes at my obvious perusal.

Hmmmm... she looked older, somehow. Were there a few more lines on her forehead and around her mouth?

“Sure do.” She pointed to a stack of veggies on the table. “How about you start cutting. Thought I’d make a yummy salad to go with the lasagne.”

“Great.”

I quickly got to work on a mound of carrots and onions, wondering if she was going to tell me what she was worried about. I was also deciding whether to talk to her about what I was going through. It hadn’t gone well with Marta and I didn’t think I could handle another rejection.

“How was school today?” she asked.

“Okay. Busy as usual. How are you doing?”

“Busy, too.”

Silence. Maybe I’d imagined that she was troubled about something.

“So, what do you think about me getting married?” I decided to just go for it.

“Really?” She stopped what she was doing and stared at me, clearly dumbfounded. “But why?”

“I don’t know.”

“You have no idea as to why after all this time you want to get married?”

“Not a clue.”

“Have you and Liam decided to have children?”

“No.”

“So you’re not pregnant?”

“No.

She looked at me, a serious expression on her face.

“You *have* talked to him about this, haven’t you?”

“No.”

"Well, you do want to marry him, right?"

"Er… yes. But it doesn't matter. He doesn't want to get married anyway."

Okay, lie number five. I wasn't completely sure I wanted to marry him but no way was I going to tell her about Travis. She would think I'd really flipped, for I hadn't mentioned him in years and she'd wonder why I hadn't gone into it in any great detail back then when it happened. Of course, the two of us were also busy coping with the loss of our parents—or to be honest, I was busy burying it away—so my feelings about Travis got lost somewhere along the way. Don't get me wrong, I loved my sister a whole lot but when it came to matters of the heart, she was tough. She took after our mother whereas our father had the softer, gentler side. So I could see why I hadn't bothered to confide in her—I wasn't sure she'd even be interested.

"Do you know that for a fact?" she asked, bringing the rest of the vegetables over to the table and joining me in cutting them. "That he doesn't want to get married?"

"Well, not really. It's always been understood, though."

"Does he know you've changed your mind?"

"No."

"Don't you think you should tell him?" She stared at me, eyebrows raised.

"No. I mean, how can I? He's happy with the way things are."

"But you're not."

"And that's my problem, not his."

Carm stared at me for a few minutes, grinned, then said, “Well, Aunty Rose will be thrilled.”

That got the both of us laughing. Leave it to Carm to throw some humor in—an Avery trait, for sure. Our Aunty Rose was our mother’s eccentric sister who was totally devoted to the church. Left millions by a wealthy husband who passed away years ago, she devoted her days to funding trips to the Holy Land for devoted parishioners, hoping to save their souls from hell. She was always trying to get us to go and at times I felt I should. Maybe the problem was that my soul really did need saving, especially after all the lies I’d been spouting out lately. *Hmmmm... something else to consider.*

“Yeah, she still doesn’t know that we’re living together.”

Odd! Was that a sob I heard? I turned to look at my sister.

Oh my goodness! She was crying. Full-out sobbing.

“What happened? Did you cut your finger?”

She shook her head.

“Is it the onions I’m chopping?”

“No.”

“Well, then, what’s going on?”

Silence. Then a soft voice.

“I think David is having an affair.”

I dropped the onion and just stared.

“What? David? Your husband, David?”

“Who else?” She ran and got a Kleenex and proceeded to blow her nose.

“No way would he cheat on you.”

"I think he is," she said, dumping the tissue in the garbage and grabbing another one to wipe her eyes.

"What makes you say that?"

"Read an article in Cosmo about warning signs. He has them all. He's lost weight, is dressing better, takes phone calls and hangs up when I appear."

"Cosmo? Really, Carm? You're basing it all on an article in Cosmo? Come on."

"You come on. I'm serious."

A door slammed.

"Mommy, Mommy. Where are you?" yelled out Cindy, from the living room.

"I'm in the kitchen, honey," she said loudly, wiping her eyes even harder. "Shhhh… I don't want them to hear anything about this."

"This talk is not over," I said. "Just postponed."

"Hi, Aunty Zee," said Cindy, running in like a tiny bulldozer, all golden curls and looking adorable in her karate outfit.

"Hi yourself," I said, swinging her up in my arms." When she first started to talk, she had a hard time saying Zoey and shortened my name to just Zee. The name stuck, even though she was five now and could pronounce pretty much anything, these days.

"You staying for supper?"

"Sure am. Is that okay?"

"Yeah. I wuv you."

"I wuv you, too."

She knew how to say 'love', too, but once again, liked her version of the word. Probably because we all said how cute she sounded. I hugged her tighter. She was such a darling child and I adored her to pieces.

Hmmmm… *maybe having children was just what I needed.*

"Hi," said eight year old Cole, slowly walking in, holding something in his hands.

"Hello there," I said, swinging Cindy down to ruffle his hair. He'd made it clear the last time I saw him that he was too old for hugs. "How's my main man?"

"I'm not your main man. Liam is."

"I don't know about that," I said. "You're pretty darn special to me." It also hit me that finding out if Liam was my main man was precisely what I needed to do.

Next, David came into the kitchen with an armful of groceries. He went straight to his wife and gave her a kiss on the cheek, put the bags down, noticed me, swooped in and landed a kiss on my cheek.

As he pulled away, I stared at him, searching for any kind of possible wanderlust going on. Nope, he only seemed to have eyes for his wife. Surely, she was wrong, but I still saw tears in her eyes as she turned to empty the bags.

"Aunty Zoey. Look."

Ten year old Cole opened his hands. A green frog jumped off and landed right on my arm.

Ugh. On second thought, having children could be downright gross and dirty as anything. Not a fan of slimy things, I yelled, "Get it off me."

Cole looked surprised at my disgust.

"Cole," said David. "How many times have I told you

not to bring those creatures into the house? Now take that one out and release him into the pond."

"Awww… Dad," he said, but he quickly took the frog away from me. "C'mon, Greeny. Guess you're not wanted.

Greeny?

Immediately, I grabbed a napkin to wipe off the bit of muck left by the frog's feet.

"Don't you like him?" Cole asked, looking puzzled.

"Love him." Okay, another lie. I was cranking them out so fast and furious I wasn't counting anymore, but I didn't want to hurt his feelings. After all, he was just sharing his treasure with me. "I was startled that's all and besides, I think he's happiest with you."

He beamed. "Yeah, you're right. He and I are best buds. After supper I can show you where he lives."

"I'd like that," I yelled after him, as he ran out the door to release Greeny. I was secretly hoping he'd forget.

Carm and I finished the supper preparations but I never got a chance to ask her again about what was going on, since we were constantly interrupted by Cole and Cindy. Then, it was time to eat.

Supper was a swirl of stories and jokes and good times, but I could sense tension running through my sister. I looked over at David. Surely, she'd misunderstood but she was right about one thing. He had lost weight and looked much neater in appearance, a far cry from his usual sloppy look with baggy jeans and loose T-shirts. In fact, he was beginning to look exactly how he did when they first married, before he'd put on a few pounds. Couldn't blame him, Carm's cooking was fantastic.

"Aunty Zee—where's Liam?" asked Cindy.

"He's away," I answered, turning to look at her, hoping David hadn't noticed my scrutiny.

"Will he take me swimming sometime again?"

"I think he will." I'd forgotten that every year, Liam suggested we take Cole and Cindy for a swim at a local hotel from time to time.

"You'll have to have some of your own one day," said Carm, with a wink.

Could she see inside my heart? Something that I didn't notice?

Was that what I was longing for? Children? I'd never really wanted any before, feeling that all the kids at my school were my children. Could I really handle some of my own? Another muddle to figure out and to make it worse, when I got into my car to go home, I kept thinking of what to name my kids. Petey and Beth? Cheryl and Timmy? Mickey and Fred?

Damn.

Looked like my visit to my sister hadn't given me the peace I craved. I felt more stressed than before. Could that possibly be what I wanted? Marriage plus kids? Oh no! No way could I tell Liam that I not only was thinking of marriage but children too. He'd run away so fast, there'd be skid marks. Not even once, had we ever talked about babies.

Feeling like walls were closing in on me, thoughts of getting away were becoming increasingly more alluring. Glancing at my watch and realizing it was still early, I made a quick detour and pulled off at the lake, Liam's and my favorite place to walk. I first went into *Hutch's Restaurant On the Beach*, which boasted the best fish and chips in Hamilton, if not Ontario. Fortunately they also served ice cream and I ordered a chocolate chip cone and strolled down the path along the water. The more I walked, the urge to get away—all by myself—stayed with me, looming larger with every step. Shivering from the cold night air, I longed to feel the sun wrap around me like a cloak, making me feel safe and secure while I went for long meditative walks. With uninterrupted periods of solitude where I had time to think, I was sure I'd figure things out. It sounded like heaven, right about now.

But was it self-centered to go away? Was I just thinking only about myself? Becoming a narcissist? What about Liam? He'd be hurt as anything. Would I cause him unnecessary pain?

Could I really do this to him?

Normally, this was not like me and I'd make peace no matter what—even avoid possible arguments at a cost to myself, craving harmony at all times. My life had been so out of whack as a teenager that I struggled and worked hard to keep things on an even keel. So something must be really wrong if I had to get away. This was serious business, but I sure didn't want to hurt Liam. He was way too nice a guy to ever deserve that.

Watching a young couple snuggle on a bench, another thought hit me. *What if Liam met someone else?* He was certainly a wonderful guy—a real catch—not to mention pretty darn good-looking. I was sure some nurse would jump at the chance to move in on him—especially Nurse Jackie. I saw the way she had eyed him at that Christmas party last year, hanging around, flirting like crazy. If I hadn't come over to claim him, I swear she would have moved in to try and snag him.

So why take a break from someone so wonderful? It'd be a real risk on my part to so call 'rock the boat'. And would Liam view it as a break or end things forever? But wasn't I doing more harm in staying? When I was confused? How could I walk around pretending that everything was okay, when it wasn't?

Maybe I should talk to him about all this. But then again, I wasn't even sure what was bothering me—at least, what was the root of it all. I'd be expressing vague feelings and thoughts. Yeah, right, that'd go over well.

Should I try?

Maybe he could help me sort it all out. Nah. I'd end up being embarrassed and even more messed up. I mean, I couldn't even explain it to myself. But maybe I should just ride it out and not actually leave.

My head was spinning with arguments for and against going away. Self-doubts continued to flood me and I felt like I was drowning in them.

What about my sister? Maybe this wasn't a good time to leave her. Was David cheating on her? Carm seemed to think so. No way. I tried to wipe that horrid thought from my memory. He wouldn't do that—ever. Or at least I hoped not.

What about Marta? It was only a couple of months before her wedding. What if she needed me? Who would calm her down?

Oh, hell.

Finishing my cone, I stopped and stared at the lake, hoping its current placid state would speak to me. I closed my eyes and after a few minutes of trying to quieten my mind, I could hear my dad say, *"Sometimes you just have to step away, take a break, then you'll come back stronger than ever."* He'd said that to me once when I was struggling with my math homework. He was right—after a cookie and milk break—I'd figured out those equations in record time.

Opening my eyes, I took a deep breath as it hit me that I really did need to step away, like Dad used to say. I always put others first and was quite happy in that role. I was the caregiver, the one going to the ends of the earth to help anyone in need. That was, until my own world came crashing down. Panic surfaced. I needed to sort myself out. My confused gut was interfering in everything I did, everything I said. I was no good to anyone and besides, I could keep in touch with everyone through the internet, tweets, text messages and Skype. They could come to visit, too.

I stood up tall and a smile tripped across my face and stayed.

I'd made a decision.

For the first time in my life, I was thinking of myself first and I was going to get away for the summer—alone. It was the right thing to do. I glanced up at the heavens and whispered, "Thanks for the advice, Dad."

Feeling a skip in my step, I hurried back to my car, sure of my resolution. As I turned on the engine, getting ready to go, I felt exhilarated at finally doing something to help myself rather than just wallowing in confusion.

Glancing at my watch, I realized it was almost eleven o'clock—time for Liam's phone call. I never missed those chats but tonight I was wishing I could, for I wasn't sure I wanted to hear his voice. I felt guilty every time I thought of how great a guy he was. I didn't deserve him—certainly not now.

But maybe if I got myself sorted out, we could plan a future together.

At least I hoped so.

Six

"You can't just close your eyes and pick a random spot on the map and move there for the summer," exclaimed Marta, throwing her arms up in the air in frustration, ignoring the fact that several people were staring at her. "That's ridiculous."

I cringed. Her loud, shrill voice carried throughout the whole Tim Hortons. Even the employee working the till, peered around it to find out the source of the noise.

"I didn't," I said, softly, hoping she'd calm down. "I couldn't decide, so I picked six places I liked, wrote their names out on pieces of paper, tossed them in a bag and chose one."

Dammit!

I knew she thought I was crazy, but once again I was annoyed that she wasn't supportive of my plans. First, she'd knocked down my wedding thoughts, now my travel itinerary. Sighing loudly, I cursed myself for telling her. I understood it was a pretty strange way to pick a vacation spot but, tough, it worked for me. And it wasn't as if Marta never did anything strange.

Staring at her, watching the disgust seep across her

face, I saw her in a new light. Maybe she never really was the friend I thought she was. Maybe she just hung around because I was quieter, leaving her the full stage to emote and talk about herself, and now she couldn't seem to handle the fact I was upstaging her. Especially when her wedding was fast approaching and she obviously felt it should be the main topic of conversation, at all times. I was just glad I'd already thrown her a shower. One less thing to worry about.

Come to think of it, the same thing happened when I'd talked to my sister. I was trying to talk about what was bothering me but we soon got on the topic of her husband cheating. Okay, sure, that was huge and I did want to know what was worrying her. I also loved the role of the compassionate listener—it was a comfortable one for me—but now that I was having issues, I wanted to be heard too. Sighing again, I took another sip of coffee. One more thing to think about and another reason to set out on my own.

"But Zoey, that's ridiculous. And Port Dover? That's so far from here," said Marta, bringing me back to the present. She was still confrontational, but at least, quieter.

"It's only forty-five minutes. When I picked places, I kept it within a certain area so it wasn't too far."

"Forty-five minutes is an eternity, when I'm used to visiting you whenever I want," she said, dramatically, throwing her arms up in the air.

"You can still come there to see me or we could meet halfway. And there's always the phone and email."

"You're nuts, you know. Are you sure you're not sick

or something? Shouldn't you see a doctor? First you're having marriage thoughts, now you're taking off for the summer and all by yourself."

"I'm just fine, thank you," I said firmly.

I knew my words were terse but I couldn't help it. I was pissed. Maybe this wasn't such a good idea. I'd invited Marta out for coffee figuring I'd tell her my plans, after all she was my best friend, but I didn't expect her to react so strongly. My own sister was supportive—confused, but supportive. Mistakenly, I thought Marta would be happy for me—once again, obviously a huge mistake in judgement on my part. I should have remembered that she hated change of all kinds, at least, when it came to me, especially in the midst of her wedding plans. I was her rock, when stressed. Too bad she couldn't be that way for me.

"All this because you need to get away from Liam?"

"No. All this because of me. I need to figure out what's wrong."

"I didn't realize you were that unhappy." She looked genuinely puzzled.

"I can fake it well."

"So you have no clue as to what's bothering you?"

"Not really." No way was I going to start talking about wedding plans again, as well as, babies. And I certainly wasn't going to mention Travis. She'd have me committed for sure and besides I didn't want to risk getting hurt by Marta showing some concern, then switching it back to her own stuff. Of course, I was always interested in what was going on in her life, but my issues were just too fresh right now and I was too vulnerable.

"Have you told Liam yet?"

"No."

Her eyebrows rose.

"Well, don't you think you should?"

"He's home tonight. I'll tell him then."

"Great homecoming gift."

I leaned forward, planting my elbows on the table, saying firmly, "I'm not doing this to be mean, Marta. I need to sort out what's going on. Staying with Liam and faking it, only makes it worse."

She looked taken aback. "But he's the best guy ever. If I wasn't already engaged, I'd go after him myself." She leaned forward as well, as if squaring off. "What if you lose him? Have you thought about that?"

"That's a chance I'll have to take." But I still felt sick to my stomach, every time I considered that possibility.

Marta shook her head. "What will you tell him?"

"Just that I need some space."

"If you tell him you want to get married, this wouldn't be happening."

"If I tell him I want to get married, he'd dump me."

"You don't know that."

"Well, it's a moot point now. I've made my decision. I'm going away. The woman who owns the cottage is messaging me the key this afternoon."

"But I don't want you to leave," she whined, sounding like a little kid.

"I have to." I knew I sounded sure of myself, but I was far from that. I worried every single minute that I was making a huge mistake.

Marta looked at her watch, stood up and enveloped me in a big hug. “Have to get to work. This conversation is not over.”

“You’re not going to talk me out of it. I’ve already handed over a deposit for the cottage.”

“We’ll see.” She waved, threw down some money, and walked out the door.

Grabbing another coffee to go, I quickly headed back to work. Normally, I never took time off in the middle of the day, but I wanted to tell Marta in person and she worked nights. It turned out to be a total disaster, but her comment about my going to the doctor ate away at me. Maybe I really did need to see a counselor to help me sort stuff out. I was much better at fixing other people, than myself. Maybe Marta was right and I needed help.

Right then, I made myself a promise—if my summer holiday didn’t clear things up and I still couldn’t sort out my issues, I might look at that in the fall. Anything that would help would be welcomed.

Back at work, I settled down to finish up some paperwork, since I’d be gone for a few months. This way, I could leave knowing I was all caught up and didn’t have to hurry in during August to get things ready for the start of a new year.

“How’s it going?”

Startled, I looked up to see Principal Margaret Sheen standing in the doorway. I glanced at my watch. Wow! I’d been working for two hours straight and not once had I thought about Travis or Liam. Maybe I should just continue working all summer if it got me thinking of other things besides them. *No, I had to go. It'd all been arranged. I wasn't backing out no matter what.*

"It's going great. Come on in." I beckoned her inside the room.

She hesitated. "I'm not interrupting, am I?"

"Not one bit."

I adored Margaret, both as a person and as an administrator—not a fairer boss could be had. She ruled the school with compassion, standing firm when needed and bending when it would benefit students, as well as, staff. She was also a team player who always consulted with me before imposing new rules. I'd learned a lot from her, especially about teamwork.

"You mentioned yesterday that you were actually leaving for a holiday this summer?" she asked, closing the door and sitting down. "We got interrupted so I didn't get a chance to discuss it with you. Sounds like just what you need."

"Yes, off to a cottage. But you can email me with any issues or concerns." Funny how I felt guilty for taking time off—holidays I'd earned.

"I won't do that. Always figured you work too hard as it is." Her eyebrows creased together. "Are you doing okay? I was worried about you after that assembly the other day."

"Sorry. I got a bit emotional. Sure didn't plan on that."

"You don't need to apologize. That was a horrendous ordeal to go through as a teen. But you've been looking really tired lately and I think you definitely need a break, some down time." She smiled widely, a hint of mischief in her eyes as she leaned closer. "As a matter of fact, I came over to tell you that you are officially done today. I can handle the graduation soiree tonight for, as you know, we've hired security guards and hardly any students even show up the last day. Next week is exams and you've already organized it all. I'll just implement your plans. So you're free to take off early."

I was stunned. She must be really worried about me to go to this extreme. I shook my head. "No, I couldn't let you do that." No way did I want her to think I was a basket case—wouldn't bode well for my future in education.

"I insist." Her tone of voice brooked no argument.

"Really?"

My mind raced.

Normally, I'd argue more, wanting to be tough and let on that I could handle anything, as well as feeling the school couldn't do without me. But for once, I kept thinking of myself. It actually would be pretty great to leave as soon as possible, especially since I didn't feel I was much help to anyone with my mind off in the clouds. I was having a hard time focussing on anything else but my own issues. A first, for me.

"Yes. You deserve a break and I think you need one," she said firmly. "You can't work as much as you do and keep sane. I've said that to you before and I'm saying it again. It's just not humanly possible."

She was probably right but nevertheless, I took a few more minutes to think of what it would be like not to chaperone the dance tonight with all its possible problems, not to mention making sure the exam schedule went smoothly, which of course, it rarely did. My answer was swift—a no-brainer.

"Well, okay. I think I will take you up on this." I knew it was the right decision, for immediately a sense of peace oozed through me at not having to deal with anymore work stress. Not now, when my personal life was a mess.

"Good. Lots of families take off on holidays the minute school's out. Of course, you wouldn't know that, since you rarely go anywhere." She grinned. "But this way you can get a good week's start without dealing with the added trouble of more cars on the road."

"Thank you so much. Are you going anywhere this summer?"

"Sure am. Our whole family is going on a cruise to celebrate our thirtieth wedding anniversary. I'm already dieting to make room for the ten pounds I usually put on." She laughed. "I've been on one before and discovered that I needed two wardrobes. One at the beginning and looser, larger robes at the end, after pretty well eating twenty-four seven."

I smiled. "As if you ever have to worry about gaining weight. You work out every day. But hey, congratulations on the anniversary. I didn't realize you've been married that long."

"Best thing I ever did, was to marry Brian. But enough about me, where are you going this summer? Anywhere exciting?"

I noted the stars in her eyes when she mentioned her

husband and felt envious. After all those years, to be certain you married the right person was quite a feat. She was one lucky lady.

"I'm going to Port Dover."

"Oh, I've been there. It's beautiful." She leaned closer. "You really do seem tired lately. I sure hope there is nothing seriously wrong with you. You'd tell me, right?"

"Of course I would. But nothing's wrong, really. Just exhausted, I guess. I'm hoping sunny days and walking along a beach will cure me. You're absolutely right, I need some time to rejuvenate."

She smiled. "I always am."

"Pretty much." I grinned back.

The compassion in her eyes touched me and I considered pouring my heart out, seeking her sage advice. After all, she managed to balance family life with work and did an excellent job of both, from what I could see. But I just didn't feel comfortable going into my issues with her. After all, she was still my boss and I wanted her to think that I was the efficient vice principal she always had—just momentarily a mess.

Tears filled my eyes and I was glad the bell rang, signaling the end of the day and pulling me out of another possible meltdown. I slowly got up.

"Well, better supervise the buses." Another of my vice principal jobs—to make sure everyone got on the bus with no hassles. I just hoped there were no fights or problems today, for I wasn't sure I could deal with them at the moment.

We walked down the hall together and just before

Margaret turned off to her office, she enveloped me in a huge hug.

"Have a grand time," she whispered.

"I will."

I was sure she noticed how close I was to tears back there in my office, but I was grateful she allowed me the dignity to decide to share or not. Maybe one day, but not today.

I watched her walk away, then continued to a staff door that opened to a long line of yellow buses and a horde of students rushing out, all anxious to get home. I waved and said hello so many times my arm was sore, not to mention my mouth from smiling. I also lucked out today. No fights. A smooth transition onto the buses and I was off home.

Usually, I was excited when the day ended and I could get back to Liam. Both of us often worked late but when we saw each other after long hours apart, the condo became our refuge, our place of peace. We usually made a late dinner, or one of us brought home take-out and we always took the time to snuggle and get caught up with each other's lives. This time, however, as I drove home, butterflies flitted around and I felt nauseous. Tonight was the night I tell Liam my plans.

Sure not looking forward to that.

Seven

I'd planned the whole thing all out.

I'd get Liam a drink, initiate a chat about his conference, get him all relaxed and then just lay it straight out. No hemming and hawing. I'd even rehearsed my speech before a mirror, trying to get the right expression on my face—compassionate but firm. Then, I'd take off to the dance. But… since I didn't have to attend it now, we'd have more time to talk—a good or a bad thing. Time would tell.

Still feeling the bottom was soon to drop out of my world, I set my briefcase down by the door, and headed straight to what we called our 'cuddle chair'—an oversized green recliner that Liam had kept from his university days, where we often sat together watching movies. I curled up on the chair, huddled under my blankey, sniffing the faint scent of his cologne that lingered on the fabric—Hugo Boss—a gift I'd given him for his last birthday. I closed my eyes, thinking of the first time I'd met Liam.

It was winter and I'd been skating along the Rideau Canal in Ottawa, rushing to get to a psychology class at

Carleton University. A fresh snowfall had blanketed the trees, making them sparkle as if dressed for a special occasion. Snowflakes drifted down in slow motion, bestowing a magical, almost mystical feeling to the day. So enthralled with how beautiful everything looked, I stopped for a minute to take it all in, breathing deeply the crisp, cool air. After having my fill, I pushed off with my right foot, hit a crack and fell, bang, onto the ice, flat on my face. Gingerly rolling over and checking to make sure all my limbs were intact, for some odd reason, it struck me as funny and I couldn't stop laughing. But then again, I definitely was one to laugh during tough times—rather that than cry. I just lay there, giggling away, catching snowflakes on my tongue like a little kid.

"Hey, lady, are you okay?"

I stopped laughing long enough to look up into concerned eyes—big, gorgeous eyes the color of the sky on a summer's day, with long lashes framing them, wisps of chestnut hair escaping his Maple Leaf toque, a hint of a smile on his lips. Bathed in snowflakes, he had seemed ethereal—unreal somehow—like a ghostly snow prince from a fairytale story. He was downright gorgeous.

"Should I call an ambulance?" he asked.

"Oh, no." That got me moving fast as I struggled to get up.

The prince reached down to help me, pulled me up and wrapped his arms around my waist, making sure I was steady on my feet. I was tempted to wobble more, play it up, anything to keep his arms there. They felt so good.

"Are you all right standing on your own now?" he asked.

"Er, yeah."

He quickly let go and gathered up the papers, pens and books that had been thrown out of my backpack when I hit the ice. Turned out he was going to Carleton too and we skated together the rest of the way, chatting nonstop and by the time we'd arrived, he'd asked me out for coffee. Actually, he just beat me to it. I was going to ask him the same thing. We'd been together ever since.

I got up off the chair and started pacing around the living room, lost in memories, at least this time about Liam, for a change.

A few months later, the house I had lived in was unexpectedly sold and I was evicted. It couldn't have happened at a worse time for I'd been in the middle of term papers and exams and felt overwhelmed by having the extra stress of looking for a place on top of it all. Liam kindly invited me to move in.

"We can even get married, if you want," he'd said, shocking me.

"No way," I'd replied, shaking my head furiously. "I don't do marriage."

"Really?" He'd looked at me intensely, eyebrows furled and I was sure he was going to ask 'why', or get into a big discussion about it. Thank goodness he didn't, for I really had no explanation, but enthralled by his kindness and urged on by my workload, I'd accepted his invitation to move in. Two days later he helped me pack. There were no commitments, no ceremony, just a mutual, unspoken agreement of respect.

Surprisingly, since we hadn't known each other all that

long, our relationship worked for us, as we continued to support each other throughout our various career choices. The same year he applied to McMaster's medical school in Hamilton, I applied to do a Masters in Social Work and moved there with him when we both got accepted. Everything seemed so smooth and easy and I liked it the way it was. *Until now.*

So could I really do this to him? Leave him for the summer? Was that too much to ask?

Now that the time to tell Liam had arrived, all my doubts began to slowly filter in again.

Stop it.

I'd made my decision and needed to stick to it. I couldn't just keep going over and over the pros and cons. I'd already done that a million times and, besides, I wasn't trying to hurt Liam. I just needed to sort myself out. I hated being like this but it was my reality and I had to deal with it. Maybe then my ridiculous thoughts of weddings and Travis would settle into place and I could get back into my old life. I hoped he'd understand. I was counting on it.

Worn out from reminiscing and conflicting thoughts, I glanced at my watch and saw that I had about two hours before he arrived. I'd offered to pick him up but he was with two other doctors and one of them had left his car at the airport to drive them home. Frustrated and anxious, I decided to try and get some work done. Maybe that would get my mind off all my issues.

Grabbing a fistful of cookies to chew on, I settled in at my desk in the den, attempting to sort out a mishmash of paperwork that I was going to drop off at the school tomorrow morning before I left. I'd already contacted the lady about the cottage and she agreed to let me move in early.

Struggling to fill out forms, I was only half-concentrating, the whole time waiting for the moment when Liam would walk through that door. Even my father's painting, staring at me from across the room, couldn't seem to calm me down, as every few seconds I glanced at my watch. It was like a giant countdown and finally, at exactly eight o'clock, I heard the door open. It was time.

"Hey, Veep. You home?"

I felt like throwing up.

Usually, I would jump up to greet him, excited to have him home with me again. This time I got up slowly and walked to the living room, not anticipating this meeting in the least.

Could I go through with it?

And there he was.

Six feet tall, rumpled hair from his habit of running his fingers through it rather than use a comb, huge grin, rushing toward me, enveloping me in a big hug which made me feel even guiltier. He seemed so happy to see me.

"What a surprise! I figured you'd be at the dance," he exclaimed.

"Nope. Got the night off."

"Lucky for me. Now come and sit with me a while and tell me how work's going." He dropped down on his chair and patted the cushion beside him.

"Okay, but first a drink."

I took off to the kitchen and brought back a beer for him, a glass of pinot noir for me.

"A toast to us," said Liam, as I sat down beside him, clinking our glasses.

"So tell me all about the conference," I said, after we'd each taken a sip of our drinks.

"You first."

"No, I insist. I'd like to hear how that procedure you sat in on went down."

His eyes lit up. "Well, okay. Then you."

He launched into a thorough description of what he saw and I enjoyed witnessing how excited he was. I enjoyed even more, seeing my plan going so well—he was drinking and talking and I was watching him unwind before my eyes. Next it was my turn to chat and I prattled on about this last week of classes. Then… silence. It was time for my truth session.

I jumped up from the chair muttering, "Sorry. I have some work to finish."

Liam looked shocked but I just couldn't do it. I practically ran to my office. *No way could I tell him I was leaving.* It'd be like hurting a sweet little puppy dog. Somehow I'd find a way to handle my confusion and I'd cancel the cottage first thing tomorrow.

Sitting down at my desk, I stared at the paperwork I wanted to finish. I just couldn't seem to summon up the will to do it, especially when I couldn't get Liam's face off my mind. He looked so puzzled. Usually when he'd been gone a while, I never left his side. I was like Velcro wanting to be with him every single second. Not this time. I wanted to be as far away from him as possible. Being within five feet of him, set my mind off in spirals of confusion.

An hour ticked by, in which I'd forced myself to get my paperwork up to date. Doing something so routine, seemed to calm me down and when I was done and sure he was asleep, I crept back into the living room.

"Are you finished?"

Startled, I jumped. *Damn, he wasn't asleep after all.* He was sitting there, on his chair, in the dark, exactly where I'd left him. I flipped on a light.

Once again he patted the seat beside him, motioning me to come over and join him, but I couldn't bear to be that close. I sat on the couch facing him, trying to appear all business-like, as if he were a student in my office.

He leaned forward. "What's going on, Veep? Something's been bugging you for months. I think it's time you tell me."

I didn't realize he'd noticed. Guess I was much more transparent than I'd thought. Hell, my principal had even been worried about me.

So this was it. I was going to do it.

Truth time. It was now or never.

I took a deep breath and began, "Well… you know that time when we went camping in Peterborough? Do you remember how relaxed I was?"

His eyes lit up.

"I do, indeed. Maybe we can get away this summer and head back there."

"Er… um… I do feel I need something like that again. A chance to unwind."

"I think it'd be great. I can start researching places right now on my laptop."

He started to get up.

"No, please, sit down." I took a deep breath, then let it out slowly. "I need to go alone. For the whole summer." I felt myself slipping into my terse vice principal voice. No, it wasn't fair to Liam, but I just couldn't help it. My rehearsals had flown out the window. I was winging it and just needed to get it over with.

It hurt like crazy to see his eyes again go from sheer joy and excitement to total shock.

"What brought this on?" he said softly. "Have you met someone else?"

"No. It's not that at all. I'm just confused."

He got up and came over to sit beside me, reaching for my hand. I backed away, clenching my hands together, fearing that if I touched him now, I'd give in and take it all back.

"Are you confused about us?" he asked.

"Yes, no, I don't know. Guess so."

He sat very still—so still it alarmed me—just staring at me, his eyebrows squished together in confusion. Finally he jumped up, hurried into the bedroom, and came back with a small navy blue velvet box. Getting down on one knee, he opened it up and said, "Zoey, I love you with all my heart. Will you marry me?"

What?

There, on a tiny white satin pillow, sat the most

gorgeous ring I'd ever seen—a shiny green emerald, surrounded by a wreath of rubies and diamonds. It was absolutely stunning.

I looked up at him.

"This is so beautiful," I stammered out.

"It's one of a kind. I designed it myself."

"You did?"

"Yes. Picked a green emerald because I remembered you painted your office green, saying you found it calmed you down when you tackled paperwork late at night. Diamonds represent a touch of tradition and since your birthstone is a ruby, which I researched symbolizes happiness, love and passion, I added them as well. The wreath-effect represents our life together—a circle—continuous and never-ending. In short, forever." He paused. "It's how I feel about you."

Damn. He'd done all this for me?

His face was earnest and his words soft and sincere. A part of me wanted to scream 'yes', slip the ring on and just forget about all my issues.

"I can't, Liam. I'm so sorry."

Now, if my life were a movie and I was at Silver City watching it, I'd hate my character. I'd stand up and boo, screaming, "You idiot. The handsome, kind, sweet, loving prince is asking you to marry him and you're saying 'no'? Off with her head."

My sympathies would totally side with Liam, thinking he deserved way better than a selfish girl who 'wanted to go off and find herself.' I mean, really, that whole finding oneself was such an old cliché, anyway. Archaic, as hell.

Sigh.

But hey, wouldn't at least one person stand up and cheer? Clap for the woman who was true to herself, admitted she was mixed up and instead of glossing over her issues and bowing to her man's wishes, she chose to take the time to sort herself out? *Wasn't that just as heroic?*

Sure, I felt bad for turning him down but I was just too darn mixed-up to go along with it.

"Figured you'd say no." He snapped the case shut, got up, tucked it in his pocket and sat back down on the couch. "Just wanted you to know where I stand. I've always wanted to marry you."

"You have? But I thought you were happy, even relieved, when I said no the first time?"

"The look of horror on your face showed me where you stood, so I backed away from the subject. And I loved you way too much to want to lose you by pushing for more of a commitment. I just stayed quiet."

Curious, I asked. "How long have you had the ring?"

"Not long. Just before the conference. I was trying to decide the best venue to propose." He looked around the room. "Never figured it'd be here. I wanted something really different—a story to tell our kids."

He wanted kids?

I felt like such a creep, definitely the villain of the story.

"Oh," was all I could get out.

"So it's over?" he asked. "We've just broken up?"

The hurt look on his face crushed me. And… oh, no!

Was that a tear I saw? Was he going to cry? But he never cried. Not even once had I seen him do that. No, I must be imagining it.

Once again I wondered—*how could I do this to such a nice person?*

"I'm not looking at it as over. I just need some time." But wasn't that like the proverbial saying—that 'I wanted to have my cake and eat it too?"

Silence.

"I still don't understand why."

"I just need time to myself."

Should I tell him more?

No, I couldn't. I wasn't sure of anything these days and wasn't ready to share what I was going through, especially since I could scarcely understand it myself.

"Are you planning on dating anyone?" he asked.

"No. But if you want to, go ahead." I mean, I could hardly tell him not to.

Silence.

"Where are you going?"

"Port Dover."

"When are you leaving?"

"Tomorrow."

He looked stunned. "And you're just telling me now?"

"Yes.

"Can we stay in touch?"

"I'd rather we didn't." That hurt to say, but I needed to do this and if I was talking to him on a regular basis, I wouldn't be taking the time to sort it all out. Man, this was tough.

More silence.

"Well, I wish you all the best, Zoey." He sounded very formal, like he was choking on his words. "I really do. If you feel you need this time alone, by all means take it." He even managed a smile, weak though it was.

A part of me wanted him to beg and not let me go so easily. To yell, "Please don't. I need you." I'd be tempted to stay then, for I was an expert at putting other people's needs before my own. But I knew that Liam was not like that. He was a gentle soul who truly wanted the best for me. If I thought I needed to be alone, he would never stand in my way. That was just who he was. I truly believed that all he wanted was for me to be happy in a very unselfish way. *He was a way better person than I was.*

"It is what I need." It was hard to spit those words out and stick to what I wanted. I felt myself caving, wanting to take it all back, but it was too late. It was a done deal—a necessary done deal.

He sighed. "Well, I'll try to understand, but I can't promise I'll wait forever. Marriage and children are definitely in my game plan."

They were?

At least we were finally speaking some truths. All the same, I felt nauseous hearing his words, hoping in fact he really would wait around, but I knew that wasn't fair and after all, it was what I deserved.

But just what else could I do?

What do you do when you find yourself all mixed up?

And your mind is in a muddle? When all I could think of was the guy I loved when I was fifteen, and an array of wedding dresses. Not to mention my parents' deaths seem to be haunting me, as well.

Really, what was I to do?

Once again, I felt like I had no choice.

Just wished I hadn't hurt him so much.

Eight

So it was really happening—I was on my way.

Port Dover—here I come.

I'd slept all night on the couch and took off early this morning, not wanting to face Liam. I was afraid if I saw him again, I'd hurt all over and maybe even chicken out.

Oh, who was I trying to kid.

I'd barely slept a wink.

Especially since the last thing he did the night before was hold me in his arms, kiss me tenderly and whisper, "If this is what you want, go for it." He was so darn sweet about it all, even though I knew I'd crushed him by turning down his proposal. He then went off to bed leaving me staring at the ceiling all night until it was time to leave. I was sure glad I didn't have to go into work and was able to drop my paperwork off early before anyone got there. I was in no mood to face a slew of people, not to mention a host of problems.

But… dammit.

So far I'd hit every red light and stop sign possible on my way out of town. Was this an omen? Telling me to turn around? That I shouldn't go? Was I an idiot to rent a cottage in a small town where I knew no one? Most important, would I ever get Liam's sad face out of my mind? Should I just have accepted his ring? That beautiful, beautiful ring? Would I lose him forever? Oh crap. To do this to him, was the worst thing ever. I truly was an idiot. Definitely, the antagonist in it all.

Nope.

I banged my fist down hard on the steering wheel, willing a green light to appear so I could get going.

I really had to stop thinking like this.

Enough of the wavering.

I needed to do this—to take care of my own needs for a change. I'd packed lots of soothing music to listen to on my iPod when I went for walks and I'd even brought my exercise mat and a book on yoga. I was hoping to chill out, get relaxed and sort out my issues. I couldn't help that I was so confused. Couldn't help that my past for some reason was making a grand entrance into my present. Grand? Yeah, right. It was stomping in, loud as could be, unsettling me, and throwing me off course, even making me feel sick.

Or maybe that was just hunger pangs. I hadn't eaten anything last night or this morning. Should I stop for reinforcements? I glanced at my watch. Nine o'clock. Nah, I could wait until I got to Port Dover. After all, I'd packed a bag of goodies to bring, figuring I'd need the solace of comfort food when I got there and contrary to what Marta believed, it wasn't that far away. I turned on the radio and sang along to Carrie Underwood—better that than cry. I mean, that was the whole point of being alone. I needed the time to think. No way, was I going to chicken out and turn around.

The light finally turned green and I was on my way again. Minutes ticked by slowly, but finally, a large water tower with Port Dover written across it in blue, heralded that I'd arrived.

"Here I am," I shouted out, wishing I hadn't as I'd forgotten my window was down and I'd startled two joggers who almost tripped and fell. "Sorry!" I yelled out at them, ignoring their dirty looks.

Slowing down, I took a deep breath as I drove into the town, seeing the lake sparkling in the distance. How absolutely beautiful it looked and immediately, a wave of peace rolled through me and I felt my belly unclench. This was the right thing to do. I just knew it.

I snuck a look at the paper lying on the passenger seat that had the instructions on how to get to *Hope Cottage*. Its name was one of the reasons I'd picked it, for 'hope' was definitely what I needed right about now. Following the directions, it took about ten minutes to locate my new summer home.

And there it was.

All pink clapboard with white trim around the windows and doorway. The picture on the internet didn't do it justice, as I noted the bright purple and white flowers in full bloom trailing up and down the trellises in front, creating an almost breathtaking picture of tranquility. A wooden sign on the front yard spelled out *Hope Cottage* on it and in smaller words beneath said *where dreams come true*. I could only wish that would happen but first I needed to know what my dreams were. They'd obviously changed these past six months.

I drove into the small laneway beside the cottage and pulled my luggage and small bag of groceries out of the trunk. Glancing around, I noted that there was a cottage on either side but not unbearably close. Good, I craved solitude—free from endless responsibilities.

Anxious to get inside to check it out, I quickly opened the door, dropped my luggage and groceries inside and took a walk around.

A white wicker couch and loveseat with navy blue cushions crisscrossed with red poppies, graced the living room which consisted of a small TV and wicker coffee table. A vase of red tulips sat atop the table and along with windows decked in white lace, the whole effect was one of warmth and coziness. I wanted to curl right up on the couch and never leave.

The kitchen was a small room off the living room. Its pale yellow walls and gleaming white appliances led to a tiny table in a little breakfast nook off to the side, overlooking the backyard. A swing just begging for me to join it, hung from a large maple tree, swaying slightly in the breeze. Next door was the bedroom which held a single bed covered in a bright blue blanket, a small dresser and night table. It looked sweet and clean and inviting. Thank goodness. I'd read of many horror stories where cottages didn't turn out to be as wonderful as their advertisements proclaimed they were. I was glad mine more than lived up to its description.

Next… the beach. I'd saved the best for the last.

I quickly ran over, shoved aside the curtains and opened up the glass doors off the living room. Stepping out on the deck, which faced the lake, I took a deep breath and sucked in the fresh air. Clean with a hint of salt, it couldn't be more stunning.

The water beckoned as it glistened and shone, as if magical fairies had polished it just this morning. Blue skies hovered above so it was hard to tell where the water ended and the sky began, making it look surreal, almost like a painting. But it was real and my home for eight weeks. Excitement raced through me.

Glancing at my watch, I saw that it was only ten o'clock in the morning and already the beach was filling up. Couldn't blame everyone. I was tempted to head there as well but decided that since my stomach was still rumbling, I'd have a brief coffee break first, out on the deck, where I could continue to drink in nature's awesomeness.

Going back into the living room, I put my suitcases on the bed ready to be dealt with later and went in search of the coffeemaker. The owner had reassured me that there was a good one here. Yep, and it was filled, ready for me to just punch a button. I whispered a note of thanks to my landlady.

After a few minutes, I poured my first cup, added sugar and milk and it was good to go. Placing some yummy chocolate chip cookies on a plate, I headed back out to the deck, put my goodies on the table and plunked down on a chair.

Awww… heaven. Peace and quiet at last.

Picking up my coffee cup, I took a sip, closing my eyes, savoring its taste. I didn't think anyone would argue that there was nothing like the first taste of coffee. Sometimes I wondered if I should even bother drinking the rest as nothing compared to that initial sip—I popped open my eyes—especially heightened by cerulean skies, puffy marshmallow clouds and rippling water. Leaning my head back and letting the sun's warmth envelope me, I started to feel relaxed for the first time in ages. Maybe… if I just let my mind drift, I'd discover what had been happening to me these past few months.

What the…?

I sat straight up as a red rubber ball flew across the grass, right in front of me. Voices followed.

"I'll get it."

"No, I'll get it."

Two little boys, about six years old, raced after the ball, followed by a harried looking blonde woman, apron trailing half off her slim waist, as she tried to catch up with them.

Noticing me, she yelled out, "So sorry."

"Oh, no problem," I lied. *Dammit.* My peaceful beginning to my holiday had lasted approximately sixty seconds.

The woman stopped in front of the deck, tying her apron back on and flicking strands of hair behind her ears.

"What are you two doing here?" She glared at the boys. "You were supposed to stay in the yard."

"But Mom, it's so nice out," said one of them.

"Yeah, we wanna go to the beach," said the other. "And besides, the ball flew out of the yard. Like it had wings or something."

"Yeah, right. I just bet you helped that ball over here," said their mother, looking even sterner.

As I watched the whole scenario play out before me, I realized they were identical twins, carbon copies of each other.

"We're sorry," said one of them, head down.

"Yeah, sorry," said the other who glanced at his brother, than put his head down as well.

The picture of remorse—so adorable. I almost laughed out loud.

The lady looked at me again and shrugged her shoulders. I saw a glint of a smile on her face. Guess it struck her as funny, too.

Raising his head and noticing me for the first time, one of them trotted closer to the deck and said, "Hello, Lady. I'm Jimmy and this here is Timmy. I'm a half inch taller and have a mole on my cheek and he doesn't. That's how you can tell us apart."

"Well, hello there." Despite my frustration in having my solitude interrupted, a smile inched across my face. They were just so darn cute. Both had red hair and freckles and yes, Jimmy did have a noticeable mole and was slightly taller. They looked like the red-headed version of Dennis the Menace—cute but with impish eyes eagerly out looking for all sorts of trouble.

"What's your name?" asked Jimmy, who was obviously not shy.

"Boys. Don't be so nosy," said their mom.

"I don't mind. My name is Zoey."

"Like Zoe the Muppet on Sesame Street?" asked Jimmy.

I smiled. It wasn't the first time I'd been asked that. "No, after Zoe Laboure, a French saint. Except my name has a 'y' at the end."

"That's a funny name," said Timmy.

"Timmy, that's a rude thing to say," said his mom.

"Sorry."

"Got some extra cookies?" Jimmy asked, eyeing the one in my hand.

"Well, I might just have some." I picked up my plate and started to get up to offer them some, but their mom said, "Oh, no, you don't." She shook her finger at the boys. "Neither of you finished your breakfast. I left your toast out on the table. If you eat it all up, you can have a cookie at Charlie and Louise's place, later on."

Their faces lit up. This Charlie and Louise must have good cookies.

"Race you to the kitchen," said Jimmy.

"Okay," said Timmy.

The two of them scampered off, hollering at the top of their lungs.

"They're so adorable," I said, my anger having dissipated.

"Too adorable for their own good. I'm Izzy, by the way," the lady said, with a sort of cute half smile. "And I know you're Zoey. Sorry again. I was watching them play ball in the backyard out my kitchen window, until Jimmy decided to hurl it as far as he could. You were probably enjoying some peace and quiet until my boys showed up."

"Oh, that's okay."

Sure, I hadn't wanted to be disturbed but on the other hand, it could be a long eight weeks on my own. Maybe it was good to know my neighbors. Who knew? I might have had enough of this solitude in three days and I'd be out throwing a ball around myself, hoping the boys would come over to add some excitement to my life.

"You here for the summer?" she asked.

"Yes, you?"

"Sure am."

A voice rose up from the door of her cottage. "Mommy, Mommy, Jimmy's hogging the milk."

"Guess that's my cue to go," she said. "I also have some pies to deliver for the noon hour rush, so I'd better get them all boxed up."

"Pies? Noon hour rush?"

"Yes, I bake them. Ten a day." She pointed to the next cottage. "There's a bakery there. You'll have to check it out."

"Really? I live next door to a bakery?" My stomach rumbled in anticipation.

"Sure do. They sell goodies out of their screened in porch. The best ever. And I'm not just saying that because I bake the pies. Louise does all the rest and her cookies and brownies are to die for."

"I'll definitely have to check it out."

"Mommyyyyy…"

"Well, better get going before those boys of mine rip the place apart. Nice meeting you."

"Nice meeting you, too."

I struggled to get back into my peaceful state but about fifteen minutes later, I heard a door shut and I saw Izzy coming down the path in front of our cottages, carrying two large bags, her boys running ahead brandishing black plastic swords that they swiped the air with. Izzy looked laden down, as if the bags were way too heavy for her thin, almost fragile frame to handle.

Springing into action, I hurried off the porch to meet her.

"Do you need some help?"

"Oh, no thanks. I'm okay."

"Are you sure? This way I can check out that bakery. I'm dying to see what all is there."

"Well, in that case, okay."

She handed one of the bags over and I carefully took it, aware there were pies in them. One drop and they'd be destroyed.

"We got to be real careful we don't bang into her and break one," said Jimmy, coming up to greet me.

"Yeah," said a grinning Timmy. "I broke one once and we got to eat it."

I laughed. Judging by the excited gleam in his eye, eating crushed pie was the greatest thing ever. He eyed the bag.

"Don't even think about it," said Izzy. "Run along, you two."

Timmy looked deflated as he finally took off, once again slicing the air with his sword, Jimmy in hot pursuit.

Izzy looked over at me. "Wouldn't surprise me if he ran into them on purpose."

Curious, I opened up my bag and took a whiff. Cinnamon and apples wafted up to greet me. My stomach rumbled.

"Can't say I blame him. They smell delicious."

"Thanks, well, here we are."

Izzy turned right, leading us along a walkway that led to the large cottage next door.

It was painted a soft green color and the front door held a sign that said *Granny's Homemade Delights* spelled out in a darker shade of green. As we walked up the steps that led to the front porch, I could see a couple through the window, clenched in a passionate kiss.

I slowed down. "Should we wait for a while?" I asked. "To give them some privacy?"

"Nope. We'd be waiting all day. They're always like that."

"Newlyweds?"

"Been together for fifty years."

"Really?"

Izzy opened the door.

"Howdy," said the woman, pulling away, frantically trying to tuck her gray strands of hair back into her hairnet. She had a huge smile on her face that was so infectious, I found myself smiling back.

"I'm Louise."

"And I'm Charlie."

I took a quick look at the man standing behind her. He had his head down as if embarrassed to be caught in such a romantic clinch.

Oh my goodness, it was Santa Claus.

My smile got even wider, as I stared at his white hair, beard and portly figure, but when he raised his head and I looked into his eyes, I stopped in my tracks. My smile whipped away, my jaw dropped in shock and I did a double-take. His eyes were a bright cobalt blue… exactly like my father's.

He laughed. "Yup, I know, I look like Santa."

Realizing, I was standing there rudely staring, I quickly said, "Ahhhh… sure do."

"And I can think of no better person I'd like to resemble. He's the kindest guy in the world," he said, hitching up his pants. "I try to be just like him."

"Yeah, in your dreams," said Louise, tempering her comment with a grin.

"I *am* nice," he declared, trying to look hurt but his eyes were twinkling and I was sure he was just kidding.

"Yes, you are, dear. Anything you say. Now come on and help me unload these pies," said Louise.

"Santa is quite the hero to aspire to," I agreed, going along with Charlie, still stunned at his resemblance to my dad.

Everyone used to call my father Santa too, and he often dressed up like him, surprising us at school many the time. *Sigh.* I really didn't need to be reminded of my parents right now. It usually made me sad and I'd enough to think about.

Trying to avoid looking at him, I gratefully helped them unpack Izzy's pies and set them on the counter. Anything to keep myself occupied but, to be honest, I kept sneaking looks at Charlie. It wasn't just his eyes, hair and beard. My dad was also a jovial sort like Charlie and even the way he moved, slowly, kind of clumsy-like, was similar. So much so, that I wanted to hug him, open up to him and tell him everything that was on my mind, like I used to do when I was younger. Dad had been my sole confidant and we got to taking long walks every evening where I'd spill my guts out about everything going on in my life.

Don't think about him.

"They look good, today," said Charlie, eyeing in particular a peach one. "They look good every day but today they look even better. But maybe it's because I'm hungry."

"Charlie, honey, stay away from them. Your cholesterol is probably sky high," said Louise, but she smiled at him with affection. Anyone looking at her could tell how much she loved him and vice versa. I envied them that kind of connection.

"It's a pain getting old." He frowned. "Used to be able to eat whatever I wanted. Now heartburn has become my enemy."

"Well, it's about time you took care of yourself, the way you sample everything," Louise said in a sterner voice. "And don't give me that pathetic hound dog look. I'm just taking good care of you."

As they batted words back and forth, I felt on the verge of tears, for that too, brought back so many memories of my parents. They had acted a lot like Charlie and Louise, madly in love, but bickering constantly in a good-natured, almost comical way. It was sweet to watch. *But what was with my getting teary-eyed so much lately?* I'd never been like that before.

I looked around, searching for any kind of diversion from my thoughts. The closed-in porch that housed the bakery was large, bright and airy. Besides a long counter that boasted an assortment of every treat possible, there was even room for a few tables and chairs if someone wanted to sit down to enjoy a coffee and pastry. Everything looked delicious and enticed by the scrumptious smells, I ordered a brownie and downed it immediately. Rich, chewy and even filled with gooey chocolate chips—just how I liked it. I then ordered a dozen assorted cookies.

"Come on over one day and we can have tea together," said Louise, packaging them in a small box.

"I'll be sure to do that." At least, maybe.

"Going back now?" asked Louise to Izzy, who was folding up her bags and tucking them into the satchel she carried.

"Yes."

"Well, boys, here are your cookies." Louise handed over a chocolate chip cookie to each one of them. Guess their tradition was to get one when they left.

"What do you say?" asked Izzy.

"Thank you," said Jimmy and Timmy, chiming in at the exact same moment.

"You're very welcome," said Louise.

"I'll walk back with you," I said, anxious to get going.

"Are you staying in Hope Cottage?" asked Charlie.

"I sure am," I said, trying not to look at him.

"Well, don't be a stranger. We're usually always here," he said.

"I'll remember that."

I was glad to get away from the memories they evoked and concentrated on watching the twins who raced ahead to run along the edge of the water, picking up stones and sticks and anything that fascinated them.

"Sure hope they don't bother you too much. They're kind of noisy," said Izzy.

"Oh, that's okay." Now that I'd gotten to know them a bit, I really didn't mind and as I watched them run around with such joy and abandonment, I couldn't help but get excited too, for I was also captivated by the sparkling water and the glorious day. I was going to love it here and maybe the twins really would be a welcomed diversion from time to time.

"Well, let me know if they ever bother you."

"Oh, they won't. Have you always baked? You seem like a pro."

"Well, I probably could improve on the pies but I really do love to cook."

"They look perfect to me. Are you one of those cooks who doesn't have to measure, but always manages to get the right amount in each recipe?"

"Of course." She laughed. "Is there any other way?"

I smiled. "Louise and Charlie seem sweet."

"They are, especially Charlie. He takes a real interest in everyone and always likes to help. He was a cop, you know. Retired chief of police in Brantford, known for his diplomacy skills. He's a great sounding board, if you ever need one. He listens well and is very wise. I've poured my heart out to him many a time."

"Really?" I was still reeling from the fact he reminded me of my dad.

"Yes. If you ever need any help, he's the one to ask. If he doesn't know the answer, he'll find out who does." She paused for a second, then said, "Hey, you should come over for dinner one day."

"Oh, sure. I'd like that." I snapped out of my 'dad' thoughts to watch her eyes light up. Looked like she seemed to be craving friendship. Guess being cooped up with boys all day could leave you with a huge desire to talk to another adult, for a change. I wondered if her husband was off working or something.

"As long as you like spaghetti." She laughed. "That's about all they'll eat these days."

"Just so happens, I love every kind of pasta going."

As we arrived at my cottage, I said, "Well, see you. This is where we part ways."

"Yeah, see you. Thanks for the help with the pies."

"No problem." I got the feeling she was sad to see me leave.

"Bye," yelled out Timmy and Jimmy.

I waved at them, then hightailed it up my deck steps to put on more coffee to have with my assortment of cookies. I know I'd had some earlier, not to mention a brownie, but they were too delicious-looking to not at least try them. I bit into a peanut butter one while I checked my cell phone for messages. I had two of them—one from Marta and one from my sister. I decided to call Marta back first so that I would have more time with my sister.

"Hello?"

"Hey it's me."

"Hi me. How's it going?"

"It's only been a few hours. It's going okay."

"You sure?"

"I live beside a bakery. How amazing is that?"

"*Groan.* I'll have to stay away. I can't gain a pound until this wedding is over. My dress fits within an inch of my flesh."

"How are the plans coming along?"

"Good. I'm on track."

She went on for over an hour about every single detail. I also noticed she didn't seem to care much about what I was going through but at the moment, it was fine with me. I really didn't have much to report.

I next called my sister. No one answered so I left a message, hoping everything was okay with her.

I then headed to bed for a nap. Sure it was early, but I was wiped out from getting very little sleep these past couple of weeks and the fresh air and sunshine, not to mention a belly full of cookies, was making me yawn. Later on, I'd go for a walk on the beach.

All in all, it was a pretty great beginning to my holiday.

Nine

"Hello, world," I shouted out, as I ran into the living room and threw open the curtains.

The sun was rising in all its pink, blue and orangey glory, the water glistened and I felt the best I had in months, possibly years. I didn't think I'd slept that well in just about forever. Usually, in the morning, especially lately, I was yawning, dragging myself out of bed, heading straight for the coffee pot, wondering if I'd make it through another round of work, as well as, cope with my mixed bag of personal problems. Not today! I'd awoken refreshed, energized and eager to explore Port Dover.

I never did make it out for my walk last night and ended up sleeping right through until morning. Not once did I get jarred awake by the usual car horns beeping and sirens blaring—the way it was at my condo. What was even more exciting was that I didn't think or dream even once about weddings... or Travis.

A slice of caution hit me.

A few days ago I'd made it through the night without any confusing thoughts too, but they came racing back a few hours later.

Nah, don't think about that.

Maybe this time it was for real. Maybe this time it was Port Dover's magic that descended upon me, blanketing me in peace—or at least allowing a well-needed respite from my worries.

Glancing at my watch, I couldn't believe I was up this early and raring to go. It was only five in the morning. If Liam could see me now, he'd be stunned. Usually, it took the constant ringing of my alarm clock to rouse me, for it always seemed that I finally got to sleep, just as it was time to get up. Today I was wide awake and pumped.

Liam. Sigh. A pang of loss hit me hard, almost doubled me over. I felt like I'd been suddenly sucker-punched as his warm eyes swam before me—hurt, with a hint of tears. I didn't think I'd ever get them off my mind. I closed my eyes and his face appeared once again in a slideshow mode that constantly flicked pictures of the two of us together back and forth, back and forth.

"No way," I yelled out loud, opening my eyes wide. "No way, am I going to think about him. I have to stay strong." *Otherwise, what was the point of doing this?*

Quickly changing into shorts and a T-shirt, I brewed some coffee, poured it into a thermos and headed out to the beach. Noticing a few people leaving next door with treat bags, I walked that way, thinking a freshly baked goody was just what I needed to start the day off. Dr. Oz would disapprove, but what the hell, you needed to treat yourself once in a while. Liam was much more disciplined than I was and lived by the rule of eating ninety-five percent healthy and every once in a while throw in a five percent treat. He teased me about how I lived the exact opposite, craving tasty treats ninety-five percent and every once in a while throwing in a salad.

Stop thinking about him.

I shook my head, figuratively trying to get rid of the tangled mess of my Liam thoughts. Just great. I'd spent a night not dreaming about weddings and Travis, only to awaken and think nonstop of Liam.

"Hey, there."

Grateful to be jerked out of my thoughts, I looked over to see a grinning Charlie, a small dog beside him, obviously on a walk.

"Oh hi, Charlie."

I started to walk over to them, then stopped in my tracks, remembering how much he reminded me of my dad. Maybe seeing him again so soon was not such a good idea, for once again, I felt the horror of my parents' deaths threaten to overtake me. But his infectious grin and the antics of his dog standing on her hind legs barking at me, waving her paws as if beckoning me closer was a lure too strong to ignore.

"Hi," I said, walking over to join them. "Who do we have here?" I stared at the tiny dog, who looked like a scruffy brown ball of steel wool balancing on four skinny little legs. She had a tuft of hair on her head, standing on end like a little Mohawk.

"This here's Moxie," he said proudly. "She's a rescue dog. We've had her about three months."

Moxie trotted over to me, sniffed my outstretched hand, than delivered her paw for a shake. I smiled as I took in her quirky looks, until she nudged me again with her paw as if saying, “So, are you going to shake or not?” and I quickly obeyed. She had me trained already in the space of a few seconds.

Charlie let out a huge guffaw. “She seems to really like you. Usually, she’s quite shy around strangers and hides behind my legs.”

“I love dogs. Used to have one as a kid—Shadow—a black lab. We were inseparable.”

“Maybe she senses that. Do you have one now?”

“No. Too busy to take care of one.”

As I watched Moxie grab the ball that Charlie tossed and run around with it, I felt a tug at my heart. It’d be nice to have a pet again. Hell, it’d be nice to have a life outside of school. A shiver ran through me for this was the first time it actually registered that I was a full-blown work-a-holic. My sister kept telling me that, but I never really believed her. Often I’d call myself one, but only in jest. But it hit me hard that I never took time to walk along the beach, cuddle a dog or just let my thoughts flow out from my heart, as my dad would say, without having to organize something. No wonder I was so mixed up. I had no idea of what I felt deep down inside. No clue whatsoever. It was all paved over with my job sitting on top, blocking the way into my unconscious thought and not allowing me access to what was really going on. Maybe that was why it had burst forth these past few months—my gut was tired of being held captive with no chance of parole.

“You all right?”

Reluctantly, I pulled out of my cluttered thoughts, to see Charlie peering at me, eyebrows raised.

"Yeah, yeah, I'm okay." Yup, I was still lying—too many times and I'd now lost all count. All I knew was that if I ever had to confess them, the list would occupy a full fifty GB's of space in my computer.

He stared at me for a second, obviously not believing me, then glanced at his watch. "You're up awfully early," he added.

"Just too beautiful out to waste sleeping," I said, as I watched him pull two cookies, covered in saran wrap, out of his back pocket.

"Want one?" he asked, unwrapping them.

"Tempting but nope. I'm saving myself for one of those cinnamon rolls I saw yesterday in your bakery."

"You'll love them." He gobbled down a cookie, almost in one bite then started on the second one. Wiping crumbs from his mouth, he said, "Louise would kill me if she saw me eating these. Especially for breakfast. Let's keep it our secret."

He didn't look guilty in the least.

"Got used to sweets on my job," he continued. "There was always coffee and donuts hanging around somewhere. Just can't give them up."

"Don't worry. I'll keep your secret," I said, grinning. He looked less like Santa and more like an impish elf at the moment.

"Want to walk a bit further along the beach?" he asked. "I usually go down by those stairs to give Moxie the chance to really stretch her legs." He pointed to a staircase further down.

"Sure." Why not? To be honest, it kind of felt good having his company. It reminded me of all the walks I took with my dad who also liked to get out early before everyone else woke up. He used to say, "It's so peaceful first thing in the morning before the phone starts ringing and obligations start begging for action."

"So what's a wonderful girl like you doing here all alone?" Charlie asked after a while, a serious tone to his voice.

Feeling his eyes on me, I turned to look, drinking in the empathy radiating from him. I bet he was an awesome cop for if anyone else asked that, I'd cut them off with a curt answer, feeling they were being nosy, but with Charlie, I truly felt he was genuinely concerned. Izzy was right, he really did seem to care.

"Oh, just needed some time to myself," I said, flippantly, not really wanting to talk about anything heavy, especially on such a beautiful day.

"Must be man trouble."

Startled, I sucked in my breath, then let it out in a long, slow steady flow. I shrugged my shoulders in response but didn't say a word as we continued along the beach. After a bit, he stopped, then led me over to a bench saying, "Let's sit for a while, if you don't mind. It'll give Moxie a chance to just run around in circles which is her favorite thing to do."

But I noticed he was panting a bit and his color had gone a little gray.

"Are you okay?"

"Oh yeah, yeah. Just not as young as I used to be."

"You sure?"

"Positive."

But I thought it was more than that. *Was he sick?*

We sat in silence but I kept glancing over at him every couple of minutes, hoping he really was all right. I also thoroughly enjoyed watching Moxie looking like she was having the time of her life. She chased the ball a few times, then trotted into the lake and swam around and then did what looked like her second favorite thing—chasing seagulls, although she never got too near them before they took off.

After a few seconds, Charlie said, "So spill it, if you want."

"Pardon?"

"The man trouble. I think you need to talk about it."

Charlie's directness charmed me for once again, it seemed bathed in warmth. I barely knew the guy and yet I found myself wanting to pour my heart out. Of course, that just might be because he reminded me of my dad but then again, Izzy said she often confided in him. He projected the kind of aura that I found I instantly trusted.

Should I talk to him about my issues?

Would he blab it all around the town? Could I trust him? Would the fact he looked like my dad who I used to tell everything to, be just opening up old wounds?

Nah! What was I thinking? I hadn't said much to Marta and Carm, why would I talk to a total stranger? Anyway, it was too nice a day to talk about serious stuff. Way too nice, and besides, I just got here. I needed a few days to breathe in the fresh air, soak up the sun and try hard not to think of anything serious. No way was I talking about my stuff to someone I didn't know, especially on my first full day at Port Dover.

I turned to look at Charlie, only to find him watching me closely. I opened my mouth to tell him that I didn't want to talk about anything, but the expression in his eyes undid me. Without any warning at all, for the first time in my life, I burst into tears—and not just a gentle outpouring, either—but full-out sobs.

What the hell was going on?

I never cried in front of anyone. Not even Liam, let alone a complete stranger. I was making an utter fool of myself.

"S…s…s… sorry," I managed to mumble, turning my face away.

"Don't be. Feeling sad is natural, when you're going through a lot."

Should I tell him?

"Well… it kinda is man trouble," I found myself saying, once again falling for the wisps of compassion wafting out from him, enveloping me, encouraging me to trust him. And I did. Trust him, that is. *How weird was that?*

"Figured so."

His sympathetic voice was my undoing, not to mention those blue eyes of his and before I knew it, I started talking about Liam and Travis, just like I used to do with my dad. Except… it was with a total stranger.

"That's a lot to figure out," he said sympathetically, when I'd finished my soliloquy. I didn't mention real names or anything and didn't tell him every single detail, but basically gave him the gist of it all.

"Guess I'm just all mixed up."

Moxie, as if sensing my pain, jumped up on my lap, licked my face, and then curled up into a ball as if going for a snooze. It was sure calming to pet her though, as it soothed my mess of a mind and I found myself sharing more until finally, exhausted, I took a deep breath and sighed loudly.

Silence.

I looked over. "Sorry about burdening you with all this."

"No need to apologize. I asked, remember?" He looked deep in thought, furrowed brow and everything. "Are you hoping to get back together with your first love?"

"No. Not at all. That's what's puzzling me even more. Getting back together is not an option. Not one bit. So why is he on my mind all the time?"

"Just curious. Do you know where he is?"

"Haven't a clue."

"Hmmmm… you know, I think you need to find him and face him," he said, slowly and surely.

"Who?

"Your first love, of course."

"No way."

"If you saw him, you might be able to gauge what about him is haunting you."

Green eyes and black hair rose before me and my heart fluttered in response.

Did I want to see Travis? In the flesh? Not really. The

thought of seeing him frightened me somehow.

"You think so? I wasn't planning on it. I was just hoping it would fade away into a past memory again."

"Maybe talking to him would help you figure out why he's on your mind." He leaned closer, his eyes dead serious. "But if you do set up a meeting, make sure you're safe."

"What do you mean?"

"Maybe it's the cop in me talking but make sure you meet him in a public place—like a restaurant or even at the bakery. You haven't seen him in years so I wouldn't meet up with him alone."

"Good point." But somehow I couldn't picture Travis as anything else but the gentle person he used to be.

"That other guy—Liam—sounds like a great guy."

Yes, he was. I could vouch for that one hundred percent.

"He is." I turned to look at him, wondering about his own life, or maybe just trying to get the focus off me. "Did you know Louise was the one you wanted to marry, when you first met her?"

"The *Summer Gardens'* dance hall," he said softly.

"Pardon?"

He smiled. A hint of nostalgia evident in his eyes, as he turned and gazed back at a clump of buildings to the left of where we were sitting.

"That's where I met her. Right here in Port Dover at a sock hop at the *Summer Gardens'* dance hall."

"Really?" I squinted to see if I could make out the names of any of the businesses he was staring at. "Does the hall still exist?"

"No, not anymore. But it used to be over there."

He continued to gaze in that direction, a smile appearing and I was sure he was envisioning the first time he saw Louise. I waited him out.

"The dance hall was hopping," he finally said, turning to look at me, "and attracted big bands and singers. It was the 'hot' place to be." He smiled. "I noticed Louise right away the very first time I went there. Her long blonde hair fell to her waist and she wore a bright pink sundress covered in tiny white daisies. She'd taken off her shoes and moved effortlessly to the beat, graceful as anything and every once in a while I'd hear her laugh. It was music to my ears."

"Did you ask her to dance?"

"Nope." He grinned. "*She* asked *me*. I was too shy but I kept hanging around her, not even making an attempt to hide my interest. Guess she finally noticed."

Good for Louise.

"And you never regretted marrying her?"

"Not one day." He looked puzzled. "What's wrong with getting married? With uniting forever and celebrating that vow with friends and family?"

"Er… I guess, nothing."

"Not sure if you are aware of it, but when you said the word marry, your whole face scrunched up into a scowl."

He sure was insightful. Guess questioning all the suspects he'd met as police chief, would heighten his observational skills. I felt I couldn't hide anything and wanted to confess a crime, even though I hadn't committed one. I even felt guiltier for all the lies and half-truths I'd spouted out lately. I never used to be like that—

tactful, yes, but not downright lying.

"Just don't understand why someone would tie themselves down, that's all."

"Yeah, I know, most young people today live together, or shack up as I've heard it called. Call me old fashioned but I think the term 'shacking up' is a sad one. To call uniting in love a shack, is pathetic."

"Liam and are shacked up," I said softly.

"Really?" He looked surprised. "So I guess you're not that afraid of commitment. You won't get married, but at least decided to stay together."

"But I am. I'm just not interested in forever kind of commitments. I just moved in because it was convenient."

"Oh."

Silence. Guess he didn't know how to respond to that.

Sighing, I said, "Well, I'm hoping in time, I'll figure it all out."

"You will. But trust me, you need to seek out that Travis character and see how you feel when you're around him again. Face it head on."

"You're probably right."

I saw him glance at his watch. "Guess I'd better be going or Louise will be sending out the Coast Guard."

But I could tell by the knowing look in his eye, that he knew I'd had enough sharing for today. And he would be right. I was wiped.

"Just come visit if you ever need to talk again. Okay? Anytime, I'm always here to listen."

"Thanks, I will. That's very kind of you." I smiled. "You remind me of my dad, you know."

"Hope that's a good thing."

"It is." *Should I explain about my parents?* Nah, way too much information and I was already on overload.

"Good. Well, let's get going," he said, giving me an intense look, as if sensing I wasn't telling him something. Sure couldn't fool him. "Louise would love to see you. That bakery's been the best thing that ever happened to her and she loves her customers."

"How long has she been in business?" I asked, putting Moxie down on the ground.

"For about twenty years now. She also caters and provides food for local businesses."

"Really?"

"Yes, she thrives on it. After Thanksgiving weekend, we move back to Brantford, where she caters all winter. There's nothing she loves more than to cook for people, the larger the crowd, the better."

He led the way to the bakery, or more correctly, Moxie did. Louise was waiting at the door and greeted her husband with a huge hug.

"Hello there," she said, smiling widely.

I couldn't help but notice she looked worried—like she'd been watching out for him. Once again, I wondered—*was Charlie sick?*

"I thought you'd gotten lost or something, honey. I was getting concerned."

"Oh, you're just an old worrywart." He leaned in for another hug and added a kiss.

"That, I am," she said, noticing me for the first time and pulling away. "Oh, hi there. It's Zoey, right?"

"Right." I smiled back.

She looked down at Moxie, who was sitting at my feet, gazing at me adoringly.

"That dog sure likes you. Not that crazy about me but seems to have a crush on you."

I glanced down. She was so cute I started to laugh, registering that this was the first time I'd laughed in what seemed like weeks. But the sight of that mangy dog staring at me, almost as if flirting, got me chortling.

"She's probably hoping for a treat," said Louise.

Charlie pulled one out of his pocket. "Well, here. Give her this. But make her work for it."

"Shake a paw," I said, laughing as she solemnly reached her paw out, then gently took the cookie from my hand and gobbled it down in two seconds. She raised her paw again, looking for another one.

"No more for you," said Louise. "Now c'mon in. I've been very rude, not inviting you inside."

I followed her, Moxie hot on my trail, breathing in heavenly baking smells—a mixture of cinnamon, chocolate and vanilla.

"Are you getting settled in?" Louise asked.

"Sure am."

I watched as she immediately went to a bowl, started stirring some kind of lemony mixture, poured it into a pan and stuck it in the oven. She looked so sweet and grandmotherly with her white hair pulled back in a bun, hairnet over it, and spectacles halfway down her nose. She also had kind eyes and dammit, I found myself tearing up again.

"Do you have any cinnamon rolls, by any chance?" I blurted out when I saw that it looked like she was taking a lull out of her baking. I needed to get what I'd come for and get the hell out of here or I'd probably finding myself pouring my heart out to her, too. Hell, if I didn't watch it, I'd be positioning myself somewhere on the beach and starting to talk to anyone who walked by. I might even set up a booth, hoping people would line up to hear my woes. I grimaced at the thought. This vacation was supposed to be about quiet time and peace and here, on my first full day, I'd begun by talking almost hysterically about my issues. *To a stranger.* Crap!

"Sure thing. With icing or not?" asked Louise.

"Icing, please."

I watched as she scooped up a bun the size of a large dinner plate and slid it into a bag.

"Saw you got to meet your other neighbors," said Louise.

"Yeah, those boys are adorable."

"Sure are. Sad about Izzy though," said Louise.

"Oh?" I tried to sound nonchalant, not really wanting to know anything. I got my fill of gossip at work, for often teachers liked to chat about one another, but I also didn't want to be rude to Louise, and besides, I could tell she was going to spill it anyway.

Liam always teased me, saying I had the type of face that made people want to confide in me. Not sure about that but one thing I was sure of—he was right. No matter where I was—a gas station, convenience store or out at a function—people opened up. It was either a curse or a blessing. I wasn't sure yet.

"Her husband left her." She shook her head. "Just couldn't take the twins. Wanted all her attention. A selfish, selfish man. Now he's fighting her for sole custody, just so he doesn't have to pay child support."

"Oh, that's sad."

No wonder Izzy looked so tired, if she was dealing with all that.

"Yes, it is incredibly sad. We try to support her as best we can." She handed over the bag. "Well, here you go. Hope you enjoy it."

"Thank you."

"So come on over anytime. You might get a bit lonely all by yourself."

"I'll do that."

Yeah, right. But I knew the lure of baked goods would have me back in no time. I'd just have to guard my emotions and keep them well hidden.

Louise really did seem kind and I was sure, well-meaning. Both she and Charlie also appeared well-matched and I thought I was going to enjoy getting to know them more. However, for today, I scooted out fast before any more sad stories headed my way. I was on an emotional overload as it was and my mind was spinning. Usually compassionate by nature, I was too overwhelmed at the moment to let anything else shake me. I didn't want to get mired down in other people's problems right now for that was also a huge issue of mine—my tendency to gladly drop my own concerns to get involved with someone else's. Guess that was why mine never got sorted out. Not this summer, though. These weeks were devoted to me. I owed it to myself to get better and back to the way I used to be. I was counting on it.

After leaving the bakery, I noted the lighthouse at the end of the pier, deciding it would be the perfect place to have my breakfast, or feast, was more like it. I walked along the beach and then wound my way through a gathering of people fishing on the pier and sank down on a bench. Man, it was glorious here. Once again, I closed my eyes and took a few deep breaths of fresh air, imagining Liam and Travis floating off somewhere in space, leaving me alone. A long sigh rippled through me and I briefly went into an almost meditative state, until the sweet smell of cinnamon rose to tease me as if saying 'open the bag, open the bag.' I popped my eyes open and took out my roll, immediately taking a lick of icing. Awwww… coffee and sweets—the best breakfast ever.

Hearing shouts of joy, I watched a young family spread their towels out on the beach to get ready for a day of swimming. I thought back to all the picnics my parents used to take us on, where we'd chomp down on hamburgers and potato chips and laugh until our sides hurt. Oh no! A stream of sadness poured its way out of my heart but I quickly squashed it. I didn't want to think about my parents right now. As a matter of fact, if they were alive, I probably wouldn't be in this predicament. Dad and even Mom would have listened to my woes with Travis and helped me come to terms with it and I'd never have lived with Liam in the first place. Being staunch Catholics, they would have skinned me alive if I did. Not that I was blaming them, after all, it was my decision to move in with him, but I knew that Dad would have been the first person I turned to for help and guidance. But hindsight and wishing the past could re-write itself was a waste of time. I needed to deal with things the way they were now—just not right this moment.

Someone waving at me caught my eye and I looked over to see it was Izzy and her children, making their trek back from the bakery. I waved and Jimmy and Timmy came racing down the beach and onto the pier.

"Hi there," I said. I couldn't help but smile at their excited faces.

"You fishing?" asked Jimmy.

"No. You?"

Timmy shook his head.

"Well, we might if Daddy ever visits," said Jimmy, looking sad. "He keeps promising."

"Sorry. They're bothering you again," said Izzy, finally catching up. "They love to come down to the pier to watch the fishing going on and when they saw you, I couldn't hold them back. Looks like you're their new best friend."

"Oh, they're no problem." And they really weren't. They'd won me over with their cuteness factor and I didn't mind seeing them at all.

"They have a worm fascination and especially love to watch the baiting of the hooks." Izzy wiggled her nose in disgust.

I laughed at her expression. "Not one of my favorite things either."

She dropped down on the bench beside me while the boys were getting expert baiting advice from a lone fisherman to the right of us. "Charlie promised that he'd take us all fishing so that I can learn with the boys."

Once again, I noticed how tired she looked.

"Hey, if you ever need a sitter, let me know." I couldn't believe I'd said that, but my heart went out to her. Those black marks under her eyes signaled she was in bad shape.

"Oh, that's okay." But she looked grateful, all the same.

"I mean it. Give me a holler any time."

"Thanks."

I waited to see if she'd offer more but she didn't, seemingly content with having some quiet time. So stuffing the last of my bun in my mouth, washed down by coffee, I got up, leaving her to enjoy the peace. Time to do some more exploring.

"Well, better get going. See you later," I said.

"Enjoy the day," said Izzy, still gazing off into space.

I looked over to say bye to the twins, but they were so engrossed in studying one of the fisherman's catches that they didn't notice I was leaving.

Wandering around the streets and in and out of stores, I was not really looking for anything in particular, just checking out what they had. I also took note of *Willies* where I could get an ice cream and *The Arbor* where I could get a red hot and a peach glow. I was already lining up my meals for the week. I needed to get back to some healthy eating at some point, but for now I was enjoying having whatever I wanted, whenever I wanted. Just for a while, at least. After all, I was on vacation. Wasn't that the time to relax the rules and just enjoy?

When I got back to the cottage, there was one thing I

was dying to do. Grabbing my laptop, I quickly powered it up and did a Google search on Charlie. I was curious about him. I mean, anyone who could get me to cry like that, must be a pretty amazing person.

"Wow," was all I could say as I stared at page after page about Police Chief Charlie Donnelly. Looked like he'd been awarded every medal possible and the common description about him was that he was 'relentless in protecting the innocent by putting criminals behind bars.' He also was the one who cracked a serial killing spree years ago. One newspaper reporter had me giggling, when he quoted a jewel thief moaning that "Donnelly's eyes rip right through you down to your very soul. He had me confessing in no time." Boy, I knew that feeling well.

I spent the rest of the day, lying on my deck soaking in the sun, just taking it easy. It was exactly what I needed.

After a supper of a grilled cheese sandwich, I wandered down to *Willies* for a chocolate ice cream and then came back and tried out the swing in the back yard. As I swung back and forth, allowing the movement to lull me into a state of contentment, I tried not to let anything too serious cross my mind. I needed a break from that, after all the emoting I did today. I certainly planned on not letting that happen again. I needed solutions not just aimlessly spilling my guts to possibly anyone and everyone. That was why I was here—for answers, not more questions.

Ten

What? An email from Liam?

Taking a sip of coffee, I just stared at the title—*Please open.* He'd respected my wishes not to stay in touch, so why write now? After all, I'd only been gone a little over a week. Fear raced down my spine. Had something happened?

Too scared to open it up, I continued to drink my coffee until I'd drained the cup, then put it down on the coffee table.

Was he saying goodbye? Was this it? Did my leaving destroy everything?

C'mon, Zoey. Just do it.

I clicked it open.

> *Dear Zoey,*
>
> *Sorry to bother you, but I was given the opportunity to go with Doctors Without Borders for a month in Mali, West Africa. I decided to accept. Just wanted you to know in case you needed to get hold of me. I may not have access to the internet but if you*

ever need me, you can call Wayne Nix—our director—and he'll get your message through to me. Hope everything is going well.

Liam

Whew! At least he hadn't dumped me, but I couldn't help but notice he hadn't added 'Love' before his name.

Doctors Without Borders?

He'd looked into that once, thinking he'd like to offer his services at some point. Usually you had to commit for a year but with surgeons it was a month. Guess it was too good an opportunity to give up. I was happy for him, *so why did I feel that a knife had sliced through my heart?* Just knowing he was out of the country unnerved me, for I liked to think of him as always there for me. Talk about being selfish. After all, I was the one who'd changed the rules. I really did hope he would have an incredible experience there. He deserved it and so did all the people he'd be helping. They were lucky. Liam was damn good at his job.

What the...?

Was that a dog barking?

Struggling to put my troubled thoughts on hold, I padded over to the door and peered out the peephole.

Oh my goodness, there was Moxie. Guess she sensed my movements, for she let out another round of sharp barks, followed by a long whine. Opening the door, she came bounding in, placing her two paws up against my knees, wagging her tail like crazy.

"Hey, girl. What are you doing here?" I glanced behind her. No Charlie. Had something happened to him? Or had she just gotten loose and come for a visit? Nah, she'd be more frantic than this, if something was wrong. I picked her up and cuddled her and she leaned in to lick my face.

"Do you want to go for a walk, Moxie? Is that it?"

She wiggled out of my arms and when I put her on the floor, she ran to the door, and pawed at it.

"Okay, okay." I laughed at her antics, amazed at how she managed to get across her wishes, even without the ability to speak. "I'll go get ready." I glanced at my watch. It was a bit early, so my guess was that she somehow escaped Charlie's notice and decided to come get me.

Exactly ten days had passed, and except for a couple of times when I'd slept in, I'd gotten into the habit of joining Charlie and Moxie on their morning walks. Here I thought I had wanted to avoid everyone but instead I was loving the interactions with my new neighbors. I still had lots of time to myself but it was fun to chat with people on a daily basis. Moxie and I had become the best of pals and she seemed to dote on me, often ignoring Charlie and wanting only me to throw the ball for her. This was the first time she'd come to my door, though. It was new but welcomed behavior.

Having quickly changed out of my pajamas into more suitable attire, I stepped out into the sunshine and saw Charlie headed my way, a huge smile on his face. Good. I was glad there was nothing wrong.

"Figured Moxie was here. Guess the gate in the backyard wasn't closed tightly and she nosed it open. I swear she'd move in with you if I let her."

He didn't seem the least concerned about that.

"Louise isn't that into dogs much," he continued. "Just too busy to care for one and I'm glad that Moxie is getting to know a female well. That'll help, for I find she barks at women and little girls, on the beach. Hopefully, your presence will help her learn to like the female species."

"Well, she's welcome to visit anytime." In truth, I adored her. This quirky little dog had wormed herself into my heart and I looked forward to seeing her every day.

We headed off along the lake, Moxie running in and out of the water chasing the ball I threw. She didn't like to give it up though, for she had her own game and plans in mind. She'd bring it back and drop it close to me and when I'd reach for it, she'd grab it again and run away, thinking her antics were hilarious. Only after three tries, according to her rules, would she let me have it.

"We've been lucky this past week. No rain so far but unfortunately, we're in for some later today," said Charlie, glancing over at a darkened sky, still way off in the distance.

"Oh, no. My sister and her children are coming for lunch. We're planning on having a picnic on the beach."

"Well, I think the day will be fine. It's not supposed to arrive until after supper."

"Good. She'll be long gone by then. Hey would you mind popping over with Moxie? Cindy and Cole, my niece and nephew, love dogs."

"I'd be glad to. The more socializing I do with that dog, the better she'll be, especially since there are a lot of people coming in and out of the bakery. I want her to get along with everyone. Kids, included."

"Thanks, Charlie. It'll make their day."

We walked for a while, just enjoying each other's quiet companionship. I was still amazed at how much I loved being with him, since I usually had a hard time drawing close to people. Oh sure, I was always friendly and nice, but I kept everyone at a distance. But Charlie was like a peaceful refuge in my confused life and someone I looked forward to spending time with. Guess some things defied explanations. I mean, he did look like my dad but still, he was an absolute stranger and I was continually surprised that I opened up to him so quickly. By now, I had even told him about my parents and I rarely talked about them.

"So… did you look him up?" asked Charlie.

I looked over at him, seeing the mischievous look on his face.

"Who?" I knew darn well who he meant but was just stalling. I'd managed to put Travis out of my mind the past week or so and sure didn't want it dredged up again. On the other hand, I didn't really mind that Charlie brought him up. With his gentle ways and genuine interest, he soothed me, yet challenged me at the same time. And besides, this was the first time he'd mentioned what I had shared a while back.

"Your old love, of course."

"Er… no."

"So you think the problem's solved?"

"Not really. I'm just putting it away for a while."

He shook his head. "Avoiding the issue is not going to solve it."

"You're right. But I'm still not sure I want to see him."

"I think you should. As I said before, face to face is the only way you'll resolve your feelings towards him and Liam. Otherwise you'll always wonder. You may be able to stuff it back in the past again, but I guarantee it'll flare up again somewhere down the road."

"Guess so."

Silence.

"Have you heard from your boyfriend?"

"Funny you should ask that. I heard from him this morning." I explained where he was going.

"Is that okay with you?"

"Of course. I took off. I have no hold on him."

"Aren't you worried he'll find someone else?"

"Yes, of course I'm worried."

"Well, don't let him drift along in limbo too long. You have to discover what's in your heart and reach out for what you want. If an old crush is standing between you and your man, you need to see him and straighten things out. You gotta grab life with both hands and hang onto it. Build bridges with your past."

"Bridges?"

"Yes. Roadways of peace. Sounds like you have lots of dams there instead, creating a stockpile of garbage."

Well, that was one way of looking at things.

"You might be right, Charlie. Hey, look at that big ship out there." I pointed out to the lake.

Charlie gave me a piercing look at my sudden change of topic.

"It won't help running away from problems but yes, that's a big ship."

He knew me too well.

We both stared at the boat for a while.

"Will you at least think about it?" asked Charlie. "I hate to see you look so sad at times. You think you can hide it, but you don't fool me. I can see the gloom on your face when you think I'm not looking. I know you're going through a lot at the moment."

It was uncanny—like he could read my mind as well as see into my heart.

"Okay, I promise to think about it."

"Well, my grandchildren make me pinky swear when it comes to a promise." He held out his baby finger. "Would you humor an old man?"

"Sure." I laughed, as I grabbed hold of his finger with mine and we clenched the deal.

"Going to the bakery today?"

"Sure am. I need to load up with goodies for our picnic."

"Well, Louise's the place to do it."

"No kidding." I patted my stomach. "My waistline is sure showing it. I swear I've gained five pounds since I got here."

He laughed. "You can afford to put on weight. You're way too thin as it is." He patted his own belly. "I'm the one who needs to go on a diet."

"Well, I think you look wonderful." Although, in truth, I was always worried about him. The color of his face was ashen, too many times to count.

He whistled for Moxie to come out of the water and we walked up the path to the bakery.

"Hi there," said Louise, as we opened up the door. "If I didn't know that Charlie adored me, I'd be jealous." She grinned.

"Oh, you don't have to worry about that." But I knew she wasn't. He was completely devoted to her and let her know at every possible moment. Right now he was staring at her, love evident in his eyes.

"So what would you like today?" she asked, after leaning over to give Charlie a kiss on the cheek.

"Hmmmmm…. How about a dozen chocolate chip cookies and two dozen cupcakes?"

"Hungry, are you?"

I laughed. "Very. But they're not just for me. I have company. My sister and her children are visiting."

"How nice. You must get lonely sometimes."

"Not really. After working in a school where noise is at its premium every single day and my hours are filled with dealing with problems, it's nice to be away from all the chaos for a while. But it will be great, for sure, to see my sister."

"Well, as I always say, family is where it's at."

And she was right about that. I often wondered where I'd be and what I'd be doing if my sister hadn't taken me in. I shook my head in protest. I sure didn't want to think of that either, but once again I gave up a silent thank you that Carm became my guardian all those years ago. I was a lucky girl.

I watched as Louise boxed my goodies, while I salivated on cue, already anticipating a feast later on.

"There you go," she said, handing me a large bag with a handle on it, making it easier to carry. "Enjoy the day."

I looked around and not seeing Charlie, I said quietly, “I noticed that Charlie sometimes doesn’t look that well. Is he okay?”

Worry etched across her face. “So you’ve seen it too? I’m scared for him but he won’t go to the doctor.”

“No? Well, if I can help in any way, just let me know.”

“Thanks.” She gave me a hug just as Charlie walked back in the room. “Have a great day.”

“I will, for sure. See you.” I waved to Charlie, while I leaned down to pat Moxie on the head. She whimpered a bit, no doubt wanting to join me. “See you later.” And she wagged her tail so hard, I swear it was going to fall off. *Who needed a man? I could just get a dog.* Smiling at the thought, I headed back to my cottage where I saw Izzy walking towards me, the twins running around excitedly on the beach.

“Hi there,” I said.

“Hi, Zoey.”

Jimmy and Timmy also yelled out “Hi”, simultaneously. They were both so darn sweet in their superman T-shirts wearing towels for capes as they pretended they were flying.

“We’re catching criminals,” yelled out Jimmy.

“Yeah, bad guys,” chimed in Timmy.

Grinning at their antics, a pang of yearning flared through me. Maybe I really did have a secret soft spot for kids. *Stop that.* I couldn’t even begin to think again about that subject without sorting out all the rest of my problems.

“How are you doing?” I asked Izzy, to get my mind off myself.

"Okay." But she looked worried.

"Really? You seem concerned about something."

"Oh, just that Timmy isn't himself." He looked fine to me, but then again, a mother's eyes would obviously be more alert to any change, however small, in their child's demeanors.

"Oh? What's wrong?"

"Not sure. I'm taking him to the doctor's office today."

"Well, let me know if I can help." That was the second time I'd said that today. I could see myself reverting to my old self—anxious to help others and not myself. I'd have to be careful. Sure, I wanted to be there for them, but I had to make sure I just didn't toss my own concerns aside. Obviously, I was famous for that.

"Thanks." But she looked even more stressed as she hurried off to the bakery.

I walked up to my deck, thinking about how hard it must be to raise two little boys, especially by yourself. I'd probably be worried all the time and there would be no downtime ever, unless you hired a babysitter or had a slew of family members committed to helping out. No husband would be available to even relieve you for a few hours. Hmmmm… maybe I needed to be more forceful when offering my services. Spending time with the twins on a daily basis, even for a few minutes, might help me discover if I really did have a maternal instinct or whether I'd steer clear of all children except my niece and nephew, for the rest of my life. Maybe I could also learn to continue to help others, as well as, take care of my own needs. That would be a huge lesson to learn and one that could help me my whole life.

Glancing at my watch, I realized it was getting closer to when my sister would arrive. Excited, I arranged the food I'd prepared in two large baskets. One held peanut butter sandwiches and cut-up veggies and dip, the other held sweets. I then went back to lounging on the deck, soaking in the sunshine, while I waited for Carm. Ahhh… this was the life.

At exactly 11:30 she arrived, all smiles and looking much more relaxed than I'd seen her in years.

"Auntie Zee," screamed Cindy, racing toward me, arms outstretched.

As per tradition, I picked her up and twirled her around, her excited eyes making me feel like a million bucks or at least, the best aunt ever.

"Any frogs around here?" said Cole, looking around. I could see he was still into his animals.

"Haven't seen any, but then again, haven't been looking. Maybe one will make an appearance just for you. Lots of birds, though."

"I like birds, too. They're cool." He grinned, then came over and surprisingly gave me a hug as well. Holding onto the both of them, I glanced over at Carm.

"How are you doing?"

"Good," she said with a grin. "I have some news to tell you. We'll talk later."

I noticed she didn't ask me about myself and for some reason that irked me. Then again, I'd only recently acknowledged that most of my relationships were all about them, never about me. So I guess I was more in tune with that behavior in the middle of this heavy-duty soul-searching vacation. Now what to do about it, was a whole other avenue to think about.

"C'mon, Auntie Zee," said Cindy, tugging on my arm. "Let's go swimming."

"Please, Mom," said Cole. "Can we eat later and go in the water now?"

She glanced at me and I nodded. "Fine with me."

I led them in through the deck to the living room, pointing out the bedroom and bathroom where they could all change. I was wearing my swimsuit under a long T-shirt cover-up, so I just needed to yank it off and grab a towel.

"This is the sweetest cottage, ever," exclaimed Carm, who had changed quickly and was walking in and out of all the rooms.

"It is, isn't it?"

"Does the landlady rent it out often?"

"Maybe. Why?"

"Well, judging on how good you look, I'd love to come here sometime."

"You think I look good? I feel like I've put on a ton of weight."

She looked me up and down. "No, don't think you have. Maybe all that walking you said you do is helping. You look tanned and healthy and happy."

"I do?"

"Certainly a lot better than a few weeks ago."

"Really?" I hadn't thought she'd even notice, but our conversation was stopped short when Cindy and Cole came racing out in their bathing suits.

"All ready?" I asked, looking at their excited faces.

"Aye, aye, sir," said Cole, hamming it up.

"Well, let's get going."

Carm and I picked up the food baskets and searched for a nice place to settle in by the lake.

"Race you to the water," yelled Cindy, after we laid out a blanket and piled our towels up beside the baskets.

"I'll win!" shouted Cole, who did indeed lead the way.

Carm and I joined them and I had to admit, I had the time of my life, splashing and playing and frolicking in the water with my niece and nephew. Carefree activities were definitely good for the soul and I needed to do more of this.

Next on the agenda was a huge sandcastle and once again it was the most fun I'd had in ages. There was just simply nothing like the excitement of children, loads of sand to dig your fingers into and the challenge to build the biggest castle ever. With much laughter and experimentation, we managed to produce a building worthy of a king and queen, equipped with three moats. By the time we were done, we had a crowd standing around, cheering us on. Cindy and Cole looked quite proud of themselves, but I was sure I looked the proudest.

"Now, lunchtime," said Carm firmly. "Otherwise it'll be five o'clock before we get home and the both of you will be crabby and starved by then. But don't eat too much. Don't forget, Daddy is taking us all out for pizza tonight."

"Hurray for pizza," said Cole, stuffing a peanut butter sandwich down his throat in pretty well one gulp.

"Please chew your food," admonished Carm, watching over them, making sure they ate a balance of healthy food and a few sweets.

"Heyyyyy, who's that?" yelled an excited Cindy. I turned to see Charlie and Moxie making their way over to us.

"I'd like you to meet my friends," I said proudly, jumping up to greet them. "This here is Charlie and Moxie."

Moxie strutted around as if making sure we all knew that this was *her* beach but then stopped, allowing the children to fawn all over her with pets on her wiry fur and paw shakes, in return for offerings of little crusts of bread.

"So you own the bakery Zoey keeps talking about?" asked Carm, warming up to Charlie. I'd mentioned that he reminded me of Dad and at one point she caught my eye and nodded. Guess she too, felt his magic.

"I sure do. You should come on over sometime."

"Next visit, for sure. I have a hard time saying no to a bakery and my hips show it."

"Don't think you have to worry about that too much," he said. Then he glanced at his watch. "Well, I'd better get going. I'm helping Louise roll some dough for butter tarts."

The children were reluctant to see Moxie go, especially when she allowed them to hug her goodbye.

"You'll see her again," I promised.

As soon as they finished eating, Cindy and Cole raced back to add even more rooms to their sand castle, after receiving orders they were not to swim so as to give their stomachs a chance to digest their food. Especially all the cookies they'd ingested, sneaked when Carm wasn't looking.

This time I let them work alone, wanting to talk to Carm by herself.

"You're looking happier," I said. "Have things improved with Dave?"

"Yes," she said, a huge smile on her face. "Just found out two nights ago that he isn't having an affair. That's why I was anxious to come out and see you today, to let you know." She breathed out a huge sigh of relief. "Thank goodness."

"Great news. So what was going on with the weight loss and the other things you noticed? The Cosmo red alarms?"

She moved closer, making sure the kids couldn't hear. "Get this! He thought *I* was having an affair."

"He did? What made him think that?" I was stunned. She barely had time to brush her teeth, let alone embark on some kind of nefarious encounter. "Was he reading Cosmo too?"

She laughed. "Nah. And I certainly haven't lost any weight, which was one of the signs. Guess I've been preoccupied lately, what with the kids, the agency and so on. I wasn't giving him as much attention as I used to and he felt I was losing interest in him, so he was trying to get in shape hoping he'd be more attractive to me again."

"*Have* you lost interest?"

"No, not at all. Just tired all the time. Owning my own business is not all it's cracked up to be. There are so many things to do and with the kids, especially when Dave's away, I'm the chief chauffeur for their numerous activities. Guess Dave was picking up on my huge influx of stress."

"Anything you can do about that?"

"Well, we discussed hiring someone else to pick up the slack at work. That's hard for me to do because I'm a control freak but I agreed to do it. I start interviewing next week."

"Good for you and I'm thrilled to see you so happy."

"And get this. He even arranged with his parents to babysit the kids for a weekend at the end of the month so we can get away by ourselves. He booked a hotel room in Niagara Falls—the exact room where we honeymooned. That was what he was doing when I caught him on the phone a few times being secretive."

"What a guy."

Silence.

Once again I noticed she didn't ask me how I was doing. This time I wasn't letting it go.

"So don't you want to know how my days are going out here?"

She looked startled. Guess my voice was a bit shrill, but too bad, I was tired of one-sided relationships. Maybe they worked when I was somewhat together but now that I was a mess, I needed to talk too.

On the other hand, I was surprised I'd spoken up.

Probably all Charlie's talk about taking charge and reaching out to embrace life was sinking in, for I even found the courage to add, "You know, you *never* ask me how I'm doing or even seem to care. It's like you think my life is wonderful and yours is so hard. And when I do talk about myself, you cut me off and bring it all back to you. And what's worse is that I let you. I shut right up. But I don't want to do that anymore. I need you as a sister—a friend and confidant."

I held my breath, instantly regretting my outburst. I loved Carm and certainly didn't want to alienate her from my life.

To my surprise, she stared at me with wide eyes, then grinned. "Well it's about time."

"What?"

"I'm glad you said something."

"You are?"

"Yes. I always have such a hard time getting you to talk about stuff going on in your life. It's like after mom and dad died, you clammed up, keeping your distance from everyone, not wanting to get too close in case they die too. Or at least that was my theory."

"I do that?"

"Yes."

Come to think of it, Liam had once said the same thing to me.

"And I used to ask you all the time how your day was," she continued, "and you'd always say 'oh, fine'. Nothing else. I guess I got tired of coaxing words out of you and stopped asking and just kept on talking. Anything to fill up the constant silences between us. Now, it's a habit. Sorry about that. I promise to make a great effort to fix that." She leaned forward. "Now, come on. Tell me why you're *really* at a cottage, all alone, without Liam. I'm all ears. Really, I want to know."

So I took a deep breath and told her all about Travis. Every dirty little detail. Well, none of the details were really dirty, but you get my point.

She leaned back in shock.

"Travis? You mean the guy who dumped you at prom?"

I winced. Nevertheless, it was the truth. "Yes." But I had never really told her all of it back then. Only that we had broken up. Although I'd kept some of the truth from Charlie and Marta, I decided to tell Carm everything. I even shared Charlie's advice.

"Really? You're thinking about all that now?"

"Yes."

"How come you didn't tell me what really went on back then?"

"I found it too darn painful to talk about. And… I was embarrassed."

She shook her head, looking sad.

"I should have insisted you see a psychologist. With our parents' deaths and this Travis thing, I think you just kept everything in until it completely messed you up. I mean look at you. In a relationship with Liam—one of the nicest guys I know—and you're off here alone thinking of someone else. It was all my fault. I should have gotten you help a long time ago."

"It wouldn't have made a difference. I wouldn't have talked much back then, anyways."

Silence.

"Well I agree with Charlie. I think you should see

Travis," said Carm. "And get it out of your system."

"You really think so?"

"Yes, definitely. You need to find out why he's on your mind so much."

"I'm beginning to think the both of you are right."

"Trust me. We are. You need to face him again to get closure."

Would it be closure? Or would I be opening myself up to new hurts?

"And you don't want to lose Liam."

Crankiness flooded me. "You know, Liam isn't the saint everyone thinks he is. He has faults too, you know. He's not perfect." I knew I sounded like a bratty kid but I didn't care. Everyone seemed to think he was some kind of prince or something. Okay, guess I did too. But it still wasn't right.

"Never thought he was perfect. As a matter of fact, he drives me crazy when he explains medical issues in such great detail." She rolled her eyes. "I just ask him a simple question about surgery or something and he goes on and on. But you have to admit, he's a decent guy and treats you well. I even get a bit jealous at how attentive he is to you. Hangs on to every word you say."

"He does?"

"Yes, and the way he looks at you—whew—it's clear he adores you."

I'd been trying so hard to block him out of my mind, but just listening to Carm talk about him sent pangs of longing through me. I didn't even know what to say to her, I missed him so much. I sure hoped he was safe where he was. I stared out at the lake, as always, wishing my confusion would just go away.

Carm grabbed my hand. “So please, keep me informed. And next time I cut you off or ignore you, point it out. Old habits die hard, you know.” She pulled me into a hug and I wanted to stay there forever, it felt so safe. “Don’t worry. You’ll get this all sorted out. Now, c’mon, I’d better get those kids of mine home and cleaned up for our big outing tonight. Let’s round them up.” She pushed away, calling out, “Cindy! Cole! We have to get going.”

After gathering up all our picnic paraphernalia and a brief moment at the cottage where everyone changed back into shorts and T-shirts, they headed home with promises to visit again.

Tired, I took a nap and awoke to rain dancing across the roof. It was a nice sound, very calming, so I stayed in bed for a while just listening to it until I began to get curious as to how the lake looked in stormy weather. Hurrying to the living room, I looked out the window. Wispy fingers of fog wafted across the beach, reducing my visibility so I couldn’t see much. Disappointed, I made myself a cup of hot cocoa, topped it with marshmallows, and settled in the living room with my laptop. I eyed my phone. I missed Liam. Should I call him? Leave a message? Nah. That would mess me up even more.

Resting my head on the back of the couch, I let my thoughts run free. My promise to Charlie came to the forefront. Then I thought of how my sister agreed with him.

Maybe I should seek out Travis. Maybe it really would help.

I sat straight up, hit my Google icon and started typing. Maybe I could at least try to find out where he was. I didn't have to go see him but maybe knowing where he was would help me make a decision.

Nervous but determined, I signed onto my Facebook account and did a search.

Nope. No Travis Terrace. But there was a Jason Terrace. His brother, maybe? I seemed to recall a little brother running around. I crossed my fingers that he hadn't made use of any privacy settings, thus blocking me from any of his information. I also held my breath, then let it out with a loud whoosh when I saw that I could get into his pictures from the past couple of years. I quickly clicked on his Christmas photos and there he was—my Travis—and he looked all grown up.

Staring at a photograph taken a year ago, I knew that I'd recognize that grin anywhere. He was still handsome—a little less hair but gorgeous all the same. And wait, what was that? Looked like a picture of Travis in front of… I peered closer—a bookstore. I squinted to read the name—*TT'S TOMES & TEA*. I laughed at the word tomes, for that was he called books. Of course, that was its meaning but no one usually used that word back in high school, except Travis who used to walk around saying that 'he had just read a tome'. Another quirk of his.

He owned a bookstore?

But really, how could I be surprised about that? With all the reading he did and his fascination with books, it'd be a surprise if he didn't. I grinned at the use of his initials as I Googled the name of the store. Clicking on images, I saw picture after picture of his business with a grinning Travis outside it, looking proud as anything. Obviously a dream come true for him.

I then found his website and looked at his contact information. The store was in Simcoe, Ontario. I gasped. Just twenty minutes away.

Was this fate at work? Coincidence? Did I subconsciously know where he lived and picked a place nearby?

But then again, not a huge surprise. Travis had never aspired to traveling far away, content in his own little world of stories. I remembered him even turning down a chance to go to Florida during March Break, wanting only to spend the week with his stack of books, saying "I'd rather travel in my mind then deal with hot, sweaty weather.' So I should have guessed he wouldn't have settled too far away from Hamilton.

Should I drop by?

Were Charlie and my sister right? Should I seek him out? Find out why I was thinking about him? Pretend to be buying a book? Yeah right, like anyone would fall for that.

Nah! Seeing him could make it all worse. I was frightened of how I felt. No telling how I'd be if I actually saw him. What I really needed to do was forget him. Yeah, that was what I was going to do. Shut him out of my mind, like I'd been trying to do the past couple of weeks.

I slammed down the lid on my laptop, making a vow that every time I thought of him I'd banish him back into my 'forget-about-him' files.

This time, for good.

Liam came back to mind and I glanced at my phone again. *Awww... what the hell.* I opened up my laptop and looked up the number he'd added to the end of his email and quickly dialed it before I chickened out. My message was simple—just wanted him to know that I'd received his email and hoped he would have a wonderfully fulfilling experience. Not sure why I did it. Just somehow wanted to feel close to him.

Eleven

My eyes popped open.

Was that a knock I heard?

I sat straight up and glanced at the clock. Four a.m. *What the hell?* I looked down to find my laptop there and discovered I was still sitting on the couch. I'd obviously never made it to bed and had dozed off in the living room. And owwwww—my neck hurt like anything. I reached up to try to massage away the pain. Guess I'd fallen asleep with my head off to the side.

The doorbell rang out.

What? I hadn't imagined that someone was at the door? No one would be visiting me this early. Not even Moxie. And besides she'd bark, not knock. As smart as she was, I didn't think she'd be able to manage that. In my sleepy state, I stifled a grin at the thought, forgetting about any noises I'd heard.

Ring! Ring!

I shook my head trying to clear out my foggy, sleep-infused brain as I cautiously put my computer down on the coffee table, tip-toed to the window and looked out. A frazzled looking Izzy was standing on the doorstep, hair askew, Timmy wrapped in her arms, Jimmy standing beside her.

I quickly opened the door.

"What's wrong?"

"It's Timmy, he's burning up. I saw your light on, figured you were up and wondered if you could maybe watch Jimmy while I go to the hospital, just until Charlie can take over. Jimmy's so worried about his brother that he won't stop crying and… " Her voice lowered to a whisper, "I can't deal with both him and his brother right now." She looked like she would keel over at any moment.

I glanced down at Jimmy's tearful face.

"I don't wanna leave my brother!" he screamed, wrapping his arms around his mom's legs.

My heart went out to him and I didn't blame him one bit. I'd want to be with my sister too, if she were sick. Instantly, my vice principal training kicked in.

"Look. Why don't I drive you? This way you can all be together and I'll be there to keep an eye on Jimmy." And besides, I didn't think Izzy could make it on her own.

Her eyes lit up.

"Really? But, I don't want to bother you that much."

"No trouble at all."

"I'll just go back to the house and get my purse."

"I'll be ready in five minutes and I'll pull up to your cottage."

Throwing on shorts and a T-shirt, I grabbed my purse and keys and drove over.

Jumping out, I helped Izzy put Timmy in the back seat

where she sat with him cuddled in her arms. Jimmy stayed up front with me.

"You okay?" I asked, taking in how scared he looked.

"Y…yeah, guess so."

"Let me know if you need anything."

"'kay."

"Where's the nearest hospital?" I asked Izzy, as I started the car.

"It's in Simcoe. Do you know where that is?"

Simcoe. Where Travis was.

"I know how to get there."

I should. I'd searched out various routes last night, in case I decided to visit TT's.

"Once we're in the city, I'll direct you," added Izzy.

The drive seemed like forever, but in fact it was only about twenty minutes before, after twisting and turning through various streets, I finally saw the sign spelling out ER in big red letters. I turned into the driveway and pulled up to the door, getting out to help Izzy and Timmy.

"I can't leave the car here," I said to Izzy. "I'll go park and come find you. Jimmy, you stay with me."

"But I want to be with Mommy and Timmy."

"I know, honey, but we'll go find them as soon as I park," I said, in my firm vice principal's voice, brooking no argument.

He looked about to protest, then shrunk down on the seat saying, "Okay."

I watched as Izzy and Timmy went into the hospital, making sure they made it, then started the car again and drove out, down the street and into the parking lot.

Luckily, it was still early enough to find a spot and within minutes, holding Jimmy's hand tightly, we were back in the Emergency ward and at the front desk.

"Excuse me. Do you know where I can find Timmy Knowles?" I asked the nurse who had her head down and was writing something on what looked like a chart.

She glanced up for a second, blinked as if surprised to see us there, and finally said, "Yes. Down the hall to the right. Room eleven."

"Thank you."

"They're checking him out, now," she smiled. "Don't worry, he's in good hands."

Guess she picked up on my anxiety.

"Good to know," I said, gratefully.

We took off down the hall, found the right room and entered to find Izzy sitting there on the edge of her seat. Jimmy ran over to her and once again wrapped his arms around her legs.

"How is he?" I asked.

"The doctor's with him now." She pointed to a curtained off bed. "And thanks again for bringing us. I remembered Charlie saying that Louise freaks if she hears the phone or doorbell ring in the middle of the night and I didn't want to scare her. I was going to call him in an hour and have him pick up Jimmy at your place."

"No problem. Have you and Jimmy had any breakfast?" I asked, noting her pale face and swinging into action mode again—a role I was comfortable with—a role I savored, for it was so much better being on the 'helper' side of things than needing help yourself, which was how

I felt lately. It'd be nice to pay a visit to my stronger self, for a change.

She shook her head. "No time for that."

"Why don't I take Jimmy and try to get some food in him and we'll bring you back a coffee and something to eat?"

"That'd be lovely." But her eyes never left Timmy. Worry lines were etched across her face.

"I wanna stay," protested Jimmy, tugging on his mom's hand.

Izzy squatted down so she was at his eye level. "I know, sweetie. But how about you go with Zoey and pick up something for me? I'd like that. Will you do that for me?"

"Okay." He reluctantly followed me out of the room.

After checking the map of the hospital, hanging on the wall near the receptionist's desk, I led Jimmy to the elevator.

"Can I press the button?" he asked.

"Certainly." I showed him which one to hit and it took three pushes but he finally got it right.

The cafeteria was just down one floor, so we were there in seconds.

"Are you hungry, Jimmy?" I asked, as we followed the blue arrows leading to the cafeteria.

"Kinda."

"Well, we'll see what they have."

The selection was small but I noticed they had a wide assortment of cereal in individualized portions.

"How would you like that?" I pointed to the rows of boxes on the counter.

His eyes lit up. "Wow! Hey, can I have two kinds and mix them all together?"

"Sure can." I laughed at how excited he sounded.

Grabbing some toast and a coffee for myself, we settled at a table in the corner and I watched as he opened up the flaps of the two small boxes and poured the cereal into the bowl, then mixed it all up with his spoon.

"Is Timmy going to be okay?" he asked, suddenly stopping what he was doing and looking over at me with worried eyes.

"I'm sure he is."

"Good. Cuz we need to practice what we learned in swimming class."

"Do you like to swim?"

"Yep."

He opened up a packet of sugar, dumped it on and started eating in earnest. In fact he was shoveling it in. Guess he really was hungry.

"Can we go see him now?" he asked, pushing his empty bowl away.

Or maybe he just didn't want to be away from his brother for very long.

"Sure. Let's go pick up some food for your mom."

"Okay."

I led him over to the counter that held about three varieties of muffins but his eyes fixated on what looked like a brownie smothered in chocolate icing.

"That's Mommy's favorite," he said.

I smiled. I could guess whose favorite it really was.

"Um, are you sure you don't want to take her a muffin?

Or maybe some toast? Cereal?"

"No. She'll like that."

"Well, okay then."

After picking up a large black coffee, I grabbed some creamers and sugar packets since I'd forgotten to ask what she took in it, if anything. When we got back to the room, I saw that Timmy was sleeping. Izzy beckoned us to the back of the room where Jimmy proudly handed over the rich dessert, saying, "Lookit, Mommy, this is for you."

"Just the kind I like." She hugged him tightly, as she winked at me. She knew her son well.

"I know. I showed Zoey. And don't worry if you can't eat it, I can do that for you." I winked back at her, stifling a giggle.

"Well, thank you."

"How is he?" I asked, when Jimmy pulled away to go over to see his brother. I was glad to note that her cheeks had a bit more color in them and she'd scraped her hair back into a ponytail presenting a less bedraggled look.

"They just finished doing x-rays and blood tests. They think it's a virus. They're considering admitting him, so they can keep an eye on him overnight."

"But didn't he just get checked out by a doctor the other day?"

"Yes, and he had started a round of antibiotics but somehow it just hit him hard last night. Guess I waited too long to take him."

"Oh, don't blame yourself. It must be so hard to decide when to go or not. Here's your coffee. Do you take anything in it?"

"No, just black."

I noticed Izzy's eyes bouncing between both her twins. "Don't touch that, Jimmy."

I grimaced as I saw Jimmy pick up some tubing and twirl it around. As much as he was concerned about his brother I could see how restless he was, especially if he had to stay here all day. That seemed way too hard for a six year old.

"Why don't I take Jimmy back with me and we'll go swimming and come back later?" I asked.

I saw the reluctance in her eyes and I didn't blame her. After all, I was a total stranger. She'd been thinking of leaving him with me this morning when she was in crisis mode, but only until she could get in touch with Charlie. Now she was probably calmer and thinking straighter, wondering if it was the right thing to do.

"Well… Charlie likes you and said you are a vice principal in a high school..."

I could almost hear her mind ticking away.

"Sure am."

She looked worried and about to refuse but just then Jimmy dropped a box of Band-Aids he'd found on a shelf and they flew all over the floor. Fortunately, Timmy kept on sleeping. As she helped me pick them up, she whispered, "I think that would be a good idea." Guess she figured it would be hard to keep an eye on Jimmy and focus on Timmy, as well.

"Wouldn't that be nice, Jimmy? To go swimming? Then you can bring back some books to read to your brother," she said.

"I'd love you to visit with me for a while. It'll be such fun," I added.

Jimmy stared at his brother, then at his mom. She nodded her approval. Smart woman—she'd given Jimmy a job to do.

"Um, okay."

"Call if you need us." I wrote my cell phone number down on a piece of paper and handed it to her.

"I will and… thanks."

"No problem."

We hung around for a few more minutes, then I led Jimmy to the door.

I must admit I was enjoying his company. He was so full of questions and enthusiastic about everything, it was fun to have him around. Especially since it made me start to view everything through his childlike eyes which was a real eye-opener for me and so darn refreshing. I definitely had to spend more time with my niece and nephew when I got back to Hamilton.

"Would you like an ice cream cone?" I asked, thinking all children liked ice cream and it would provide a great diversion for his worried thoughts about his brother. It was also eleven o'clock and I figured the stores would be opened by now.

He clapped his hands. "Yeah, do I get to pick out my favorite kind?"

"Of course, what is it?"

"Bubble gum."

"Oh, I like that too." And I did. I was a bubble-gum addict, not being able to enter a store without getting a gum out of the gumball machine. A silly quirk of mine, but a habit well ingrained. Liam teased me mercilessly about it and even offered to buy me my own machine. *Liam, sigh.* Seemed like everything reminded me of him. I quickly pushed him out of my mind.

I wasn't being completely honest, though. I had a secret reason for the ice cream. I knew I was trying to relegate Travis to the back of my mind, but now that I was actually in Simcoe, I was dying to see *TT's*. From all the research I'd done, I'd noticed on a map that there was an ice cream store called *Flavors* down the road from the bookstore and I figured while I was here, I might as well check it out. No way was I going to go into *TT's,* but I could at least see how it looked from the outside.

We parked near the ice cream store and Jimmy was thrilled to find out his favorite flavor was there.

"Cool," he said, licking his cone feverishly, a blissful expression on his face.

I went for a scoop of butterscotch.

"Want to walk for a bit?" I asked.

"Okay."

I could have taken him anywhere, for his compete devotion was centered on that cone, but I knew exactly where I was going. I led him down the street to *TT's*, then panicked. What if Jimmy wanted to go in the store? How would I say no, especially since he was upset about his brother and promised to bring back books? I glanced down and figured that would be the least of his concerns, as I watched him still working his cone and making sure he savored every bit of it.

But what if we ran into Travis? What would I do?

No way. The chances of that happening were very slim, weren't they? But just in case, I led Jimmy across the road so that I could get a good look at the store but not be near the entrance, just in case he walked out or in the door the minute we were in front.

Stopping to look at it, I had to admit—it looked fantastic. Quaint, sweet, intriguing and fascinating came to mind.

It was painted a soft gray with a burgundy-colored door and burgundy trim around the windows. The front window was enticing. *TT's Tomes and Tea* was written in burgundy across the window and a large wooden rocking chair with a green and white throw tossed over it, was lined up beside a small round table with a teapot, cup and saucer on top of it. A display of various books—a rainbow of color—were spread around the chair. The caption read: *Curl up with a cup of sweet tea and a good book.*

A lady walked out the front door swinging a bag and the mouth-watering smell of baked goods wafted out, reaching me across the road. Immediately, I sensed that Travis' store was special—a combination of cozy reading and treats—decadence at its finest. However, it left me with mixed feelings, thrilled that his business looked like a success but annoyed that everything looked great in his world while mine was a total mess. Sure, I knew that was a lousy thought to have, but I just couldn't help it.

Feeling a bit shaky being so close to Travis, I wondered if I should just brave it out and go in? Was I ready for that? Nah. Judging by the instantaneous speeding up of my heart, I figured now was not the time. I hadn't the courage plus I certainly wasn't looking my best, since I hadn't even taken the time to comb my hair this morning—just slung it back into a ponytail. Maybe one day but certainly not today. If I did venture in to see him, I wanted to dazzle him. Wasn't that the rule when you see an old love? You always make sure you look your best?

"What next?" asked Jimmy, swallowing the last bit of his cone.

Pulling out of a fog full of Travis memories, I stared at Jimmy who looked up at me, eyes all excited.

"Well, let's get home and go swimming."

"Yeah, goody." He grabbed my hand and we took off to the car but just before we set off home, I glanced back at *TT's*. Hmmmmm… maybe one day I'd venture in. It just depended on how curious I got.

Jimmy was silent on the way back until we arrived in Port Dover and pulled up to my cottage.

Even before unbuckling his seatbelt, he looked up at me, a tear drifting down his cheek. "Will Timmy be home soon?"

Guess his brother was never far from his mind.

"I'm sure he will. The doctors will take good care of him and get him all better."

Silence.

"Would you like to have a picnic after we go swimming?" I was hoping that would divert him from his sad thoughts.

"With peanut butter and jelly sandwiches?"

"Sure."

"Can we have it on your deck?"

"Fine with me." They didn't have one, so I guess it was exciting to eat on one.

"But can I go to Charlie's and have a cookie after we swim? As a treat for lunch?" Right, his daily treat. He'd just had ice cream, but what the heck. If it made him happy, I was all for it.

"Sure can."

"Goody." He unhooked his seatbelt and practically jumped out of the car.

I dug out the key his mom gave me and we walked over to his cottage to retrieve his swimsuit, towel and some books and then went back to my place so we could both change and head to the beach.

Jimmy turned out to be a pretty amazing swimmer.

"I take lots and lots of lessons," he said proudly, after showing off what he'd learned. "Me and Timmy race each other all the time."

At the mention of Timmy's name, he started to look sad again.

"Hey, are you hungry yet?" I asked, paddling over, trying to divert his attention to something else.

"Yeah. Can we go see Charlie and Louise now?

"Great idea."

After drying off and wrapping towels around us, he skipped all the way to the bakery. When we got there, he hurried in the door and ran right over to Louise and Charlie who were cutting slices of cake and putting them in the display case.

"Timmy's sick," he announced.

Alarmed, Louise looked at me. “Is he okay?”

“Yes. They’re just running tests.” I certainly didn’t want to show any worry in front of Jimmy.

“And we’re having a picnic on Zoey’s deck,” said Jimmy.

“Well, that sounds like a great idea. And I bet you’d like some cookies for that?” asked Charlie, with a wink.

“Yeah, chocolate chip, my favorite.”

“Of course.” Louise scooped about a dozen of them into a bag.

“How’s he really doing?” asked Charlie, pulling me aside while Louise occupied Jimmy.

“Not sure yet. It might be a virus. Guess we’ll have to wait and find out.”

“Are you going to the hospital later?

“Yes. I’m planning on it.”

“How about I drive you?” asked Charlie. “I’d like to see the wee boy.”

“Sure, that’d be great.”

“And one word of advice.”

“Yes?”

“Watch how much sugar Jimmy eats or he’ll be bouncing off walls.” He winked. “I know that from experience.”

“Good point.” I laughed. “I never even thought of that.”

He grinned. “Figured so.”

“I’ll try to keep it in control.” But I knew the battle had already been lost.

When Jimmy re-joined us, Charlie explained that he’d be taking us later.

"Can we ride in your van?" asked Jimmy, both hands clutching onto the cookies.

"Sure can," said Charlie, looking over at me. "How about I pick you up at your house?"

"That works for me." Charlie's calm influence would be the best thing ever at the hospital. For Izzy and for me, not to mention the twins.

Jimmy and I went back to the cottage and I had to run to keep up with him. He seemed so excited about our deck picnic and after we both changed back into shorts and T-shirts, he even helped me make sandwiches and arranged them on a plate. He put the cookies on another platter and carried them out to the table on the deck, while I brought out a pitcher of lemonade.

"Dig in," I said, when I realized he was waiting for me.

He hesitated. "Can I eat them in any kind of order?" he asked.

I laughed. "Sure. Go ahead. But let's limit it to two cookies, okay?"

"Only two?" He looked like the world had ended.

"For now."

"All right. I can save some for later, right?"

"Right." Although I'd try to steer clear of that, if possible.

I watched as he picked up a sandwich with one hand, a cookie with the other and alternated eating them.

"This is the best ever," he said a few minutes later, grinning at me, peanut butter and chocolate smeared all over his face.

I couldn't help but smile, but a few minutes later, I

noticed his eyes were droopy and within ten seconds he was asleep. Guess his early start to the day had finally caught up. I carried him inside and over to the couch, wrapped a blanket around him, then stood and watched. *Nothing could be more peaceful than a sleeping child,* I thought as I turned and went back to the deck, cleaned up, then stretched out on a chair where I could keep an eye on him.

Now that I had some time to think, *TT's* flew into my mind again. I'd been so close to Travis today and a bundle of emotions ripped through me—excitement, joy, fear, worry and yes, even a tiny bit of anger. Should I have gone in? I still wasn't sure I could handle seeing him. *Who knew that I was such a wimp?* As a vice principal, I made tough decision on a daily basis and nothing scared me. But the thought of seeing Travis reduced me to a frightened little kid.

"How's it going?"

I jerked upright to see Charlie coming up the deck stairs. Glancing at my watch, I saw that it was 4:00 pm and realized I must have dozed off as well. My last thoughts had been about *TT's*. *Groan.*

"Okay." I wiped my eyes, trying to wake up as he pulled over a chair and sat down beside me. "I saw Travis' store," I blurted out, albeit softly so as not to wake Jimmy.

"Pardon?" He looked puzzled.

"Travis owns a bookstore in Simcoe."

"*TT's*?"

"You know it?"

"Of course. Everyone around here does. Louise

provides their baked goods." He looked surprised. "So Travis is your old love? You never mentioned his name before."

"Yes. Have you met him?"

"Of course. He's the owner."

"What's he like?"

"A lot like you described him. Nice guy. I can now understand why you can't forget him. He's certainly well loved by his community and is always involved in some local cause. Even raises the most food for the Simcoe food bank. Did you go in?"

I shook my head. "Nope. Not ready for that yet."

"Mommy…"

I jumped up and rushed over to the couch. Jimmy was awake.

"I'm here, Jimmy. Time to go visit your mom and Timmy."

"Oh." He initially looked startled to see both Charlie and me but then did a half yawn, half grin as he slid off the couch. "Did you bring your van?"

"Certainly did."

"Goody."

After getting Jimmy cleaned up and remembering to pack the books for Timmy, we all piled into the van and it was a short trip to the hospital with Charlie pointing out local places of interest and Jimmy chattering on about anything and everything. Soon we were there and I led them to where Timmy and Izzy were. I noticed with relief that the boy was looking a whole lot better, less pale and more alert. He smiled when he saw Jimmy and Charlie.

"He's doing okay," said Izzy. "They're definitely still keeping him overnight, but it does looks like it's some kind of virus."

"How about I keep Jimmy with me tonight so you can stay here?" I asked.

"That's a great idea," said Charlie, definitely putting his stamp of approval on the arrangements.

Izzy looked relieved. "That'd be wonderful. I called his father but he said he can't make it down here." She rolled her eyes. "Not like I expected him to or anything."

Guess there was no good feelings there, I thought as she went over to tell Jimmy the plan.

Jimmy looked tired and didn't protest. Probably all the excitement of the day was finally catching up with him again.

"Can we watch a movie?" he asked.

"Sure can." I smiled.

And that was what we did.

After Charlie dropped us off, we went to his cottage and picked up some DVD's and watched the story about a pig called *Babe* which totally enthralled him in between, of course, chowing down on the popcorn I'd made. Sure seemed like his stomach was a bottomless pit but then again, I was matching him kernel for kernel. At least there was no sugar involved. Did butter count?

Finally, he fell asleep on the couch and I took up my perch on the chair, not wanting him to wake up in the middle of the night and be frightened. I was totally wiped out but had to admit, I had a smile on my face that just wouldn't stop, thoroughly enjoying having the boy around. The possibility of being a mother was the one thing I'd never explored. It was fun having a little person in the cottage—sure brightened it up. I couldn't wait to spend more time with him. Usually with my niece and nephew, it was a few hours here and there and mostly other people were around. Maybe I should start spending whole weekends or days with them. I was sure my sister would love that and it would give me more time to be around Cindy and Cole and children in general—something I was finding I loved. They were way more innocent than the teenagers I dealt with—less tarnished by life. I was having a blast.

Twelve

"So he's okay?" I asked, hearing the excitement in Izzy's voice clearly through the phone, as she explained that Timmy's fever had broken and he would be released that day.

"Great! That's a huge relief."

"Is Timmy all right?" asked Jimmy, who'd obviously heard the phone ring and came racing into the living room. We had just eaten breakfast and he was in the washroom getting changed.

"Sure is," I said, as I handed my cell phone over. Figured hearing it from his mom would make it all seem so much better. Sure enough, his eyes lit up and he couldn't stop smiling as he listened to the good news. He then handed it back.

"Mommy wants to talk to you."

"Thanks, Jimmy." He scooted to the hallway to retrieve his running shoes.

I listened for a few minutes, then said, "We'll be right over."

"Can I make my brother a card?" he asked, after I hung up the phone.

"Sure can."

I dug out some crayons from the box of toys and stuff we'd brought over from his cottage and pulled out some paper from my own stash. While I got ready, Jimmy got to work, spreading the paper on the coffee table and carefully selecting various colors to depict his thoughts. Sneaking a peek, I saw that he had drawn two young boys on a swing and had written 'I miss you' under the picture. Sweet!

"Great job," I exclaimed, enthusiastically.

"Can I take him some cookies too? These are his favorite," he said, getting up and reaching for the bakery bag on the countertop.

"Another wonderful idea." I pulled out saran wrap for him to cover them in, as well as some green ribbon I'd noticed in the kitchen drawer the other day. That was very thoughtful of him. Izzy was sure doing a good job teaching him compassion, sometimes a rarity in people these days.

After we were both ready, we piled in the car and took off. Jimmy was proudly holding the card he'd made and the cookies, practically sitting on the edge of his seat or at least as far as the seatbelt allowed him.

"I'm never going to fight with Timmy ever again," he promised, fervently.

I smiled. "That's a good idea."

"Whatever he wants to do, I'll do it."

My grin grew. *Yeah, like that would ever last.* My guess would be maybe for a day or two, if that. Nevertheless, it was a kind thought.

After parking, I trailed Jimmy as he raced into the hospital and had the elevator button pressed before I got there.

"See? I'm getting good at this."

"You sure are."

He practically danced in the elevator waiting for the doors to open and then he flew down the hall and into Timmy's room. A beaming Izzy greeted us and Jimmy ran into her arms, hugging her tightly. I wished I'd had a camera to record the moment. I'd entitle it '*True Love*.'

"Hi," Timmy said with a grin, sitting up on the bed, eyeing the cookies Jimmy had in his hand. "You got something for me?"

Jimmy ran over to hug him as well, then presented him with the card and the goodies.

"Cool," said Timmy, holding the card, but his eyes were on the cookies. "Can I have one now, Mom?"

"Well, all right," said Izzy. She looked at me, laughing. "I know he must be feeling better since he wants to eat."

While Timmy told Jimmy all about his medical tests, making a big fuss over the needles he'd gotten, Izzy and I sat nearby, watching the two of them.

"You okay?" I asked. "You must be so exhausted. I bet you didn't sleep one wink last night."

"You're right. I am tired but so happy that Timmy is okay and it's nothing serious."

"Do they know what caused it?"

"No. Just one of those things, I guess. Definitely a virus he picked up. Could be from anywhere."

"Well, let's hope that's the end of it, now." I reached

into my purse. "Oh, by the way, I brought your mail. Just in case it might be important or something."

She leafed through it, extracted a brown envelope, ripped it open and read the contents of the paper.

A worried look crossed her face.

"What's wrong?"

"Oh, it's their dad," she whispered. "He's going for full custody. At first it was just for more visitation rights, now he wants total control. I get paper work from him almost weekly."

"Really?"

"Yeah, he couldn't care less about them. Wouldn't even come to the hospital but his new girlfriend loves kids and wants them. I mean, that's ridiculous. That's why he left me." She shook her head. "He likes to be the center of attention at all times. I'm sure once his girlfriend shows the twins even more attention, he'll leave her too. Louise thinks he's doing this so he doesn't have to pay child support but I also think he's just trying to hook his girlfriend in even more. Give her everything she wants now, come across like a nice guy, then crush her later on."

I felt guilty. Here she'd been looking so happy and now she was worried again. Guess I should have left the mail at home.

"Are you going to fight him?"

"Of course. But he's a lawyer. He'll get good representation and I have little money to hire the best to fight him. Charlie gave me the name of a local lawyer and I've set up an appointment later this week. I'm basically just scraping by with funds I earn from my children's books, baking and my waitress job last year."

My heart broke at how sad she looked.

"What about child support?"

"Oh, I do get some but he's whittled it down to the smallest amount possible. After I pay for shoes and clothes, since they're constantly growing, there's little left over."

"That's a shame."

Wait a second...

"You write children's books?"

"Yes." She smiled.

"That's huge."

"Oh, nothing much. A series about Coon, the rocking raccoon."

"Rocking?"

She grinned. "Yup, rocking. He's a singer in a rock band with a baboon, a snake, and a sloth that travel around from forest to forest doing concerts for environmental concerns."

"What a great idea."

Were they in TT's, I wondered?

"How did you get started?"

"It began with bedtime stories. I was being creative about getting the boys to care about their environment and they loved the tales so much that I sat down and put them on paper. Then one day, I decided to publish them. They're self-published and a friend of mine does the illustrations but," she rolled her eyes, "they're not bringing in much money. I put them in quite a few bookstores on consignment, but I just don't have the time to do much advertising or seek out an agent to try to get them with bigger publishers where I might make more money. I'm also not sure they're good enough but it'd be nice to have some extra cash for the twins."

"I bet they're terrific."

"Who do we have here?" asked a booming voice.

Startled, we both jumped and turned towards the door. And there was a smiling Charlie holding a tray of coffees, chocolate milk and muffins. Squealing, Jimmy ran over, helped himself to a chocolate milk and took one over to Timmy while Izzy and I gratefully helped ourselves to a coffee.

"Phoned the hospital and heard the good news. Figure you'll travel better in the van and besides, Zoey has a visit to make," he said.

"I do?" *What was he talking about?*

"Yes. I think you need to pay a certain bookstore a visit."

"Books?" screamed Timmy from his bed. "I want some books."

Oh crap. Now I might have to visit Travis' store just to get some books, since I could hardly disappoint a sick child. I glared at Charlie who glared back, then winked, his eyes softening. Ahhh… it was hard to stay mad at him and besides, he was probably right. I needed to get this over with. Travis was right here, only a few blocks away, a perfect opportunity for me to face him and see what was going on.

"I just might." I winked back.

"What's this about?" asked Izzy, looking puzzled.

"Oh, nothing. I'll tell you later."

"Well, might as well make yourself at home." Izzy pointed to a row of chairs lined up across the back of the room. "We have to wait for the doctor to release Timmy. Could be a while."

We all sat around chatting and I thoroughly enjoyed listening to Charlie's stories about the bakery and how they began. He had a soothing voice and a colorful way of describing scenarios that wrapped you up in his spell. I was amazed to hear that Louise began by selling baked goods just out of their kitchen until she had a huge demand for whatever desserts she could come up with. So they added on to both their cottage and their home to accommodate the increased load of baking. It was a true success story.

After about an hour, the doctor finally arrived and released Timmy. I walked them out to the van and waved goodbye. Just before he got in, Charlie looked at me, waggled his finger and said, "Go."

Some people might have viewed Charlie's interference as negative, but I knew he was only trying to help, giving me the extra push I needed. That somehow this so-called 'together' vice principal was not clear-headed in the least, to solve her own problems.

So now I was left behind. Alone in the same town as Travis' bookstore.

Should I do it? *Could I do it?* Well, I could at least go there and figure out what to do later. Yeah, that sounded like a viable plan.

I drove over and parked down the street. Yesterday,

when Jimmy and I were across the road from the store, I had noticed a bench there, so I bought a coffee at a Tim Hortons nearby and headed there where I sat, sipped and stared at the bookstore. For some reason, I just couldn't bring myself to go in.

Hmmmm… I tried to get a handle on my thoughts.

What was I really thinking? Or feeling?

What was going on in my gut or heart, as my dad would say?

Well, for one, I was happy Travis had realized his dream, but did I really need to see him? After all, it'd been well over ten years. It'd be like getting to know a whole other person, for surely he would have changed as much as I had. I also wondered what Travis would think of seeing me after all this time? Would he even remember me? Would he have forgotten about prom night and his announcement? Maybe it had no effect on him whatsoever. Maybe he had just continued on with his life, not giving me a second thought. *How would I feel if that were the case?* And if he did remember me, would he even want to talk to me? After all, we'd left on pretty bad terms. Or at least, I had. I'd been damned rude to him.

I sat on the bench just staring, wondering if any of the people I saw go in, or walking past the window on the inside, was him. A few had dark hair but I couldn't see their faces.

I closed my eyes, trying to figure out what to do but all I could see was a kaleidoscope of photos of all the good times we'd had, while Adele's song *Someone like You* provided the soundtrack running in the background. In fact, I felt I was re-living the lyrics where someone went back to re-visit an ex realizing how wonderful he was and that she hoped to find someone like him. Was Liam like Travis? Nah, I didn't think so.

"Zoey? Is that you?"

My eyes flew open and I stared at a vision of shiny raven hair, sparkling green eyes, big toothy grin and, of course, at that particular moment, the clouds just had to open up. The sun shone down, encapsulating his image in a blinding, shimmery, floating cylinder, making him appear other-worldly—an extra-terrestrial or at the very least an angel.

I blinked, then peered closer. Oh no! It was Travis, looking as handsome as he always did. My heart raced as I looked around for some place to hide. Could I just get up and hightail it down the street? Pretend I'd never been here? Should I act indignant and say *you've got the wrong person, buddy* and walk away shaking my head as if he were a lunatic? Should I…?

"Zoey Avery? Is that really you?" the vision repeated, this time louder.

Mesmerized, I stood up, legs shaking.

"Er, yes." Should I have pretended I didn't know him? Nah, that'd be silly and I was sure he wouldn't believe that.

"It's Travis. Travis Terrace."

"Yeah, I know."

"I thought I saw you yesterday, walking up the street with a little boy. I figured I'd imagined it, but then Charlie called to say that I should keep watch, for you might be showing up today. It's great to see you." And he smiled wider, if that was even possible.

Charlie told him?

Damn.

"Good to see you, too." And again, all I could think about was—wow, the years had certainly been kind to him. He looked amazing.

I knew it was rude but I just stared. Soaking him in and …whoosh—*all the feelings I used to feel way back then, came crashing through me*. So much so, I started to sway. Worried I was going to faint, I grabbed hold of the back of the bench.

"Are you okay?" Travis asked, looking alarmed, as he reached out to take hold of my arm.

Crap. That was all I needed—his touch. Shrugging him off, I sank down on the bench. "Yeah, I'm okay."

"You sure?"

"Yes. I just stood up too soon, that's all."

"Well, can I treat you to a coffee?" he asked, pointing to my cup. "I see that you still love it. I remember how you once ordered four of them to go at Hortons and slurped them down as if they were some kind of life force or something." He grinned and I almost swooned. Did he still have to have those sparkly white teeth, too?

"Er… sure."

Damn. I sounded like the teenager I once was around him—nervous, jittery and in danger of making a fool of myself. And to think he remembered my caffeine addiction—hard to believe.

I got up slowly, dropped my cup in the trash can,

ignored his proffered arm and followed him across the street and into the store.

The delicious aroma of coffee and pastry hit me hard. I knew those smells too well from being at Charlie and Louise's almost every day. I looked around. The store was much larger than it seemed from the outside and the tall bookshelves were arranged artistically among comfy sofas, tables and chairs. The café was set off to the side with a long counter showcasing a variety of goodies. The whole scenario made me want to drop everything, grab a book, coffee, a cookie and settle in for the day. I also noticed a bulletin board with events posted on it. I moved closer to take a look and saw that Travis ran several fundraisers for local charities. Seemed like he was as involved in causes as I was.

Finally, noticing Travis staring at me, I quickly said, "It's beautiful. So it's all yours?"

"Yes, it is." He looked proud and well he should be.

"Your dream come true."

He looked surprised. "You remembered that I was always into books?"

"Sure do. I could probably recount all those stories you told, too." Hell, I remembered every little thing about him. I even knew how many freckles he had across his nose—an even dozen.

He reddened. "Guess I did overdo it somewhat."

I laughed. "You think?"

"I definitely had a wild imagination back then." He led me to the coffee pot. "Same as always? One milk? Two sugars?"

He remembered?

"Yes, please. I never did break my sugar habit."

I followed, as he carried two coffees to a little sitting area off to the side, the whole way there greeting customers. Everyone seemed to love him as I watched their faces light up when they saw him. He put the coffees down on a small table, left and returned with a plate of cookies.

"You still like sweets, right?"

"Of course. Some things never change. And especially since I heard they come from Louise's bakery in Port Dover."

"Sure do. They're the best. Here you go." He handed me one of the coffees after I sat down. "Now, what brings you to Simcoe?" he asked. "I don't flatter myself that it's to see me."

Guess he'd be surprised to know that I'd been thinking of him nonstop for months. I almost started to laugh picturing his shocked face if I told him that. But it was my little secret.

"Well, I'm staying in the area and just thought I'd look you up." *Lie number five hundred. I was sure I was up to that by now.*

"Really?" But his eyebrows raised. "Did you know I live in Simcoe now?"

"No. But I was looking for some books to read and a friend mentioned *TT's* and I wondered if it was you." I just couldn't admit that I was seeking him out on purpose and tracked him down via Facebook. He would think that was odd as hell—even I thought it was odd and I was the one who did it.

"You remembered that initial phase of mine, did you? That for a while I called myself TT?" He laughed and I wondered if he was nervous too. He didn't seem to be but he did have that little eye tic thing going on, which he used to get when he was antsy about something. Usually he was pretty unflappable, taking everything in his stride. I didn't think seeing me would be able to throw him off.

"Sure do. I was visiting someone at the hospital and decided this would be a good time to pop in, grab some books and see how you are doing."

"Hope your friend at the hospital is okay."

"He is."

"Good."

I looked around at the busy store where some people were curled up reading and sipping hot drinks, while others were scanning shelves searching for various books. "Looks like you're doing really well."

"Just lucky, I guess. I work hard at creating an atmosphere people seem to love. Like guilty pleasures—taking time to read a good book and enjoy a treat all at the same time."

"Excuse me, Travis. Do you have Marcia Muller's latest?" We both looked up to see a woman staring at Travis with adoration in her eyes. I didn't blame her. He inspired that in people.

"Sure do. It came in last week."

"Sorry to bother you but I can't seem to find it."

"No problem, Janet. I know right where it is."

"Excuse me," he said to me, with a wink. "I'll be back in a minute."

"No problem."

I watched as he helped the lady. He seemed born to do this as I observed his relaxed posture, even taking the time to discuss the book with her, telling her how wonderful it was. I glanced around at the thousands of books the store held. I bet he'd read every one of them. No wonder his clients came back again and again for I was sure his enthusiasm was an adrenaline rush for them. Another flood of emotion surfaced. Sigh. We had so much fun together. Like the time we ran out of gas, right in the middle of the country. Did Travis care? No way. He grabbed some cookies he'd brought and led me to a broken down old barn nearby and we had a picnic, the whole time swapping stories and watching the graceful gaits of the horses nearby as they trotted around the field. Two hours passed before he called his parents to come and bail us out with a gas can. How sad that those times had all ended so dramatically.

I had to get out of here.

I wasn't prone to panic attacks, but I was sure I would have a full-out one if I stayed here any longer. The memories combined with the present were colliding and I was overwhelmed—even felt faint again. I stood up.

"Are you going somewhere?"

I turned to find Travis standing behind me, looking alarmed.

I took a deep breath to steady myself. "Yes. I have to be getting back, and besides you're busy. Guess I shouldn't bother you when you're at work." I desperately needed to stop this jaunt down memory lane.

"Well, it is busy, but then again it usually always is. But I have time for you." And there was that smile again. Damn. But at least I felt a bit calmer and less panicky.

"Well, I won't keep you and besides I really do have to go. Could you point me in the direction of children's books?" I figured that wouldn't be so rude since I could then buy something and exit quickly.

"Oh, all right." He looked a bit puzzled but stayed quiet and led me over to a section equipped with tiny chairs and tables.

"Do you have any rocking raccoon stories?

He grinned. "Do you mean the adventures of Coon?"

"Yes." I smiled. "My cottage is next to the author."

"Really? She lives near you?" He looked surprised.

"Sure does."

"I'd love to meet her. I wasn't here the day she brought them in, so she dealt with an associate of mine. I can't keep those books on the shelves. I think I have only one left. I've tried to get hold of her, even left messages, but she never answers back."

"She's been busy. I'll let her know, though." It could mean more money for her.

"Please do."

He showed me where to find her books and we discovered there really was only one left, so I grabbed it. I then picked up several others about various animals for Timmy and on the way to the customer service counter, I snagged a few mysteries for myself, paid for them and quickly headed to the door.

Travis followed me out.

"I'd love to have you over for dinner," he said. "We have a lot to get caught up on. I want to hear all about what's going on with you these days."

Oh crap. Not sure if I could handle that.

"Maybe."

He looked at me oddly.

"Please think about it. I'd love to spend more time with you. I've been meaning to look you up for years." He handed me his business card with all his phone numbers on them. "It'd be just like old times."

"Okay. I'll think about it." But it was those old times I wanted to forget. And had he really meant to look me up? Somehow, I doubted it.

I left the bookstore in a hurry, glad to get out of there.

Was it a mistake to come?

Did it just stir up old feelings better forgotten?

Guess time would tell.

Thirteen

Where am I?

Panicking, I sat straight up in bed, heart pounding, before I realized I was in my bedroom in Port Dover. I hated when that happened—you wake up and forget where you are for a moment. I took deep breaths to get my heart rate back to normal.

Tossing and turning all night and alternately thinking of Liam and Travis, I hadn't gotten much rest and when I'd finally drifted off, I'd obviously fallen into a deep sleep—but only for an hour. That was all. Not a great way to start the day.

Glancing at my watch, I realized I'd better get a move on. Marta was coming to visit and I had something I wanted to do first.

Slowly climbing out of bed, still fuzzy-headed with fatigue, I pulled on shorts and a T-shirt and forgoing my coffee and walk, headed over to Izzy's. I was concerned about how Timmy was and if they'd made it through the night okay. I knocked on the door lightly so as not to wake anyone if they were still asleep, but Izzy answered, looking rested and grinning ear to ear. Relief flooded me. Looked like all was well.

"I come bearing gifts," I said, as I held up the bag of books I'd purchased from *TT's*. "Except I plan on keeping my copy of Coon. Hope you'll autograph it for me."

She blushed, saying, "Sure I will."

"And by the way, before I forget, TT's is out of your books. I bought the very last copy. You might want to give them a call so they can order more."

"Really?" She looked pleased.

"Yes, the owner said he left a few messages for you to call him back."

"Oh." Her face reddened. "Jimmy figured out how to work the message machine and I bet he erased them. I've caught him fiddling around with it a few times. I'll call today."

"Good. It might mean more sales."

"Great. I need that. Hey, do you have time for a coffee?"

I glanced at my watch. "Sure. Can't say no to coffee."

She stepped back so I could enter the living room, then follow her into the kitchen where the aroma of freshly baked pies greeted me.

"So Timmy's still doing okay?" I asked, looking around, as I settled down on a chair at the kitchen table. The few times I'd been here with Jimmy, I hadn't really paid much attention since my total focus was on the boy, but I now realized the layout of the cottage was similar to mine but with no wicker. Everything was made out of wood and very rustic looking plus a lot more durable to hold up against small children. Izzy had made it even cozier with the addition of framed photos of the boys, scattered throughout. It was warm and inviting.

"Sure is. Actually, they're both sleeping right now since they stayed up wrestling with each other late into the night." She shook her head. "Guess that's their way of showing how much they missed each other."

"Seems like they have that special twin magic going on. I've seen it with students at school. It's like they read each other's thoughts, finish each other's sentences and are in tune with what each other is going through. Like if one stubs his toe, the other feels a twinge of pain."

"Yup. They've been that way since birth."

"Can't believe you found the time to bake," I said, as she placed a mug in front of me, along with a pitcher of cream and sugar.

"I need the money."

"Heard any more from your husband?" Wasn't sure if I was being too nosy or not. Sometimes people wanted you to ask and sometimes they didn't. Figured I'd take a chance. Actually, I couldn't help myself. I was really worried about her.

"No. Just waiting for the lawyers to finalize the date for the case conference with the judge. I figure it'll be in the next couple of weeks."

"Does he spend much time with the twins at all?"

"Very little. Mostly he makes lots of promises but doesn't follow through. But I'm blessed with Charlie. At least he's been a well-needed male influence this summer. The boys adore him and hang on to every word he says."

I nodded. "Charlie's great. When are you meeting with your lawyer?"

"Tomorrow. I also arranged to re-mortgage my home to pay for it."

"What a shame. Where is your house?"

"In Caledonia."

"Well, I live in Hamilton, not far at all."

"I went to school in Hamilton—McMaster. Got my undergraduate degree and was accepted into law school in Toronto."

"That's quite a feat."

"Dropped out though when I got pregnant with the twins." She sighed. "It was hard to study, especially with a controlling husband who likes being the center of attention. He wanted me home and the house to be run like we were starring in *Leave it to Beaver* or something. I was always supposed to be dressed nicely, hair perfect, the house clean with quiet children when he arrived home. Like—dream on."

"Would you consider going back to law school?"

"Can't afford it."

But I saw the longing in her eyes.

"Or maybe, you can't afford not to," I said softly.

"You may be right. I sure miss the whole experience of studying, learning new things, being around adults who aren't demanding, wanting me to do something for them every minute. I love my children but a break now and then would be good. And I could definitely make a better life for them if I had more money."

"With student loans, it might work for you in the long run. I could help you look into it, if you'd like. I could check with our guidance head to find out the process of applying."

She looked stunned. "That's very kind of you. If it's not a bother, I wouldn't mind at least gathering more facts. I really can't even afford to rent this cottage but the boys had such a rough year that I just felt they needed time away from where the separation and divorce all took place."

"Any family to help?"

"Nah, not really. Foster parents, but they retired and moved out west to live near their daughter."

"Oh." Wasn't sure whether to ask more questions or not.

"Yeah, I was a foster kid. Taken from my mother at the age of ten, when the police found her passed out drunk in a park. Basically, just went from home to home for a while."

Liam popped into mind. That'd been his experience, too. Would have been mine as well if it weren't for my sister.

"Sorry to hear that."

"Well, my story had a happy ending. I lucked out in my third house."

"Thank goodness."

"Yes, found some foster parents I really hit it off with."

"A friend of mine had a similar experience," I blurted out, without thinking. Wow—since when did I refer to Liam as just a friend? I'd surprised myself but the word just slipped out.

"Really?"

"Yes, well actually, he's my boyfriend. Liam's his name. Or I think he's still my boyfriend."

I decided to be honest but once again, I was surprised I was talking about him with a total stranger. Guess going through a crisis together makes you closer, or maybe it was the Port Dover magic hovering around, making me open up to my new neighbors.

"So he was a foster kid, too?"

"Yes. Doesn't talk too much about it. Apparently, he was a bit of a bully back then, angry at the world because his mom died. He kept picking fights with everyone and after moving him from house to house, they put him in a group home."

"Must have ended up okay, if you're with him."

"He was lucky, too. He met a guidance counselor he adored in grade eleven. She reminded him of his mother, managed to secure his trust and with her assistance, he got his act together. From then on, he excelled at school and went on to be a doctor."

"It's always great to hear success stories."

"Sure is."

Silence.

"What's up?" asked Izzy. "You look lost."

"Ahh… well… it's just that I came close to being in one as well."

"Really? What happened?"

Surprisingly, I explained all about my parents—in sketchy detail, but more than I'd usually say.

"Wow. You've been through a lot. You're lucky to have your sister."

"Very lucky. Did you ever re-connect with your mom?"

"Nah. She died shortly after that incident with the police.

"Sorry to hear that."

She sighed. "She just couldn't give up the booze and although I loved my foster parents, it made me long for a family… a stable, happy, loving family like a lot of my friends had. Unfortunately," she shook her head, "I took up with the first man who promised me that. Everyone I knew told me Roger was too possessive but I was just as determined to see what I wanted to see. Never waited to figure out if our love was real or not. Turned out he was the wrong guy completely."

I wondered if Liam felt the same. That he wanted a real home? The forever kind and one that was warm and cozy and with a bit more color then all that beige we had going on in the condo. After all, he apparently did have one when he was younger and his mother was still alive. *He'd also asked me to marry him*. Here I'd always thought that he was kidding and never really wanted to do the whole ceremony thing and all along he'd been designing a ring. Had he always been afraid to talk to me about it because I was so against marriage? And then he mentioned that he wanted children—a complete surprise. But come to think of it. He was the one who wanted to spend more time with my niece and nephew—more than I even did.

Maybe I hadn't really known him at all.

Damn. Another thing to worry about, as guilt hit me hard.

"That's so sad that your marriage didn't work out," I said, shrugging my own thoughts away. Izzy needed some kind of response. I couldn't just ignore her.

"Well, guess that's life. I'll get it together somehow."

But she sighed again—a long and painful one. “Just wish the boys had a father who was involved in their lives, though.”

“And to think he’s taking you to court for total custody.”

“Yeah, go figure.”

The pain evident on her face was hard to bear and the more I watched her, I could see that she had a thick coat of make-up on over dark black circles under her eyes.

“Do you have any close friends? Who stuck by you?”

She shook her head. “Not even one. I was a textbook case of living with a controller. He kept me isolated from everyone I was close to, only approving friendships with people he knew. And of course, they all deserted me after the divorce. I was left with nothing.”

“That’s so awful.”

“I still keep in touch with my foster parents, though. But enough about me. How are you liking Port Dover?” She poured more coffee into our mugs.

“Loving it.” I wanted to ask more questions, but figured she’d probably had enough of her own issues and was switching off to another topic. I should know, I was famous for doing the same.

“I can’t believe you bought a book of mine. I would have given you one for free.”

“You’ll never make money that way and besides, I’m proud to know an author.” I pulled it out of the bag. “Signature, please.”

She smiled, got up, rooted around for a pen in one of her kitchen drawers, then came back and signed it.

"Thank you so much for all your help. I don't know what I would have done if you hadn't been around. Jimmy said he had the best time ever with you."

"He's a great little boy."

"Thanks. I think so too." She leaned closer. "Hey, I see you out walking with Charlie in the morning. Bet he's a big help."

"Sure is. He's a good listener. But so are you." I grinned and then, seemingly out of the blue, found myself sharing the whole Liam and Travis saga. Actually, I was quite curious to get her take on it all.

"Wow. That's a lot of sorting out to do. So Travis, the one who called me, is the owner of *TT's*?"

"Yes."

"Well… I say you go for dinner with him."

"I'm sure Charlie would agree with you. Guess I'm just afraid to face my feelings."

"Better than regretting anything later on."

"You're probably right."

"I think you know deep down that you should go."

"Maybe." I smiled. "Just not willing to commit yet."

"Mommy, where are you?"

I heard Timmy's voice. That was my cue to go, so I quickly stood up. "I'll drop the pies off, if you'd like."

"You would? That would be a huge help."

"No problem. And don't forget to call TT's about your books."

"I will, for sure. Thanks."

I left shortly after, not even waiting for the twins to find me there, so as not to disturb Izzy's morning routine.

I was sure she was trying to keep things calm for her boys. As I walked to the bakery, I kept an eye out for Charlie and Moxie on the beach, but I didn't see them.

"I'm the pie-deliverer today," I called out to Louise, as I entered the sunroom.

Louise looked up. "Great. I have a customer who has already laid claim to them. She'll be here in an hour."

"How's Timmy doing?" asked Charlie, who was sitting at the table drinking a coffee and not looking too well at all—very pale—and I noticed the hand holding his mug was shaking.

"Oh, didn't see you there. You okay?"

"Just a little under the weather."

"You're totally out of shape, if you ask me," said Louise. "You came back after walking Moxie huffing and puffing. I think we need to get you to the doctor." She looked towards me and I figured that she brought it up in front of me on purpose, wanting my help.

"I agree," I added, in my firmest voice. "You need to go."

"No, no. I'm fine. No use you two ganging up on me. I ain't budging and besides, you didn't answer me. Do you know how Timmy's doing?"

Damn, he was stubborn.

"He's doing well. So far, so good." I looked around. "Hey, where is Moxie, by the way? Thought I'd say hello to her, since I've missed our walk the past couple of days."

"In the yard. Come on, I'll show you. She'd hate for you to be here and not visit."

"Oh, you don't have to come," I said, worried over how tired he looked. "Why don't you sit there and rest."

"Nah. I want to talk to you and besides, I'm not an invalid."

He led me to the fenced-off grassy area at the front of the house, which faced away from the lake.

As Moxie came over yipping and yapping and wanting a cuddle, he asked, "So? Don't keep me in suspense. Did you visit *TT's*?"

"Yes, I did." I picked up Moxie who was determined to lick my face in her joy to see me.

"And…?"

"It was okay."

"Just okay?"

"Yes."

"Any questions answered?"

I shook my head. "I'm still not really sure how I feel about it all." I then shared what went on, figuring he deserved details after helping me out so much.

"I think you need to go to that dinner and see how the evening transpires."

"I knew you'd say that." I smiled. "Still not convinced it'd be a good thing to do. I feel so fragile lately. Like anything could set me off."

"It might help, though. That was the point of this summer escape, wasn't it? To sort things out? Could be you need to be around him longer. Don't let your fear stop you."

"Well, you're probably right."

"You're agonizing about him for a reason. Might as well find out why."

"I'll think about it."

"Promise?" He held out his baby finger.

Laughing, I clasped his finger with mine. "Promise."

After giving Moxie a final pat, I said my goodbyes and headed back to my cottage to scurry around and clean up before Marta arrived. I'd gotten really messy lately—throwing my clothes over chairs and not putting stuff away. My kitchen counter was covered with groceries I hadn't even bothered to stick in the cupboards, wanting to be outdoors all the time. I just never took the time to tidy up, only doing the minimum of housecleaning.

It took about an hour to make a dent in the mess but the cottage at least looked neater, so I now rushed to change into cleaner shorts and a T-shirt. What the… ? *My pants were tight.* Crap. Guess I'd have to cut back on all the sweets I was eating. Living beside a bakery was just too tempting and my stomach rumbled almost every time I thought about Louise's treats. They were proving hard to resist.

Promptly at twelve o'clock, I heard Marta's car pull up and she got out, looking chic as ever in matching fuchsia shorts, blouse and sandals, complete with a yellow straw hat which sported a flower the same color. She was adorable like—Barbie at the beach.

"Well this is a quaint set up," she said, touring the cottage. "Not my thing, but very nice."

"I love it."

She turned to eye me up and down. "I can see that. You look good, too. It must be agreeing with you."

"Thanks. Now, are you ready for lunch?"

"Sure am. Any swanky restaurants around?"

"I have a real treat in store for you. I'm taking you to the *Arbor* for a red hot and a glow."

"A what?"

"You'll see. I decided to give you a true Port Dover experience and apparently the tradition here is that at one point you must dine at the *Arbor*. It's been here for almost a hundred years. I thought we'd get our food and take it out to the pier and enjoy the gorgeous weather."

"Really?" Her eyebrows were raised in doubt.

"Really." I laughed. I could tell Marta was out of sorts about the whole thing, for she liked fine dining in very expensive restaurants, but tough, I figured it'd be fun and besides, it was a stand for me. Usually, we did things her way and I'd find a place that would suit her but this time, I was taking charge and doing it my way. I also hadn't been there yet and was dying to go.

We walked down to the *Arbor,* which was nestled by the lake, ordered and I laughed as Marta's eyes grew huge at the foot long red-hot hot dog. She also struggled over which glow fruit drink to have and settled on the peach one while I chose the cherry. We both added French fries to our order.

Carrying our cardboard boxes of food out to the pier, we found an empty bench where we spread out our feast. I giggled like a kid, as I watched Marta try to eat the hot dog loaded down with relish and mustard. It was the highlight of my day and I even laughed hysterically when she shrieked at the blob of green and yellow stuff that had the nerve to make its way to her shorts and stay there.

"I'll never get this out," she exclaimed, dabbing at it repeatedly.

"Of course you will. It's just a bit of relish and a small price to pay for such a delicious experience."

"Yeah, you're right." She grinned. "That was absolutely scrumptious." She shook her index finger at me. "But if I don't fit into my wedding dress, it'll be your fault."

"Oh, I'm not worried. I'm sure you'll be at the gym first thing tomorrow, running off the calories."

"I think you should be doing that too." I saw her eye my growing waist line.

"You're right, but living next to a bakery is tough."

"Awww… just kidding. You look great. You're always so skinny, it's nice to see a few pounds on you. Just surprising, that's all. And along with that tan, you look like a different person altogether. Healthier, by far. How are you really doing?" she asked, looking genuinely interested. "I've been so caught up in all my own stuff that I've forgotten about your issues."

That sounded like the old Marta. The supportive friend who really cared about me. Lulled by her interest, I decided to share. After all, I'd poured my heart out to total strangers, I figured I should at least tell my best friend. I was also mighty curious over what she'd say. It was like I was running a poll—trying to see what everyone thought about my having another visit with Travis. Then, I'd make my decision.

After my rant was over, there was total silence for a few minutes while Marta just stared at me, looking shocked.

"Go see him," she said, leaning forward, piercing me with her eyes.

"Really?"

"Yes. I had no idea things were this chaotic for you. No wonder you needed to get away. But go, spend more time with him, get it out of your system, then hightail it back to Liam fast."

"What? Go back to Liam?"

"Yes, of course. You love him."

Did I?

"Er, have you seen him around, by the way? Before he left for Mali?"

"Yes. We've been in touch. After all, he's Raymond's best man, but don't worry, we don't talk about you. I tried to but he shut right up and changed the subject. How are you going to handle him at the wedding?"

"I'll be okay. That day is all about you." Yeah, right. I was nervous as anything about being around him.

"But it's in three weeks."

"I know."

She hemmed, hawed, then said, "Wasn't sure if I should tell you but I saw him at Starbucks a few days after you left." She paused, then added, "With a woman and they looked kind of cozy together."

Could hearts really sink? I'd heard that expression before but never felt it until now. I thought my heart now resided somewhere around my toes.

Was Liam dating someone? So soon?

"Blonde hair?"

"Yes."

Bet it was Nurse Jackie.

I looked out at the water, not wanting Marta to see how crushed I was. But, then again, I was the one who'd left suddenly and dramatically. I guess I couldn't blame him.

"Sorry, I didn't mean to upset you."

"No, I'm okay. It was a risk I took."

"So go see Travis. Get it out of your system. Then run fast back to Liam. You haven't been gone that long for him to get too involved with someone else."

"I'll think about it." But it sure hurt like hell to imagine the possibility of him moving on so quickly.

Marta tried to get me to talk more about Liam, but I was all talked out between Izzy, Charlie, and now Marta. She got the point and we spent the rest of our visit snapping photos of each other in front of the lighthouse, on the beach and on the deck of the cottage. I then walked her to her car.

"Raymond and I have a meeting with the priest tonight." She sighed. "You know, I'll be glad to have my wedding all over with. Seems like planning it is like a full-time job in itself."

"After all the work you put into it, it'll be amazing. The event of the year. Don't you worry."

"You will make it to the practice run the day before, right? Even though Liam will be there?"

"Of course." I wasn't looking forward to it, but I'd be there. No way would I let Marta down.

After hugs and promises to see each other soon, she left and I sat out on the deck nursing a glass of white wine.

Should I go see Travis again? The consensus was yes. Would it help? Or just bring back old hurts again? And what about that panic attack I'd almost had at his store?

I gazed at the lake, seeking inspiration, when it suddenly hit me how odd it was that I was out here trying to sort out my thoughts about marriage and stuff and here I was situated in a cottage between two extremes. On one side, I had Izzy facing a painful divorce and a custody hearing. Divorce, of course, would be my worst nightmare, especially with little children involved. How hellish her life must be, dealing with a father trying to take her kids away. On other side, were Charlie and Louise who had been together forever and still seemed so in love after all these years. They certainly made a good plug for marriage.

Both sides of the equation were presented to me. Fate? Providence? Serendipity? Or a coincidence designed to drive me crazy?

Then there was Marta who was about to get married and my sister who had just gone through hell, thinking her husband was having an affair. Not to mention the other coincidence about Izzy being a foster child—the same as Liam.

I was in the middle of it all, messed up and confused, trying to sort out my thoughts while being confronted with all sorts of possibilities of what could happen in relationships.

My aunt would say it was God at work showing me the way through all kinds of examples of 'what could be', but I wasn't too sure about that. Or maybe, as my dad used to say—*"Opportunities to grow are all around us. We just have to open our eyes and hearts to them and find out what works best for us. Only then, will decisions be clear."*

Maybe I'd just been too busy with work to notice anything else all these years—like signs, opportunities, guidance. But I was sure noticing now. If I could only figure out what I wanted in life and what all my confused thoughts meant. I thought I lived for my job—that it was a calling, a ministry.

Now, I wasn't too sure.

Fourteen

So I did it!

I got up the courage to set up a supper date with Travis and tonight was the night. Currently, I was prowling through all the shops in Port Dover, looking for that perfect outfit. Usually, I was not much into clothes, mainly dressing in plain pantsuits for school, but I wanted something spectacular to wear to dinner. Something smashing. Something that would cry out 'I'm doing great without you in my life.' Sure it was silly, but what the hell. I mean, I could understand if it was a breakup just a few years ago, but I think my crush at fifteen couldn't care less that I was doing great without him. But at least it would make me feel better.

"May I help you?" asked a smiling, pleasant-looking lady in a store called the *Sandalmaker*, one of the trendy shops around the corner from *Willie's*. I wasn't crazy about salespeople bothering me when I shopped, but I'd already been to a few stores and found lots of nice stuff, just not something that grabbed me. I was ready to throw myself into someone else's hands.

"Well, I'm looking for something with a wow

factor." I grinned. "Something to wear when meeting up with one's ex."

"I get the picture." She laughed. "Formal or casual?"

"Somewhere in the middle." I eyed her flowery sundress that looked great with her blonde hair. "Maybe similar to what you have on."

She thought for a minute, then clapped her hands. "I have just the outfit. Came in this morning and I haven't even put it out yet."

She went in the back and emerged with a black halter dress splattered with green vines woven throughout the material.

"How about you pair it with this pale green shawl," she said, leading me to a dressing room. "The green will look stunning with your hair."

Wasn't sure about that, but I liked the dress and tried it on. Staring in the mirror, I twisted and turned around, catching what it looked like from every angle. Not bad. It actually was okay. Not too dressy, just right.

"How's it going?" called out the saleslady.

I stepped out, feeling a bit shy.

"That's definitely the outfit for you."

"You think so?"

"I do. Though," she winked, "you might want to loosen the straps to show more cleavage."

"Ahhh… don't think so."

"Oh, okay. It looks good the way it is, too."

Hmmmm… would it work? Give off the right image? Did I look like I'd made it in life? I smiled. If so, I should wear it all the time.

"I'll take it. Thanks for your help."

"You're very welcome. Drop in anytime, even just to say hello."

"I'll do that."

That was what I adored about Port Dover. Everyone was so genuinely friendly.

After paying, I celebrated with a banana yogurt ice cream at *Willies,* then headed home to do the usual stuff, shave my legs, do my nails, try and fix my hair into some semblance of a style and even paint on some makeup.

Two hours drifted by and a glance at the clock showed it was time to leave or I'd be late. I stared at myself in the mirror one last time before heading out. At one point I'd even chickened out and tried on my old standby pantsuit, but then decided what the heck and put on the dress I'd bought which I paired with black, strappy sandals. I left my hair down, not tied back in its usual ponytail and had even attempted some curls with the curling iron. Not sure I achieved anything great, but figured I'd pass.

Travis told me not to bring anything but I had picked up a bottle of wine earlier today, my mother having ingrained in me that it was impolite to arrive empty-handed. I'd also dropped into the bakery to see Charlie, hoping for a boost of encouragement, but unfortunately he wasn't there. That was a huge disappointment, for I knew he'd be thrilled that I was going and I would have loved one of his pep talks.

Suddenly feeling a burst of guilt so strong it took my breath away, I sat down on the bed for a minute. The one thing I was trying to avoid thinking about slammed into me hard—Liam. Oh boy!

Was this cheating?

Not really, I guess. It was just visiting an old friend. And after all, Liam might be seeing Jackie. For all I knew, they were even having a heated long distance relationship. I shook my head. I just couldn't deal with my Liam feelings too. Everyone was right—I had to do this—to see Travis on his own turf. Just being with him that one time hadn't solved anything. I needed to interact with him in his own home, be surrounded with everything that was Travis, and then I'd definitely get more a handle on what was going on inside my gut. Hoped so, anyhow. Also hoped I didn't do two things—faint or panic.

So I needed to put my Liam feelings away—at least for tonight.

Setting off to Simcoe, I turned the radio up loud to crowd out my thoughts and keep the fear at bay. I also kept stealing glimpses at the paper on the passenger seat where I'd written the directions. Sure wish I hadn't forgotten my GPS back in Hamilton. I was never that great at finding places, probably inherited my dad's bad sense of direction, for I always managed to get twisted around especially in subdivisions and I certainly didn't want to be late tonight. Turn left at Queenston, right at Simard and left at Chantry.

And there it was.

One forty-five Chantry Avenue—Travis' home.

I got out of the car and stood a few minutes, just breathing it in. It was absolutely adorable—like a quaint English cottage I'd seen in one of Marta's architectural magazines. She was always looking at homes, searching for her dream house and often I'd leaf through them while waiting for her to get dressed. This style had always appealed to me—simple, sweet and pleasing to the eye.

The graystone house had a thatched roof, brown trim and every color of flower imaginable flourished in the window boxes. Walking down the sidewalk leading to the front door, I spotted pansies but wasn't sure about the rest. Neatly trimmed shrubs were scattered across the yard and you could tell by the obvious care, that a lot of work had gone into this property. And there was Travis at the front door, smiling widely as he came out to greet me.

"You look beautiful," he said.

"So do you." And he did—crisp green shirt tucked into jeans—sorta like me, not too dressed up but an effort had been made, not to mention we even matched with both of us wearing green hues. It reminded me of all the work we'd put into blending together at prom. *Don't think about that.* The horrible feelings it evoked would ruin the evening.

"Glad you decided to come."

"Wouldn't miss it." *Okay, a mild lie.*

I looked around, mostly to stop looking at him.

When we were teens, his crinkled up smile made him look like a mischievous imp on the verge of doing something crazy at any possible moment. He could also swing into serious mode fast. It did me in all the time for often he'd say something funny in class, sporting a huge grin, then as I burst into laughter, his face would go all deadpan and I'd be the one who'd get into trouble with the teacher. He thought it was hilarious.

Thinking of those times, now had me on the verge of giggling. *Control yourself,* I thought. Didn't think Travis would take too kindly to my raucous laughter after all these years, especially since it would look like it was over nothing.

"Do you do the gardening yourself?" I asked, gathering up some semblance of control.

"Mostly. It's my meditative/Zen experience. I relax when I'm out putting my hands in dirt and making things grow. I even have a vegetable garden in the backyard."

"Really?"

"Sure. Come around and I'll show you."

We walked to the back where a colorful array of squash, tomatoes and corn were thriving.

"You do all this?" I was in awe.

"Yes." He sounded proud.

"And you run a business, too. You're amazing."

He grinned. "Well, thank you for thinking that. Not too amazing though. Just a hobby I love. You're the one who was always amazing, scoring straight A's on every test you ever took. And now look at you—Charlie said you're a vice principal."

I was amazing? I think not. I could think of several other adjectives that described me—confused, mixed up—to name a few. But this was the same old Travis—he never could take a compliment and immediately paid homage to the person saying it. At least that was familiar territory.

"But you own a bookstore, and I still think you're the one who's amazing."

He laughed as he led me back to the front door and into a large living room filled with an overstuffed couch, loveseat and several comfy chairs, all in muted blue. Colorful throws were tossed over them in that artistic way that looks just right and paintings of various scenery lined one of the walls. Cozy, was my first thought. Certainly no beige here.

"I'll just take the wine to the kitchen," he said.

All alone, I began to peruse the room, searching for more details of Travis' life. You sure could tell a lot about someone by how they decorated their room, as I took in the three wall-to-wall bookcases definitely showcasing his love of books. I moved closer to take a look, noting that he had a large number of Shakespeare's works, encyclopaedias, various biographies and best-sellers but it was mostly filled with noir mystery books and yes, I did remember that it was mostly mysteries he read. He also had what looked like the complete set of the Hardy Boys, as well as Agatha Christie and several that looked like rare editions.

"You've become quite the collector," I said, when Travis walked back into the room.

"Another hobby of mine. Started as a kid. After I began all that storytelling, my mother tried to get me to stop. She was worried that I couldn't tell the difference between fact and fiction, reality and fantasy. She may have been right." He smiled. "Anyhow, I kept on buying books and hiding them all over my room, under the mattress, at the back of my drawers and even in the basement, so she wouldn't find them. Now it's a relief to display them. A lot of them are ones I've had forever."

"Very impressive. How is your mom, by the way?"

"Doing well. She and Dad are currently on a cruise."

"Good for them. Didn't she have arthritis or something?"

"A few aches and pains here and there, but nothing as serious as she'd lead you to believe. They've been lucky." His eyes clouded over. "Sorry. I still feel bad about what happened to your mom and dad."

"Yeah, it was pretty awful." There, I was honest for a change and it felt good. Charlie would be proud. Usually, I'd just brush off a comment like that and say something trite like 'oh well, it's in the past.'

"It must always hurt."

"Yes. And I'm not sure I ever thanked you for being there for me."

"Don't worry about that. You didn't have to thank me. I wanted to help."

Okay, I was being honest, but I sure didn't want to talk about it much. I was afraid I'd burst into tears or something.

"This rug is gorgeous," I said, staring down at the blues and golds I was standing on, hoping he hadn't noticed my wet eyes.

"Picked it up pretty cheap at an auction."

Good. He'd gotten my message to switch topics.

I continued looking around, noticing the antique model cars on the mantelpiece above the fireplace. This looked like a real home and once again, it struck me how stark my own condo was. My mother's blanket was about the only spot of color there. If our homes reflected who we were, what did mine say about me?

Noticing Travis watching me, probably smiling at how nosy I was, I was sure he remembered past visits to various places and how I always liked to check everything out. He was right—I was nosy. I quickly said, “This is a beautiful home.”

“I’m happy here.”

I heard a noise coming from the kitchen. Raising my eyebrows in surprise, I turned to Travis, whose eyes lit up.

“And this is Bob. Bob Chalmers.”

I stared at the tall, portly man walking in from the other room carrying three glasses of white wine on a platter. He was ginning ear to ear and I noticed his eyes lit up as well, when he looked at Travis. Much to my surprise, he went right over and planted a kiss on his cheek.

Prom memories blazed a path through me and this time I was helpless to stop them.

“I’m gay,” whispered Travis, holding me close as we moved to the first slow dance of the night. “I never really knew when or how to tell you, but I can’t seem to hold it in any longer.”

“What?” I leaned back, staring into his eyes. Surely, I’d heard him wrong.

“I’m gay,” he repeated, his eyes dead serious.

My mind raced, struggling to understand.

“Is this a joke? A dare? A bet?” I asked, as I stopped dancing and pulled away. “Did someone put you up to this?”

He shook his head. “No. I just didn’t want you to get

the wrong impression. Everyone thinks we're a couple and we're not. We can never be and you need to know that."

I searched his face, still looking for a glint in his eye, telling me this was all a joke. Nope. Nothing.

"You're telling the truth, aren't you?"

"Yes."

"Are... are you seeing anyone?"

He blushed. "No."

"But there's someone in the picture?"

"Yes."

"Do I know him?"

"Maybe. Bob Chalmers."

"The guy whose parents own the karate place?" I didn't know him, but I did remember Travis mentioning him once.

"Yes."

He couldn't help himself. His eyes sparkled when mentioning Bob and it was at that precise moment I understood another old saying—'my heart broke'—for mine shattered in a million pieces. To find out the person I loved more than anything, didn't love me back the same way and, as a matter of fact, liked someone else—it hurt like hell.

I pushed away, running out of the room as fast as I could, spending a good hour in the washroom crying my eyes out.

I was in love with him.

Okay, I was young and most people would wonder what I even knew about love, but all I knew was that he was my soul mate, my best friend, the person I wanted to be with for the rest of my life. Oh sure, I admit it was a bit weird that we'd never kissed, but Dad always said the best relationships were built from friendships and that was what we had, a solid friendship. Besides, we were both shy and I figured intimacy would grow in time. Never in a million years did I clue in that he might not be interested in me the same way I was in him.

I glanced down at my sweet yellow dress. I was so excited when I tried it on for the first time. Now I just wanted to rip it off. It marked the second worst night of my life. The first being when my parents died.

"Nice to finally meet you. I've heard wonderful things about you." Bob reached out his hand.

Struggling to blast out of my horrid gut-wrenching thoughts, I shook it, registering his kind face and Travis' worried one. Maybe he too was off in the past, wondering how I'd take it.

"Nice to meet you," I said. *So they had gotten together and stayed together all these years.*

I tried to mask my feelings with a smile but a million thoughts raced through my mind. Oh, don't get me wrong. I had nothing against gay people whatsoever. I practically grew up with Marta's brother who was gay and I adored him. I mean, who wouldn't? Hell, he used to take us for ice cream all the time when we were kids. I also dealt with many students over the years, who were grappling with their sexuality. My upset at the prom was not about whether he was gay or not, it was just that as a teen I was in love with someone not attainable and it hurt—a lot.

Watching Bob and Travis together definitely showed

how much they adored each other. It was apparent in the looks they gave to one another and the ease they seemed in each other's company. I couldn't help but feel a twinge of sadness for that girl whose prom night signified the end of all her dreams of a happy ever after with the boy she loved. In fact, I never saw him again after that. Travis had tried to get hold of me several times, even showed up at my door, but I ignored him. On overload with my parents' deaths as well, I was just trying to survive day to day. Then before I knew it, he had transferred schools. Prom was our final moment together—a true disaster—or at least for me.

"Well, shall we eat? The food is ready," said Bob, obviously not sensing the tension, or just ignoring it.

"Bob's a gourmet cook," offered Travis. "Hope you brought your appetite."

"I did." But I wasn't sure I could eat anything. My stomach felt in a jumble.

Travis held out my chair for me to sit down, just like he used to years ago. Tentatively, I picked up my spoon to attempt some soup. Fortunately, the two of them were very comfortable at keeping the conversation flowing and I found myself relaxing and deciding I could eat after all. Good—because the food was to die for. And, as a matter of fact, I quite enjoyed the banter between the two of them—light-hearted, informative and fun. Not sure if they babbled on as a plan in case conversation was stilted, but they seemed perfect for each other as they told tale after tale about their trips. Guess Travis got over his not wanting to go anywhere for it sounded like they had been to almost every country possible. I sighed. And here I hadn't even been outside Canada.

"Bob's a literary agent, you know," said a beaming Travis. "I met him at a book signing."

"Really?" I immediately thought of Izzy. "Are you taking on new authors by any chance?"

"Zoey knows the author of the Raccoon Children series I have in the store," said Travis. "They're very popular. Can't keep them on the shelves."

"Really?"

"She self-publishes," I added, joining in, ecstatic to get outside myself to think of someone else for a change. Maybe with his help, Izzy could make some money, which would sure help her financial situation.

"I'd love to see her books. If Travis says they're great, they must be." Bob leaned over, squeezed Travis' hand, then pulled a card out of his pocket and handed it to me. "Have her call me and we could set up a meeting."

"Oh, wow, that would help her so much." I tried to ignore the fact that Travis squeezed his hand back.

"I'm always eager to discover a new author," said Bob.

"Great." I tucked the card in my purse.

After coffee and pecan pie, Travis asked, "Would you like to go for a walk?"

"I'd love to."

And we did. Alone, thank goodness. Bob stayed behind to clean up, declaring that we needed some time to get caught up and he'd only be in the way. I was grateful for that, for it'd be nice to have Travis all to myself. Certainly might help with my self-searching.

He led me through several winding streets to picturesque Wellington Park in downtown Simcoe, explaining that in the winter they had a gorgeous display of Christmas lights here. Apparently, it was quite the tourist attraction and people from all over travelled to the town to view them.

"You'll have to come visit in December to see them."

"Maybe I will."

Walking side by side was just like old times and I sighed, finding myself beginning to relax. Not for long though, for suddenly, seemingly out of the blue, a question popped into mind. One that was deep-rooted, hidden away, obviously festering, for I recognized it as the same question I'd asked myself again and again, way back when I was fifteen.

Should I ask it?

After all, this could be my only chance for an answer. Yeah, it was bringing up the past and I wasn't sure he'd want to talk about it, but who knew if I'd ever see him again?

Charlie's face tripped across my mind. That was all the impetus I needed, for he'd definitely urge me on to get answers. Taking a deep breath, I let it out, saying, "So why didn't you tell me you were gay when we first met? We talked for hours at Linda Lewis' party. You could have told me then."

He stopped in his tracks.

I kept my head down, pretending to be engrossed in watching the Canada geese who lined the river, fight over French fries left behind by a picnicker. I wondered if Travis would just get angry and walk away.

To my surprise, he took hold of my hand.

"I should have," he said, softly.

Damn. A tear rolled down my cheek.

"So why didn't you?"

Silence.

"Guess I was being selfish." He sighed. "I really liked you and I was afraid you'd have nothing to do with me if I told you."

"No way. I liked you, too. We could have remained the best of friends."

"Didn't want to take the chance, I guess. And I loved the way you looked at me—as if I were some kind of superhero or something." His hand tightened. "We had so much fun together and I enjoyed pretending we were a couple, hoping the whole gay thing would just go away. You see…"

I looked up at him. His eyes were full of pain.

"You see… what?" I asked.

"I was still coming to terms with being gay, equally trying to pretend it was okay, and then hating that part of myself. I did love you, you know. Just not in that boyfriend/girlfriend kind of way."

"So why pick prom night, of all nights?" That was another question I often wondered about.

This time, he lowered his eyes. "Well, it was really insensitive, that's a given. Especially, since your parents had just died." He hesitated, then continued, "For weeks before, the guys were talking about renting hotel rooms and getting lucky that night. Everyone was pushing me to get a room too and I wasn't sure of your expectations and

I just felt it was time to end the pretense." He shrugged his shoulders "Oh, I don't know, it was just so crass of me to pick that night of all nights. After all, we'd both been so excited to go and I ruined everything."

"Oh." Not a great comeback, but it was all I had. At least I had some answers, but something else was niggling away at me.

"Well, I need to apologise too," I burst out.

Wow—I didn't even know I was going to say that.

"For what? I was the villain at the time."

Hell, I knew what that felt like.

"I should have talked it over with you after the prom. You tried so many times but I just couldn't handle it. If I had, I'm sure we would have remained good friends."

He grinned. "Well, you're here now and we finally got to have the talk we needed years ago."

He opened his arms for a hug and I gladly obliged.

Was this it? What I needed? To get clarification and also apologise for my rudeness all those years ago?

"Do you have someone in your life?" asked Travis, as we pulled apart and continued our walk.

And I ended up telling him all about Liam.

"Sounds like a great guy."

"He is."

"Why is he not with you?"

"Oh, I just need some time to myself."

He raised his eyebrows. "Are you breaking up?"

I shook my head. "Not sure yet. Just so confused lately."

"Have you met someone else?"

"No." *Just obsessed with you,* but no way would I tell him that.

I saw that we had come full circle back to his house and I was glad. I was starting to feel worn out from all the emotional ups and downs of the day and didn't want to get into much of a discussion about Liam. "Guess I should get going."

"I'd love to see you again," said Travis. "Maybe we could recapture those lost moments."

"Well, er, maybe. I'm only here for a few more weeks, then it's back to work."

"Just think about it."

But did I?

Did I really want to see him again? Or was it just enough to touch base, find some closure, then move on.

I had a lot of thinking to do, I thought as I bid him goodbye and headed back to Hope Cottage, praying my refuge would help me sort out my feelings once and for all. I was fast losing patience with my constant swirl of emotions.

Fifteen

"Stop it," I screamed at the bright light flooding my bedroom. Dammit. I'd forgotten to shut the curtains.

Rubbing my eyes, I eased out of bed, not wanting to knock over the array of junk food scattered about the sheets, and yanked the pieces of material together so hard I almost ripped them down. How dare there be shimmering rays of gold, when I was so upset.

A loud beeping sounded out. "You, too, phone." I ran over, picked up the receiver and banged it down. "Enough."

With the exception of occasional forays into the kitchen for food—mostly chocolate and cupcakes—I had stayed in bed ever since I went to Travis' for dinner. I wasn't even sure how many days it was now. Five? Six? I didn't answer my door, phone, emails, and texts. Okay, yeah I was being totally selfish but I was hoping everyone would just think I was super busy. All I craved was alone time—all by myself—to figure out what was going on. I desperately needed to sort myself out, not get involved in conversations because of my tendency to shut down my own issues and focus on other people's problems. I took a stand by coming here and I wanted to honor my objective by tuning into my heart, even though it was painful to do.

So I saw Travis. Now what?

Sure, I was glad he was happy and I finally got some answers to questions from long ago that obviously had still bothered me. I even apologized for my own behavior. Could I now tuck that chapter away and just move on?

If so, why did I still feel so sad?

Damn.

Moaning and with a horrific headache pounding a drum beat in my head, I got up again and shuffled my way into the kitchen, took some aspirin, poured some coffee that I kept ready at all times and grabbed the bag of marshmallows I'd bought earlier this summer in case I had a campfire. Should I sit out on the deck? Get some fresh air? Nah, I headed right back to bed. Dark and gloomy was more my style at the moment. Some people drank, some did drugs when depressed, I pulled the curtains, made a nest of junk food and ate myself into a stupor.

Groaning, I grabbed a bag of cookies that was resting on the end of the bed and started making and eating marshmallow cookie sandwiches—two cookies with marshmallows stuffed in between them. *Yum.*

I felt like I was still lost, once again thrust back into a high school mentality—fifteen again—immersed in my love for Travis. Everywhere I looked, I pictured the two of us together talking and laughing. Next, I was re-living the pain of his announcement, while drowning in sentiment, wondering what could have been if we had been able to stay together.

Was I still in love with him?

Was that what this was all about? Was that why I could never commit to Liam? Were all those years with him a total waste of time when my heart belonged to my childhood sweetheart?

I didn't believe that. Not one bit.

I had no guarantee that Travis and I would have stayed together, even if we were officially boyfriend and girlfriend back then. Teenagers change so much and the odds were higher that we would have broken up. Besides, I was happy with Liam. Or at least I thought I was, until lately.

So what was it?

I shoveled the rest of my marshmallow cookies down my throat, even amazing myself that I could eat so many. My poor stomach. It was probably exhausted from the huge array of junk I was woofing down.

Hey, what was that…?

Whimpering? Scratching? Barking?

Was Moxie here for a visit? I hoped so. I'd welcome her any day. At least I wouldn't have to talk to her or explain anything.

Flicking food wrappers out of my way, I got out of bed and snuck up to the door to take a look out the peephole. Crap. Moxie was there, but Charlie as well. *Again.* Why didn't he just leave me alone? No way was I going to let him in. If Moxie was by herself, I'd open the door but Charlie would want to talk and I was not into that at the moment. I could just ignore him like the last time but damn, this time his knock was louder, more insistent.

Next, he started ringing the bell over and over.

"Zoey. Open up. I know you're in there. If you don't open the door, I'll break it down or call the police. I'm *really* worried about you. Are you okay?"

Call the police? Break down my door? Oh, right. Charlie was a retired cop. He'd probably just call up some of his friends on the Force.

"I mean it. Open up," he called out again, even louder.

That was all I needed—police officers questioning me. What could I say to them? "Oh, I'm just upset over my first love." They'd think I was crazy.

Feeling I had no other alternative, I opened the door and judging by the shocked look on Charlie's face, I must have looked a mess. I turned and caught a glimpse of myself in the mirror off to the side—globs of greasy hair every which way, pale face that highlighted huge black bags under my eyes, dirty stained pajamas and coffee-drenched robe with bits of marshmallow stuck all over it. Yep, I looked certifiably insane.

"Are you okay?" he asked, as Moxie kept barking, placing her front paws on my knees, trying to get my full attention. I picked her up and she immediately started licking my face, then snuggled into my arms.

"I'm okay," I managed to get out. I didn't blame him for being concerned. If the situation was reversed, I'd probably pick up the phone and commit me.

"No, you're not." He held up coffee and a brown bag. "I come bearing treats. Cinnamon rolls."

The way to my heart—sweets.

"Well, come on in."

No way could I say no to one of Louise's cinnamon rolls. They were way too good to pass up and besides, I figured I wasn't getting rid of them anytime soon. Charlie was too persistent to let up and now that the door was opened, he was going to use it to his full advantage. I wouldn't have been surprised if he had picked me up and carried me to the couch, just to make sure I didn't slam the door in his face.

We settled in the living room and I gratefully latched onto the hot drink. It was way better than mine as I tasted a touch of vanilla in it. *Mmmmmm…* I next took a bite of my roll. Delicious.

"So I take it the supper with Travis didn't go so well?" asked Charlie.

I shrugged my shoulders. "It wasn't too bad."

"No answers?"

Silence. I was grateful that he didn't babble on and gave me time to think.

"A few," I finally said, shaking my head. "You knew about Bob, didn't you?"

"Yes."

"Why didn't you tell me?"

"Didn't feel it was my place." His eyebrows rose. "You said no before, but were you really hoping to get back together with Travis? Was that what this is all about? Didn't you know he was gay?"

She sighed. "Yeah, I knew. Just didn't want to tell you because I thought you'd think I was crazy, mooning over an old love who was completely unattainable. And no, this is not about my wanting to get back together again."

He watched me closely, and I could almost hear the wheels turning in his head, but he stayed quiet.

Brushing strands of hair off my face, I asked, "What's wrong with me, Charlie? Lots of people get dumped and break-up. Why am I still crushed over this all these years later? Hell, it was so long ago."

"Did you cry when your parents died?" he asked, taking hold of my hand.

"What?"

"You heard me."

"What do my parents have to do with this?" I pulled my hand back.

"Did you cry?"

"Ah… not much." No, as a matter of fact, I remembered smiling all the time at the funeral home—trying to make everyone else feel better. Trying hard not to face the fact that Mom and Dad were gone and never coming back.

"And how much time passed before their deaths and the prom?"

"Two weeks. I almost didn't go but my sister insisted. After all, we had the dress and everything."

"So you were already in mourning when Travis shared his secret?"

"Yes."

"You do realize that you weren't in the best mental shape to receive his news. Did you talk about Travis to anyone?"

"Ahhh…. no. It hurt way too much."

"Did you cry over the fact it was the end of your happy

ever after dream with the boy you loved?"

"No."

"So you kept it all in. Not only the death of your parents but the end of your love affair."

"It was no affair."

"You know what I mean."

A mental image rose up in my mind—of a 'box' holding all those old hurts and pains that I'd locked away.

"Guess so."

He smiled. "Well, can you take some advice from an old man?"

"Sure. But who would that be?" I grinned, slowly pulling out of my foul mood. Couldn't help myself, he was just such a dear person, sitting there quietly, those mischievous eyes locked with mine.

"Me, of course." He continued to stare, as if gauging how I felt. He then took hold of my hand again, squeezed it and I squeezed back, now welcoming the strength I found in his touch.

"From what you've said, you had two sad events happen close together. One of them tragic and the other incredibly sad. Seems to me you never mourned anything—not the loss of your parents, nor the loss of your first love."

And... *he was right.*

"Guess I haven't. But why is it bugging me now? After all these years? I feel like such an idiot."

"Oh my dear, you are far from being an idiot. It was probably way too much for you back then, so you did what a lot of us do, just pushed your problems way off to the back of your mind. Unfortunately, that never works. They fester, grow blisters and ooze toxins. Usually, somewhere along the line, they creep up on us and demand attention. I think that's what's happening to you. Those old issues have finally burst free and are now refusing to go back into exile."

I nodded. "That's for darn sure."

"You're grief-stricken, Zoey. You've kept too many pieces of your life scattered about and now it's time to bring them all together. You also need a big good old cry about it all."

Cry? Yeah, right. Not going to happen.

"That might not be so easy to do. With the exception of that time I let loose in front of you, I usually don't cry at all."

"Not even in private?"

"Nope, not even then. If I ever feel the urge, I just get busy and do something to get my mind off it all."

"Well, I think it would do you the world of good, if you did."

Once again it hit me that I could solve everyone else's problems, but not my own.

"But when will it all end, Charlie? When will I have some clarity?"

My mind knew it would take time, but I was desperate for some reassurance that this sadness would go away at some point.

"Hard to tell, since it's different for everyone. It's like peeling an onion. You remove each layer at a time to get to the innermost part of it all." He pulled his hand away and held up his baby finger, grinning, "But one day, I promise that you'll wake up and the pieces will all fit together like a giant jigsaw puzzle—perfect and complete."

I entwined his baby finger with mine. "Promise?"

"Promise. I think you're doing what you should have done years ago—mourn all you'd lost when you were that happy teenager dreaming dreams and believing they'd come true. You need to face those feelings, in order to let them go. Oh, of course you'll be sad at times for I imagine you'll think of your parents all your life, but it will no longer rule you and mess you up."

"But what about Liam? Where does he fit in all of this?"

"I don't think you'll really know that until you've laid to rest your past."

"You do know that it has nothing to do with Travis being gay, right? I'm not a prejudicial, judging kind of person."

He smiled. "I know that."

Silence.

"Well, maybe you're right," I finally said. "I'll certainly give it some thought."

"I hope so. I hate to see you look so sad." He smiled as he stood up. "Just think about it. I have to get back to help Louise. How would you like to keep Moxie for a few days? She's been really missing you."

"You wouldn't mind?"

"Not at all. Looks like she's content where she is."

Moxie was still all curled up in my lap and I glanced

down to see her eyes firmly shut, fast asleep.

"I'd love her company."

He was half out the door before he turned and said, "Oh, and Zoey?"

"Yes?"

"Maybe you really are in love with Liam but are just too afraid to reach out and accept his love. Maybe you feel you don't deserve it."

"What?"

"You heard me. You need to take down all your walls before you find the truth."

Was he right? Did I feel I didn't deserve kind, sweet Liam?

I didn't have much time to think of that, though. Moxie heard the door shut and jumped off my lap and ran repeatedly back and forth between the door and me, probably wanting a walk. I think Charlie knew exactly what he was doing when he left her here. He knew that she'd get me out the door and in a sense, out of my prison, for she sure had me trained. No way could I deny her a walk. I hurried to change, quickly washing my face and dragging a comb through my hair.

Opening the deck door, I blinked, blinded for a moment by the brilliant sunshine which I'd been avoiding for days. Feeling shaky, but determined, I stepped out on the deck.

"C'mon, Moxie. I made it this far. Let's get going before I chicken out."

We had just landed on the beach when I heard a loud, "Yoooohoooo."

I turned to see Izzy and the boys trudging back to the

cottage after their pie delivery. I didn't feel like talking but I could hardly ignore them.

She ran towards me, saying, "I hope I'm not intruding. But I saw Charlie just leave and was hoping you were ready for visitors now. I was going to pop in after I delivered the pies. I've been worried about you."

"Yeah, you okay?" asked Jimmy, coming up to stare at me.

"Feeling better?" chimed in Timmy.

Izzy leaned over and whispered, "I told them you were sick."

I smiled at their concerned faces.

"Yes, I'm okay."

"Need me to take care of you?" asked Jimmy. "We could build a sand castle."

Now, how sweet was that?

"You're very kind, Jimmy, and thank you, but I'm doing all right." Yeah, sure. I was lying again. But one thing was definite—even in the midst of my sadness, I registered that I was lucky I had formed such a great community here in Port Dover with caring people surrounding me. Damn lucky.

While the boys played ball with Moxie, Izzy said, "Haven't seen you around in a while. Did the dinner not go so well?"

So I told her the truth. Might as well get it all out of my system even though I felt a twinge of guilt since I hadn't even told my sister or Marta. But Carm was newly in love again and Marta's wedding was in a few weeks. I didn't want to bother either of them with my sad news.

"So the visit didn't make you feel better?" she asked.

"Not much."

"What a shame. Glad you went, though. Charlie's been after me to make sure I face all my divorce issues. Guess it eats away at you if you don't."

"That's what happened to me. I ran away from it all."

"Easy to do. Er… hate to tell you, but I got a call from Travis. He showed Bob the books I dropped off and he wants to meet me."

"Great. Some happy news for a change. You could get a book deal out of all this."

"Um… do you want me to skip it? Seeing as how you feel?"

I blinked.

"You know, Roger was a real ass to lose you. Can't believe you'd be this loyal to me and we've only known each other a little over a month."

A tear rolled down Izzy's cheek.

"You were there when I needed you. That's someone I will value forever."

I was touched.

"Well, thank you. But of course go ahead and meet Bob. This could be your lucky break."

"Guess I should try anything that might help pay my lawyer bills."

"Definitely. Has the date been set for the case conference?"

"Yes, it's in three days. Charlie's coming."

"Would you like me to be there too?"

Her eyes lit up. "Would you?"

"Wouldn't miss it."

"That'd be wonderful." She wiped her face with her sleeve. "Well, I won't keep you, then. You need your walk, it'll get the color back in your face. And I promised I'd take these boys swimming."

"Well, I'm sure I'll see you over the next couple of days. If not, I'll meet you at the courthouse."

"Thank you."

I watched as she and the twins made their way back to their cottage, then Moxie and I headed down to the beach. It did feel good to be outside again but after about thirty minutes I was exhausted. All that sugar I'd consumed drained my energy, so I headed back home and to bed, Moxie curled up beside me after, of course, I cleaned up all the junk food lying all over my blankets. But every time I closed my eyes, sleep evaded me.

Was Charlie right?

Was I in mourning? Not just for my parents but for Travis and the end of my adolescent dreams? *Dad, sigh.* He was on my mind constantly—more so since meeting Charlie. Suddenly wanting to feel close to my parents, I jumped out of bed and fired up my computer, searching for my sister's Facebook, knowing she had a ton of family pictures there. Of course, I never added any to mine, for it hurt too much.

I stared at a photo of my parents' wedding day.

They had died so young—only in their fifties—and they had so much to live for—my dad's paintings were starting to take off and my mom had just gotten a new job with a law firm, after staying home to raise us. A pang of longing hit me so hard, it was like a slap across the face. I really missed them.

Thinking over my conversation with Charlie, I realized that I sure seemed to be running the gamut of Elisabeth Kubler-Ross' five stages of grief, especially the first four—*denial, anger, bargaining and depression.* I seemed to be flying through them at breakneck speed. Maybe my thoughts of Travis stirred up thoughts of my parents or maybe it was the other way round. *Sigh.* Guess I never did cry for my parents or for the loss of Travis. That part of my life was still frozen over—deeply preserved in ice. The last stage entitled *acceptance* seemed out of my grasp altogether. *Could I somehow help it along?*

Moxie, who had left the bed and wormed her way onto my lap, stretched and her front paws hit me in the face. I laughed.

"You'll help, right?" I asked, giving her the belly rub she clearly wanted.

Her soft *woof* of contentment was a good answer. I was sure having her around was the therapeutic effect I needed. Charlie was a wise, wise man.

Sixteen

"Oh no!"

Frustrated, I pounded hard on the steering wheel when an SUV plowed into the parking space I was counting on. I came close to flipping the driver the bird but managed to get myself back in control. Usually, I had way more patience than this but lately I'd been really short-tempered and anything set me off. Parking was so darn hard to find near the courthouse. Guess it was a busy place. Glancing at my watch, I decided I'd better find a space soon or I'd be late.

I drove up and down nearby streets, until finally someone pulled out and I scooted in right away, ignoring the other two cars vying for the same spot. I'd gotten there first. Shrugging my shoulders, trying to show a little empathy, I still felt a real sense of accomplishment. I was going to get there on time. Thank goodness.

Quickly walking the three blocks to the John Sopinka Courthouse to meet Izzy and Charlie for the case conference, once again it felt good to be helping someone else for a change. It took the focus off my own issues—a respite I needed. I'd even looked up who Sopinka was and discovered he was a noted trial lawyer who had been appointed to the Supreme Court of Canada. The courthouse had been named in his honor—an interesting tidbit of information.

Walking in the door, I was in awe at how big, shiny and regal the foyer looked. It was so intimidating that if I'd committed a crime, I was sure I'd confess it on the spot. Puzzled over where to go, I walked up to the last person in a long line-up—an impeccably dressed man, probably in his forties.

"Excuse me, sir. How do I get to the fourth floor?"

He looked up briefly from his iPhone. "You have to be inspected first. That's what we're all lined-up for. Did you think we were all just standing here for fun?" His head dropped back to his phone.

"Thank you," I spit out, as I stood behind him. I could think of a million other things I wanted to say but they involved swear words and I'd been raised to be polite. What an ass this guy was.

Tapping my foot in frustration that I still might be late, I finally made it to the front of the line.

"Please drop everything in your pockets in this bowl," barked out the security guard.

Damn.

It'd been cool out, so I'd grabbed my jean jacket which had pockets full of coin. Yes, I was a change-a-holic. Not sure why, but I hated paying with coins and always used bills or credit cards. Needless to say, my pockets were always filled with loonies and toonies until I emptied them out about once a week, which I'd obviously forgotten to do.

My face reddened, as I fished out my cell phone, a silver barrette, packet of gum and then… the huge fistfuls of coin I had in both pockets, dropping it all in the bowl, filling it to the brim.

Snotty guy turned to see what the clatter was, rolled his eyes and kept moving. He'd only had a cell phone to declare. *Show off!*

The guard, stifling a grin, checked my bowl, even fished through it until I was finally whisked through the turnstile where my stuff was returned to me.

Now chuckling loudly, he asked, "Going gambling?"

"Pardon?"

"Noticed all your change. Figured you were hitting up the casinos when you left here."

"You guessed my dirty little secret," I whispered. I was glad he was thinking that, rather than that I was a slob who never cleaned her pockets. And you should see my purse! Not to mention my car! Yikes.

"I do the same thing." He winked. "Maybe I'll see you there some time."

"Maybe." I waved at him as I hurried off down the hall, as if we were conspirators in some kind of plot.

Finally finding the elevators, as per Izzy's instructions, I took it up to the fourth floor and looked for conference room number three, where the meeting was to take place. I'd done a bit of research to see what happened at these types of gatherings and I guess it was an informal meeting where both parents outlined the issues and the judge then gave his point of view. The plan was that the case would be stopped here and resolutions would take place, without it going any further. I hoped it would all work out in Izzy's favor. I was keeping my fingers crossed.

I had just passed room number two, when someone yelled out, "Excuse me, are you Izzy Knowles?"

Startled, I turned to see a tall, blonde lady calling to me as she hurried to catch up. She seemed really nervous, repeatedly biting her lip and her eyes had a hard time focusing on mine. She also looked familiar, but I couldn't seem to place her.

"No. Izzy's over there." I pointed down the hall to where she was standing beside Charlie, outside what I assumed was door number three.

The lady finally looked at me dead on, seemed surprised, then smiled. "No way. Miss Avery?"

I stared at her. I did know her. Ann-Marie Parker. Got caught smoking dope in the washroom and I got her into drug rehab. She was graduating that year, an excellent student too. I wondered what she was doing here? And what she wanted with Izzy?

"Ann-Marie?"

"Sure is." She reached out to hug me. "Great to see you."

"How are you doing?"

"Wonderful, thanks to all your help. You got me on the straight and narrow. I'm a lawyer with Knowles and Wells. Soon to be partner."

"Well, congratulations." Knowles? The same last name as Izzy? Was she her ex husband's lawyer?

"What brings you here?" she asked.

"Oh, I'm with a friend. Just helping her get through a case conference."

Her smile dropped. “Not Izzy Knowles, by any chance?”

“Yes. Are you her husband’s lawyer?”

“No. Fiancée.” She flashed her ring.

“Oh.” I couldn’t even summon up another word to say. *Ann-Marie was the girlfriend who liked children? She was the reason Izzy’s ex was fighting for full custody?*

She leaned closer. “What’s Izzy like?”

“Absolutely fantastic,” I said firmly. “She’s a terrific person, wonderful mother and it’s totally wrong what her ex is putting her through.”

Stunned, Ann-Marie took a step back.

“But he’s a great dad and has way more money to make sure the twins are well taken care of. I think he should have full custody.”

Great dad? Boy, was she misguided.

“You’re wrong, Ann-Marie.”

Her face darkened and she looked miffed. “Please, Miss Avery. I don’t want to argue with you. You helped me way too much. Let’s just agree to disagree. But I would like to meet Izzy. It’d be nice to put a face to a name when the boys talk about her.”

“Well, follow me. I’ll introduce you.”

As we drew nearer, Izzy hurried to meet me. “Thank you so much for coming. It means a lot.”

“No problem. Er, there’s someone here to meet you.”

“There is?”

Ann-Marie stepped out from behind, reaching out her hand.

"Hello, Izzy. I'm Ann-Marie, Roger's fiancée. I was hoping to see you before the judge arrived. I just want you to know that you have lovely children and I absolutely adore them. And don't worry, I'll take good care of them."

Izzy looked shocked and kept her arm down, making it clear there was no way she was shaking that woman's hand and I didn't blame her one bit. Ann-Marie exuded confidence and I remembered her as a strong person—one who pulled herself out of a world of drugs, got it together and went on to pursue her dreams. She was a tough cookie and the enemy as far as Izzy was concerned.

"Oh, okay, thanks," said Izzy, her voice reeking of sarcasm.

"I heard Timmy was sick? Is he okay now?"

By the look in her eyes, Ann-Marie seemed to really care—that was at least good to see.

"Yes, he's fine."

"Oh, that's great. Well, I'll see you in there." She opened the door and looked back, saying, "Just glad I finally got to meet you." She smiled, turned and walked into the room.

"That was odd," said Izzy. "She even seemed kind of nice."

"She is. She's a former student of mine."

"Really? Do you have any pull with her?

"Doubt it. I did give you a glowing reference though."

"Thanks. Anything might help at this point."

"Who knows," said Charlie. "Maybe she'll be able to change Roger's stance, now that she's met you."

"Hope so," said Izzy, but she looked skeptical.

"How are you holding up?" I asked, noting her pale face, not to mention she looked like she'd dropped some weight and she had nothing to lose in the first place.

"Scared as anything."

"Is your lawyer here?"

"Yes. He's in there already."

"Hopefully everything will go okay."

"I hope so, too." She looked at her watch, took a deep breath and said, "Well, let's do this."

She opened the door, we walked in and settled ourselves down on the empty side of the table. Empty, except of course, for whom I presume was Izzy's lawyer.

"Is that your husband?" I whispered to her, nodding towards the man across from us.

"Yes, that's Roger."

I stared at him and watched as he turned his head to stare daggers at Izzy, probably trying to intimidate her. *What the... ? Get out! It was that snooty man from the lobby. That was Izzy's husband? Should have guessed. Once an ass, always an ass.* He also looked mean, a huge contrast to Ann-Marie who was by nature mighty but sweet. Right now, she was wringing her hands and kept darting puzzling looks in my direction. Her confidant air seemed to have evaporated and it looked like she wished she were anywhere else but here.

The door opened and in walked the judge—or at least I assumed it was him, for Roger stood immediately. We did, as well.

"Hello, Jim," said Roger.

He was on a first name basis with the judge? But, of

course. I guess being a lawyer, he'd probably know all the judges. That didn't fare well for Izzy.

"It's Judge Smith," he said curtly. "Please sit."

He didn't even look at Roger. Good. Hopefully, that meant he wouldn't play favorites. Roger looked taken aback but not for long. Soon that smug look was back on his face. I'm not an advocate of violence, but at the moment I wished I had a gun. Oh, not to kill, but to scare that anal expression off his face.

"So let's get on with this. You are looking for sole custody?" he asked Roger, who was apparently representing himself.

"Yes," he said firmly.

"Reasons please?"

"Two valid ones. First, I make more money and can provide better for them. Second, I'm engaged and will be married soon. They will then have a mother and father at all times."

Ann-Marie gave a weak smile, but kept her head down.

I looked at Charlie and rolled my eyes, then did a double-take. Once again, he didn't look that well. Guess we didn't help matters by dumping all our problems on him. Never thought about that before, but we probably stressed him out on a regular basis. I made a mental note to be more careful that I didn't bother him too much anymore. I didn't think his health was that great and the less stress he had, the better.

Turning back to listen to the proceedings, I was continually stunned at how loud, arrogant and over the top Roger was as he went on and on about how great he was and how the boys would be better off with him. Even Ann Marie looked disgusted for I could see her visibly cringe at times and even tried to slip down more and more on her chair. If she kept going, next thing you know, she'd be under the table. I chuckled at the thought, caught myself, and willed myself to pay attention but I was sure Ann Marie would agree with us—that Roger was coming across like a bonafide jerk. She was way too smart to be fooled. But then again, maybe not. After all, she was engaged to him so some kind of fooling was going on.

Then, it was Izzy's turn.

Fred Smith, Izzy's lawyer and Charlie's friend, looked like everyone's grandfather with his gray hair, hazel eyes and wide smile. However, when he started to talk, he was all business about what a good job Izzy was doing, listing her credits which were plentiful and detailed. He closed his argument by saying, "Just recently, little Timmy was in the hospital with a virus. Ms. Knowles notified her ex-husband immediately but he said he was too busy to come to the hospital. Ms. Knowles stayed with the boy every single minute, round the clock. She also arranged for the healthy twin to stay with Ms. Avery, a respected Hamilton vice principal, currently at Maitland High School. However, it should have been the father who was there, taking care of his sick child as well as the healthy one." He paused to let that sink in. His words were effective and packed a powerful punch. He then added, "So I think we know who the better parent is. It's easy to be with children when everything is going well, but when they are sick, that's when they need us the most."

Silence. Then, a loud gasp from Ann-Marie got us all twisting our heads to stare at her.

"What?" she said, pale-faced and staring at Fred. "That can't be true."

"It's the absolute truth, Ms. Parker," exclaimed Fred, indignant at being questioned.

Tears poured down her face as she stood up and stared at Roger.

"How dare you!" she screamed.

"What?" he asked, looking startled. "Sit down. You're causing a scene."

"I will not sit down," she barked out with a disgusted look on her face. "You lied to me. You said Izzy never told you that Timmy was sick until after he was released. I can't believe you never went to see your own son while he was in the hospital. What kind of animal are you?"

To my shock, she then stared right at me.

"If there is one thing I learned from you, Miss Avery, it's to always face the facts and take a stand for truth and all that is good. You made me face my demons back in high school and I'll never forget that about you." She turned again to glare at Roger. "I've been blinded by you. Totally missed out on clues that you are a scumbag. Sounds to me like you've put on a show to win me over and here in court, I see the real you. You're an arrogant fool who can't even be there when your children need you. Those truths are heightened by the fact that a person I respect," she nodded in my direction, "is sitting on the opposite side of you with someone who *is* worthy. Izzy is not the monster you make her out to be. *You* are and the best thing for these children is to stay with their mother." She pulled off her ring. "I've had enough and this is the last straw. This engagement is over."

Like the climax of a good movie, she threw the ring at his face, clipping him on the nose, wiped away her tears, stood up tall and marched right up to the judge, who looked stunned at the turn of events. After all, I assumed she was a respected lawyer as well and he would already know her.

"Please stop this, your honor." She looked back at Roger. "I will no longer be party to tearing those adorable children away from their mother. Forget it! I'm so out of here." She glanced back at Izzy. "Ms. Avery is right. You're a wonderful mom. You should be so proud of those beautiful twins of yours."

She then opened the door and slammed it hard as she left, making an exit Steven Spielberg would be proud of. I imagined she was thinking she was crushing Roger's face in the door jam, as she went. I wanted to stand up, applaud and yell, "You go, girl." But I kept myself under control.

Roger looked mortified and I thoroughly enjoyed the shocked look on his face. I was sure this wasn't too good for his reputation as a lawyer, either. I glanced at Izzy. She looked stunned but I could see a twinkle make an appearance in her eyes and I knew that she was enjoying the show, as much as I was. Charlie started to clap until the judge hit his gavel hard on the table, shouting out, "Order here."

The judge then glared at Roger. "Is this true?"

"Is what true?" said a loud, obviously angry Roger.

"Please remember that you are addressing a judge.

"Sorry, sorry," said Roger, but he didn't look too sorry. "Is what true, your honor?"

I bet he was just stalling for time, trying to come up with excuses for the behavior his girlfriend accused him of.

"Have you not been listening? Let me spell it out for you. Is it true that you didn't go to the hospital when your son was sick?"

"I'm a busy man, sir."

The judge rolled his eyes.

"Your honor, may I speak?" asked Fred, standing up. The term 'steely' eyed came to mind. He looked determined and forceful.

"Certainly," said the judge.

"In light of the recent update of Mr. Knowles' life and the engagement termination, I believe the boys would be better off with the arrangement the way it is, with sole custody given to Ms. Knowles. It is not like he really cares, as his ex-fiancée made clear, he is only doing this for her. Apparently, according to the twins, even when they're there, he leaves them with babysitters, his mother or girlfriend. They rarely see him at all. Not to mention he's always late with his child support cheques."

"Is this true, Mr. Knowles? That you are late with monetary support and you rarely see your children even when they're visiting?"

"Er…" he cleared his throat. "Guess so." *Pause.* "I'll try to be a better father."

"Please answer my questions and be specific."

"Yes," he said softly.

"Pardon?"

"Yes, my payments are often late. And yes, I rarely see them. I'm working all the time. Come on, your honor. You of all people should understand."

"No, I don't. That is no excuse and a shocking display of fatherhood. And you were only going for full custody due to your girlfriend's wishes?"

"Yes," yelled Ann-Marie from the doorway. "Don't you dare lie, Roger."

Guess she hadn't taken off after all. I hadn't noticed that she'd re-opened the door to listen in on the proceedings.

"Well?" asked the judge.

Roger took a minute, then nodded.

"Say it," said the judge.

"Yes, sir. I was only doing this for my girlfriend."

"This case is closed," barked out the judge, banging his gavel for emphasis. "Full custody will remain with the mother. And please be warned, Mr. Knowles. If I ever hear of you being late with a payment and not spending time with your children, I will ban you from ever seeing them again."

Izzy's mouth hung open and she looked stunned.

"You won, you won," I said, elbowing her.

"I really did?" Her eyes grew huge.

"Yes," said an excited Charlie.

"Oh, thank you, thank you, Judge Smith," she gushed.

He smiled, the first time ever in this meeting. "Just keep taking such good care of them."

"I promise, I will."

We all stood as he left, then Roger stormed out with a loud 'humph' but not before looking back and saying "This is all your fault, Izzy." Then he took off, probably in search of Ann-Marie to give her a real mouthful. He wouldn't take too kindly to being humiliated, that was a given.

"Thank goodness I'm no longer with that overbearing jerk," spat out Izzy. "This is my fault? Yeah, right."

I couldn't agree with her more.

"I say we celebrate," I said.

"I second that," said Charlie. "How about I pick up some pizza and we'll meet back at my house so we can tell Louise and the boys. I have champagne on ice since I was optimistic about a happy outcome."

"That's a great idea," said Izzy as we all filed out to the hall. I could see Ann-Marie and Roger arguing down the hall. We all tried to tip-toe past them but when she saw us, she walked away from Roger.

"I'm so sorry," said Ann-Marie to Izzy. "I put you through all this for nothing."

"What made you change your mind?" Izzy asked.

"For two reasons. First, you're friends with Ms. Avery, who I trust explicitly and second, I never knew that Roger refused to go to the hospital when little Timmy was sick. He's so damn selfish."

"Well, thank you for telling the truth," said Izzy. "You helped me enormously but most important, you helped the twins."

"You're obviously a good mom. Your children are well-behaved and very loveable."

"That's kind of you to say."

"Please," she handed over her card. "I've grown rather close to them. I'd be thrilled if you'd let me see them every once in a while."

Izzy took the card. "I'll think about it and give you a call."

Ann-Marie was beaming as she walked away, saw Roger, and then turned in the other direction. Good for her. I wanted to clap my approval. Looked like that relationship may definitely be over. I hoped so. Ann-Marie was way too good for him. How in the world did that jack-ass manage to win the love of two great women—Izzy and Ann Marie? He must pile on the charm at the beginning—until he got them, that is. And to think he blamed everyone else, not once stopping to fix his own shortcomings. But then again, how many times have I seen that? People just constantly found fault with others so they never had to change. I mean, why would they change? It was never their fault in the first place—or so they thought.

"Thank you," said Izzy, pulling me into a hug. "I knew it was serendipity when I met you this summer."

"Don't thank me. You're a great mom. It was all your own doing." But it sure felt good to have helped in some small way. It made me feel really happy for a change.

"Don't be so humble. You being here was an absolute God-send," gushed Izzy.

"I only spoke the truth." But my words were lost in the bear hug Izzy gave me.

"So, we'll all meet at my place?" asked Charlie, coming to join us. He'd stayed behind to chat with Fred for a while.

"Great," said Izzy, finally pulling away, only to pull Charlie into the hug.

"I'll be there a bit later," I said, when our group hug was finally over. "I have an errand to run first, then I'll get there as fast as I can."

Charlie raised his eyebrows and I smiled back. "I'll tell you later," I said, leaning over to whisper in his ear. "Don't worry. You'll approve."

Seventeen

Should I go?

Now that it was time, I wasn't so sure anymore. In fact, I was scared—wanting to run away.

"No, don't chicken out now," I screamed, then quickly looked around hoping no-one could hear me and come running over to help. I was alone, thank goodness.

But I'd made a decision and I was sticking to it. My determination over-rode my fear. I was going. I wasn't taking off this time.

I turned my key to start the car and wound my way through the city to the *Gateway to Heaven Cemetery* on the border of Burlington and Hamilton. I hadn't been there since we'd buried Mom and Dad over ten years ago. Sure, I knew that people visited their loved ones' graves on a regular basis, but I never had. Just couldn't handle that kind of pain. I'd rather just forget about it all. However, today, I felt I needed to be there. Not sure why but I was just going by a gut feeling that wouldn't go away, especially after Charlie insisted I'd never mourned my parents. My stomach was doing flip-flops, but I still wanted to see how I felt traveling down this memory lane that led to a burial plot. I was not looking forward to it but felt it was a must in my whole healing process. At least it was worth a try.

Driving through the gate and seeing the array of tombstones, I started to get nervous all over again. Cemeteries weren't the greatest places to visit at the best of times. No wonder they were the scene of many horror movies. I felt uneasy and I hadn't even stepped outside the car.

I glanced around. To make things worse, rain drizzled down making it all look even grayer and duller. Pulling into a parking space, I sat and stared off in space, wracking my brain, not even sure I would remember where their headstone was. I closed my eyes, getting my bearings, remembering arriving here that day and where we went. Thinking I could figure it out, I finally got out of the car, grabbed an umbrella and as if by rote, found myself walking right to where they were—up a small hill, down about ten feet, left then right, then right again and there it was—my parent's headstone.

Beth and John Avery—1946-2001. Best friends forever.

They were exactly the same age when they died—fifty-five—way too young.

I stood there for a while, just allowing my thoughts and emotions to surface, remembering how awful it felt when they lowered both coffins into the ground. So upset, I had felt like screaming my head off, but managed to control how I felt. And that seemed to be the pattern all these years—controlling my feelings, shoving them away, not facing them—*when my gut would rather scream its head off.*

Suddenly overcome with emotion, I sank to my knees, just staring at their names. The stone was pinkish in color, with two angels imprinted at the top and that was exactly who they were to me—angels—especially my dad. He was definitely my guardian angel.

Warm, vibrant memories tip-toed across my heart—Mom taking me shopping and buying me the exact pair of UGGS I'd always wanted … teaching me how to cook her signature cranberry cake with its secret ingredient which I was sworn never to reveal… Dad staying up all night to take care of a puppy, putting him in a huge box with a bow and listening to our hoots and hollers when we unwrapped him on Christmas Day… Easter when Dad dressed up as the Easter Bunny, hopping into our breakfast with baskets of chocolate eggs, and… all those long walks and talks with him, which usually always ended up with an ice cream cone.

Then… it finally happened.

At first I didn't realize it, for it was only a few tears escaping down my cheeks—next there was a flood. If I'd thought I'd cried a lot in front of Charlie, it was nothing compared to now. Tears poured out and I slumped over in total agony, dropping the umbrella, my fists pounding the ground while I screamed, "Why, why, why?"

Why did it have to happen? Why did they have to die?

Wrapping my arms around myself, I rocked back and forth, remembering the horror of the police showing up at our house. The knock at the door, my sister screaming, and my running out to see what was going on. The man and woman at the door, in police uniforms, told me everything I needed to know. My parents were dead—gone forever. I'd been eating a Popsicle at the time and I recall it melting, the juice running down my hand and onto the floor creating a purple, sticky mess. I was shattered, feeling as if I'd lost everything. To this day, I had never eaten another Popsicle again.

My Mom and Dad were gone. I was an orphan.

All through the viewing and funeral, I felt stuck in frozen mode. Not being able to cope with my horrid feelings, I tried to focus on others, making sure they were 'okay'. In fact, I was just going through the motions, feeling like a robot, trying not to show I cared—trying to be stoic and strong.

I looked around, envisioning the final burial, and picturing how surprised I was at seeing Travis there. Most of my friends were too scared to come—not wanting to think of their own mom or dad dying—but there he was, dressed in a black suit, his eyes staring at me, full of compassion. After it was over, he came up and gave me a hug, whispering, "I'm here for you, always."

Two weeks later our relationship crashed.

Charlie was right.

I'd never mourned my parents, nor the end of me and Travis.

It was way too much back then—a double whammy that hit hard. So I could now see clearly how I had figuratively stuffed my feelings away, locking them in a box.

And I was bitter... so very bitter.

It just oozed through me.

Because of what happened, I no longer believed in fairy tales, long-lasting love, families and happy endings. I no longer aspired to be married and kept my distance from people, for fear they'd die or leave me or tell me their secrets that would destroy our friendship forever. Instead, I turned into a work-a-holic at the young age of fifteen—first with schoolwork, then with my job. I planted a fake smile on my face and made like the energizer bunny, never stopping to think, to face my gut, to allow emotions to surface, to deal with them and move on. I became the ice woman, presenting a glistening, polished surface of competency with my prevalent smiles and hard work. Inside I was a frozen mess and it finally all caught up with me. It was inevitable.

Stretching my arms towards their tombstone, I screamed at the top of my lungs, "I love you, Mom and Dad and I'm damn sad you're gone. I miss you so much."

It felt so good to speak the truth for once—to acknowledge all my pain, all my love and how I was really feeling.

Then… *seemingly out of nowhere, a shot of rage roared through me.*

Damn that kid!

My hands curled into fists and now all I could think about was how much I hated that teenager who smashed into them.

Shaking, I allowed my anger to surface. Didn't even realize it was there.

"Hope he rots in hell," I spat out, surprising myself with the venom I exuded.

Once again, wanting to run away from all the pain, I forced myself to sit there, allowing wave after wave of buried emotion to surface, squeezing its way through the waves of confusion.

Then… a moment of clarity, as my father's face rose before me.

"Smile, baby girl," he'd say. "Live life to the fullest.

Funny how his words of wisdom always came to the forefront whenever I was sad. I remember him saying this to me several times, for I was always such a sensitive child, ready to back off when the going got tough, but Dad wouldn't let me. He'd always be there with encouraging words, urging me onwards.

Beginning to relax, I pictured him smiling at me. Recalling his incredible *'joie de vivre'*, it also became clear that I'd been living as if I were only half-alive and I needed to get on with my life—live it to the fullest—like Dad said.

A brainwave struck. Unclipping one of my earrings—a small golden cross—I buried it in the ground at the base of the tombstone. I then slipped the other one in my wallet.

I smiled, picturing my parents' faces, saying softly, "This way, I'll always feel connected to you and it'll be a solid reminder never to hide from what's bothering me, ever again." But I also knew that beginning in September, I was going to seek out counseling—just to make sure I dealt with it properly. No way did I want to bury things ever again.

Excited now, I couldn't wait to tell Charlie that this

sorting out stuff really worked. I felt the best I had in a long time.

Heading back to my car, I again felt uneasy—like there was something I'd forgotten to do.

I knew what it was.

Staring up at the heavens, I winked.

"Hey, I really don't hate that young boy who killed my parents. I was just angry. I hope he's also moving on with his life, wiser and more careful."

Somehow, I couldn't just leave my parents with all that rage floating around them and who knew? I might even find out where the boy lived and pay him a visit too. I knew forgiveness was an important part of healing and it might help—anything to get me going again.

Finally ready to leave, I took off to Port Dover. There was a celebration to be had—an important one and I wanted to be there.

To my surprise, after stopping at my cottage to clean up a bit, I pulled in just as Izzy and Charlie did. Guess their stopping for pizza equaled the time it took for me to stop at the cemetery.

Louise rushed out to greet us. "I can tell by the look in your eyes, Izzy Knowles, that you did well," she said, enveloping her in a huge hug.

"Sure did," said a grinning Izzy. "Mainly thanks to Zoey."

"Don't think so." I shook my head. "It's thanks to you for being an awesome person."

"You underestimate yourself. You had quite a lot of influence with Ann-Marie."

"Well, you're the great mom and today we saw true justice."

"Amen to that," said Louise. "How about some champagne?"

"I'd love some," said Izzy. "Are the boys out with Moxie?"

"Where else?" said Louise. "She entertained them all day."

"Well, I'll go get them and tell them the good news. They've been freaking out that they might have to stay with their dad all the time."

After the boys joined us, we ate and drank and partied. Charlie even got up and danced a jig, proud to be showing off his Irish heritage. Unfortunately, he was panting like crazy when it was done and I started to worry about him all over again.

"Care to keep Moxie a few more days?" Louise asked me in private, as I got ready to leave. Charlie was off showing some photos to the twins, so he was preoccupied and couldn't hear our conversation.

"I'd love to."

"Good. I cleared it with Charlie. Hope you don't mind, I told him you were feeling lonely. Quite frankly, I'm tired of Charlie coming home huffing and puffing after those walks."

"I don't mind at all. Any luck getting him to the doctor?"

"Nope. Stubborn man just won't go."

"Oh, no. I'll try again, if you want."

"Don't bother. He'll feel we're ganging up on him. I'll

just keep on nagging." She smiled. "Hopefully he'll give in one day."

But I could tell she was really worried.

After bidding everyone goodbye and collecting Moxie, I walked out the door to head home, craving a nap. I was wiped out by all the emotion.

"Zoey, Zoey."

I turned to see Charlie rushing to catch up with me. I hurried to meet him, so he wouldn't have to run too fast. His color was still gray and I sure hoped Louse got him some medical help soon. But I could understand her frustration. After all, it wasn't like she could just pick him up and carry him off to a doctor.

"You looked peaceful when you arrived. Hope you don't think I'm too nosy, but what happened?"

Excitedly, I explained about the cemetery visit.

"Good job," he said. "I'm proud of you. You're finally getting to the root of all your issues."

I hugged him. "Hope so and thanks, Charlie. I don't know how I'd have made it this far, if it wasn't for you."

"Glad to be of help."

"Sure hope all my puzzle pieces click together soon," I said, pulling away. "I'm tired of all the confusion I've been feeling."

"You're getting close." He winked. "Soon, very soon."

"I'm counting on it and hey, thanks for letting me borrow Moxie for a while."

"No problem. She loves spending time with you. It's like going off to summer camp for her." He grinned. "Dogs are great company."

"That's for sure and don't worry, I'll take good care of her."

"I know you will." He saluted, turned and headed back home.

Yawning, I went straight to the cottage and curled in bed with Moxie cuddled beside me. Surprisingly, I immediately fell asleep, dreaming happy dreams of my parents. I was sure I was on the road to healing. I hoped so, anyway.

Eighteen

I stared into the mirror, barely recognizing myself. My hair had been scraped back into what Marta called a French twist, elaborate makeup adorned my face and somehow the seamstress had managed to zip up my dress. I looked like a caricature of myself, albeit a classier version.

Today was Marta's wedding—the day I'd see Liam for the first time in seven weeks. My legs were kind of wobbly and I sure as hell would have liked to sit down but my damn dress was too tight to risk it. That was all I needed—a big fat rip in the fabric. Marta would kill me.

How did I feel? Besides shaky legs, hadn't a clue. Did I want to see him? Wasn't sure. A part of me screamed 'yes' while another whispered 'no'. I wished I could say that I had all the answers now and I was no longer mixed up. The truth was—I still hadn't figured everything out yet. I felt I was making headway, but when it came to Liam, he was still one huge question mark in my mind. As a matter of fact, I'd been so preoccupied with mourning past tragedies that I'd relegated Liam even further to the back of my mind and tried hard not to think about him. Most of the time, not always, I was able to stick to that, since I was so overloaded with other stuff.

“Ready to go, Zoey?” yelled out Andrew, Marta’s brother.

“Just about.”

“Okay, I’ll be waiting for you at the front of the house.”

“Great. I’ll be down in a minute.”

I’d been at Marta’s parents’ house since early this morning being doted on by an army of hair dressers, makeup artists and seamstresses. The bride had already left with her parents for the church but Andrew stayed behind to take me, since I wanted to leave for Port Dover right after the ceremony. My car was also my security blanket—ready to go in case I needed to get away in a hurry. Andrew had graciously offered to drive, so that I could semi-recline in the backseat, keeping my dress pristine and rip-free. Yeah, it really was that tight, especially with the extra pounds I’d put on. Even wearing spanx, couldn’t disguise that. I’d brought jeans and a tee to slip on when the night was over. At least that way, I’d be able to drive myself home.

Glancing in the mirror one last time, trying to get used to this ‘new me’, I whispered, “Good luck.” I felt I needed it for it was already shaping up to be quite a day, filled with excitement. Seeing Liam would send it into overdrive. Well, might as well leave and get it over with. Great way of looking at a wedding, huh?

Somehow I managed to make it down the stairs, taking teeny, tiny steps, and into my car.

"You look amazing," said a grinning Andrew, as I managed to swing my legs into the back seat and stretch out. "Must have had a great designer." He patted himself on the back.

"Only the best. And hey, you look pretty great yourself."

"You don't think I look too flamboyant, do you?"

"Not in the least."

We both burst into laughter, knowing darn well that he looked outrageous—just the way he liked and planned it.

Andrew always dressed to shock, similar to Marta, and I'd gotten used to it. I wasn't sure who fed off of whom, but the two of them had been standing out in a crowd since they were kids. Their parents had always let them dress the way they wanted and their get-ups were legendary. It certainly led to their career choices. Oh, guess I forgot to mention that Andrew was a bride's 'man'. Although Marta wanted a lot of people at her wedding, she kept the wedding party small—just me and Andrew. Liam was the best man and Raymond's college roommate was the only other usher. Andrew was given a choice and elected to be with me, since he wanted to wear purple to match my dress, hence the purple tuxedo. He even had purple streaks in his hair and begged me to do the same but I drew the line at that. Definitely not my style.

"Did you get a chance to see Marta by any chance?" I asked, curious.

She'd insisted that no one see her, except her parents, until she was walking down that aisle. Her goal was to make a real appearance—wow everyone—like a movie star on the red carpet. I'd only seen her for a brief moment early this morning to give her a hug and reassure her that everything would be okay, before she was whisked off by her wedding planner to get her hair done. She was in her pajamas then and although I'd snuck a peek in her room, there was no sign of her dress.

"Nope. Haven't seen her."

"Really? Her own brother?"

"Yeah, how cruel is that? I might have been able to add some finishing touches."

"That was probably what she was hoping to avoid." I grinned. "And as for my design, why so low cut?"

"The bride's choice."

"Really?"

"Yes. I know what a prude you are." He chuckled. "I wouldn't have done that to you but Marta's the boss."

"Great, just great. Otherwise it's a lovely dress."

"Yeah, right. I know you're just saying that but thanks, anyway."

"No, really, I love the color."

"I agree. Dark purple suits you. Shows off that red hair of yours."

"Guess so. Is Justin here?"

"Sure thing. Wouldn't come without him. He's already at the church."

"Good. He's a great guy."

"That, he is."

Justin was Andrew's beau. They'd been together for over ten years and he was as quiet and down to earth as

Andrew was ostentatious. Opposites definitely were attracted in their case.

"Well, we're here," said Andrew.

He pulled into St. Basil's parking lot and I gave thanks that the church was only just down the street since I felt mighty uncomfortable sprawled out like this. However, at the realization that we had arrived, the butterflies in my stomach fluttered up a notch. Was the fact that I felt I was going to throw up significant?

Get it together, Zoey.

I was here for one reason only—for Marta. I couldn't forget that and get lost in my own baggage. This was her big day and she'd definitely need some moral support. I'd even practiced saying, "Everything will be okay" in a calm manner, which I'd already used once today but was anticipating many more anxious moments.

I slowly got out of the car, glad that Andrew was there to help me, or pull me out was more like it, and walked into the church. Every step increased my uneasy feelings. Panicking, I was grateful to see the signs for the washrooms right away. I thought I'd duck in there to pull myself together. Maybe take some Tylenol, as well, for a headache that was fast approaching.

"Thanks, Andrew. Guess I'll see you in there."

"You bet." He took off down the hall to meet up with his parents. I was glad to be alone, as I headed the opposite way. Taking a few deep breaths, I pushed open the door and *what the… ?*

It took a few seconds to figure out what I was seeing.

I started to laugh.

"Fancy meeting you here," I said, witnessing Marta trying to squeeze herself out of a stall. She looked stuck. One foot was out and her arms reached back to pull the yards and yards of silk along with her. I hurried over to help. Balancing on six inch stilettoes was not something one could do easily and she looked like she was about to topple over in a heap.

"Oh thank goodness you're here," exclaimed Marta, practically in tears. "Please help me. I had visions of spending my whole wedding day stuck in this stall."

"Everything will be okay," I said, as if by rote.

"And stop saying that," she exclaimed, obviously clearly exasperated.

Guess she was on to me.

I tugged and tucked, grunted and swore, but soon she was out in one piece.

"Did I rip anything?" she asked, looking like she was about to cry.

Walking around her, taking it all in, I said, "Nope. Everything is intact."

But I was stunned and all I could do was just stare.

Her wedding dress was over the top but absolutely gorgeous. A lavender color with lace around the neckline, surprisingly high for Marta, long sheer sleeves and a veil that trailed to the ground covered in tiny purple rosettes. Her short blonde hair was streaked with purple which looked elegant and trendy at the same time. I could see now why Andrew had his hair dyed that way. They matched. Everything from her make-up to her hair to the gown suited her perfectly, making her look like the fashion icon she was. And on top of it all, she practically glowed.

"You look beautiful," I said, reverently, in a heap of awe. "Andrew outdid himself."

"You think so?" she asked, looking worried. "I keep wondering if I should have stuck with the more traditional look—all in white."

"Are you kidding? Lavender suits you to a tee." I leaned in for a hug, making sure I didn't smudge her make-up or wrinkle her dress.

She seemed pleased. "Well, you look beautiful too and thank you for wearing that dress. I know it's not one you'd usually put on."

"Ya think?" I glanced down. "Could it be any tighter or low cut?"

At least that got Marta laughing.

"I'm trying to spruce up your image. Andrew fought me on it, but it suits you."

Thankfully, I was wearing a sheer white shawl over it all. Funny how she made me wear something low-cut while her dress was high up her neck.

"I'm just glad I can still fit into it. I swear I've put on ten pounds this summer. I'm afraid to even step on a scale."

"It suits you." I saw Marta flick her eyes up and down. "Makes you look healthier and that tan hides the pounds, if there are any, that is. Isn't that what the Kardashians say? That a tan makes you look ten pounds slimmer?"

"Not too sure about that and I hardly think I'd take the Kardashians' advice on health issues, but I've started jogging every day to make room for one of Louise's cinnamon buns which I've been craving every morning." My stomach rumbled the way it did every single time thoughts of Louise's bakery entered my mind.

"Besides, it looks good next to my dress. You, me and Andrew all blend together." She sighed. "Liam and Raymond's other usher—Jake—will look drab in black tuxedos. But guess you can't win all the battles."

"Well, you won most of them. And Raymond mentioned that at least they'd all be wearing purple ties."

"You're right. Er… " She grabbed hold of my hand. "You sure you're okay?"

"Yes, yes. I'm fine." Crap. I didn't want her looking worried on her wedding day and I could tell by the piercing look on her face that she wasn't talking about my weight gain. She meant the fact that Liam would be at the church.

"Positive?"

"Positive." I almost held out my other hand so that we could pinky swear, but I figured she'd think I was really losing it. "Now don't be concerned about me. Today's your day and that's all that should be on your mind. You and Raymond."

To be honest, I was not okay. I hadn't slept in days, trying to allow myself the venue to mourn as much as possible—both my parents and my juvenile relationship with Travis. I was tired and cranky. Marta had sent me a brief email that Liam had arrived back from Africa in one piece and was definitely coming to the wedding. I wasn't surprised—he took his best man duties seriously, like he did everything else. But I was upset I hadn't heard from him, after all I'd tried to make contact but then again, what did I expect? I'd been the one who'd left and needed to accept the consequences of my actions since I had told him not to get in touch with me. Also, I couldn't even be sure if he knew I'd called. I'd anticipated seeing him at the rehearsal last night but he hadn't made it due to a crisis at work. I was relieved that I'd escaped a possible confrontation but I knew he was here today. Apparently, he'd arrived at the church early this morning to get his instructions from the priest. Charlie'd said that one day it would all come together but dammit—*when!* I had been hoping I'd be a smiling 'together' kind of person at this wedding. Yeah, right.

"Thanks for everything, Zoey."

I came out of my fog to find Marta looking teary-eyed. "For what?"

"For putting up with me in all my bridezilla glory this past year. And I wasn't that supportive of you and everything you were going through, but I promise that will change."

I was surprised she'd realized that.

"It's okay." And it really was. Port Dover had been the best thing that had ever happened to me.

She smiled. "I've been so worried about this day. It's hard to believe it's really here."

This time it was Marta who leaned over to hug me and I gave thanks for these few stolen moments in the washroom together. I didn't think I'd ever felt so close to her before as I did this minute.

"Just try hard to relax and enjoy the day," I whispered. "You worked so hard to make it special and it'll be perfect. Just you watch."

That is, if I didn't pass out when I saw Liam or scream and run out of the church. I had no idea how I'd react.

Get hold of yourself, Zoey.

The beginning strains of music boomed out and I knew it was time to get myself to the back of the church, especially since I was the first one down the aisle. They couldn't start without me. I walked Marta to the room where her dad and mom were waiting. The bridal party then took our places.

"Ready?" I looked back at Marta.

"Ready," she said with a nervous smile.

"How about you?" I asked Andrew.

"Can't wait." He was prancing around, anxious to get going.

"Well, let's get this show on the road."

The Wedding March rang out. Ready or not, I had to move.

Well, here goes nothing.

I turned to wink at Marta, mouthed good luck and began my trek, slowly and carefully, the way we'd rehearsed. I knew I was supposed to be happy, but I felt I was looking at this whole situation as if I were marching to the guillotine, dreading every step, not in the least in control of my emotions. I'd planted a smile on my face, preparing myself for my first view of Liam. So far, I couldn't locate him. *Why did Marta have to pick the church with the longest aisle ever?*

Halfway down, butterflies were now doing gymnastics in my gut and I felt a stomachache moving in, as I continued to skim the crowd, searching for him, holding my breath, waiting for the moment when he came into view. But I still couldn't see him. Finally, I reached the end of the aisle, and… *there he was.*

Breathtakingly handsome in his black tuxedo, hair a bit longer curling around his collar, with that gorgeous toothy smile. Thirsty, I drank him in and waited for the moment when our eyes would meet. I was sure I'd see his usual twinkle and experience the comfort that always radiated out of him—after all, he was my rock. Also, he, of all people, knew I was shy and how nervous I would be in the maid of honor role and I was sure he'd wink and make it all better. So yep, he was staring... *right on past me. As if I didn't exist.*

Not even once did he make an effort to catch my eye.

Comfort, be damned, this was hell.

No matter how many times I'd imagined this moment, never did I expect to see that cold, frozen expression on his face.

I never thought he'd choose to ignore me.

I figured he'd still be his usual warm, loving, kind self. I was sure wrong about that. Who knew—maybe he was dating someone. After all, he had told me that he wouldn't wait forever. Crap. I wondered if Jackie was at the wedding as his date? Or had he met someone in Africa? Another doctor, perhaps? Nah, I think Marta would have told me. Hoped so, anyway.

A tear pushed itself out and I quickly brushed it away.

No way did I want Liam to see me cry, but as I walked past Raymond who smiled widely at me, once again I noticed that Liam still avoided me, keeping his eyes focused on the back of the church. Could he not even bear to look at me?

Forget him. Think of Marta.

This was her big day. Don't think of Liam, but in truth, I couldn't keep my eyes off him. If only he'd been a creep or mean to me, then I'd feel better. But nope—he was one of the nicest people I'd ever met. In a way, I didn't even blame him for ignoring me. I'd hurt him a lot. Rejecting his proposal was probably the last straw for him.

Sigh.

It sure looked like I didn't have to worry about where Liam stood in my life. He'd taken that decision away from me.

Damn.

But I just couldn't stop sneaking peeks at him. Man, he looked good. I even had a hard time tearing my eyes away to watch Marta float down the aisle. However, when she took hold of Raymond's hand, tears rolled down my cheeks full blast. They looked so in love and I was happy for them. That was what was important today—their happiness. It was all I needed to focus on.

Somehow I made it through the whole ceremony, even managing to sit down without splitting open my dress. I kept my eyes on Marta and Raymond, managing not to look over at Liam even once during the ceremony. Surprisingly, Travis' face flew across my mind a few times but I tried hard to block him out, as well. It only caused me more pain remembering I'd once wanted to marry him and who needed that thought on such a joyous occasion. I'd enough to think about.

"I now pronounce you man and wife," said the priest.

Raymond leaned in for a kiss and the joy on both their faces said it all. They headed down the aisle, huge smiles on their faces, and their obvious bliss was so noticeable, that someone started to applaud and we all joined in.

My job was to take Liam's arm and follow them. In light of how he was treating me, I was dreading this. But fake smile and all, still not looking into my eyes, he graciously stood beside me while I took his arm and we walked down the aisle together. Touching him was hard, though. It sent shivers right through me and I was not prepared for the longing that flooded me. I'd really missed him, that was a given.

"How are you doing?" I asked, trying to be the bigger person and initiate conversation.

"Okay. And you?"

"Smile," yelled out the photographer.

I didn't get a chance to answer him. We both planted smiles on our faces as flashbulbs twirled and swirled around us and then we were quickly ushered into a limo and taken to Liuna Gardens in Stoney Creek for pictures. It was also where the reception was.

I wanted to ask Liam a million things, like how his trip was, how work was going and oh, yeah, was he dating Jackie and did he miss me even a little bit? But it was obvious he was avoiding me—even managing to get in another limo so we wouldn't be together. When we got to the gardens, he cooperated fully in any picture-taking but as soon as they were finished, he walked over to chat with Raymond.

"Kinda getting the cold shoulder there," said Andrew, coming up beside me.

"So it's not just my imagination?"

"No. It's pretty obvious to me, but then again, I've been watching. Hope you don't mind. Marta explained the situation to me and wanted me to keep an eye on you."

"No, I don't mind. Thanks. It's what I deserve."

"Well, I think you did the right thing, going away to figure things out. And I thought you should know that I don't think he's totally oblivious to you. When you're not looking, he sneaks a few discreet peeks at you." He winked.

"Really?"

"Yes. I think he's much more aware of you then he's letting on. My guess is that he doesn't know how to act around you, so he's just staying away."

A pang of longing rushed through me, especially when I saw him joking with Marta and it brought back all the times we'd had a good laugh together.

"Well… I don't blame him. I never really told him what was bothering me. But thanks for telling me that, Andrew. It does make me feel a bit better. Sure don't want to think that all those years with him meant nothing." I leaned over to give him a hug, whispering in his ear, "But I swear a few times I saw him wrinkle his nose as if I had a disease or something and he'd forgotten to wear his hospital mask."

Andrew exploded in laughter just as the photographer yelled out, "One last picture."

"Duty calls," I said, as Andrew tucked my arm in his and like robots, we all assembled in front of a host of flowers. After we were directed where to stand, I found myself beside Liam. Guess he hadn't enough time to escape.

"You look good," I said, again trying to be chatty.

"In this monkey suit? It was hard to put on after a summer of jeans and T-shirts."

"I know what you mean." I searched his eyes, looking for some clue as to what he was thinking or feeling, but it was like he had shutters over them, protecting himself. From more pain, perhaps?

"Er, you look nice too."

But once again he sounded polite, as if just going through the motions.

"Thanks, how did your trip go?" I figured I'd keep trying, not wanting to give up yet.

"Good." And although his eyes lit up, he didn't elaborate like he normally would. One more sign he was consciously keeping a distance from me.

Sigh, I gave up and walked away.

"How's it going?" asked Marta, catching up with me.

"All right. How are you doing?" No way would I ruin her day by telling her anything sad.

She beamed. "Except for these shoes that are killing me, surprisingly good." She laughed. "And don't you dare say 'everything will be okay'."

I laughed as well. She really was on to me.

"Great. Keep on smiling. You deserve this."

I stared at her starry eyes. Hmmm… now that I was in the midst of a wedding, *did I still want one? Someday?*

I looked around at all the happy faces. Sure, I did. Charlie was right. What was so wrong with committing and sharing your special day with friends and family? In fact, it looked quite enticing. We all needed more of these special times where we celebrated happiness, for a change—time away from often hard days filled with grim moments—respites of joy. But enough philosophizing. *This wasn't the time to do that*, I thought, as I joined the others who were walking down the path to the reception hall.

Fortunately, once again, Liam and I didn't have to sit beside each other—Marta's touch, for sure. I was thoughtfully placed with Andrew, which made the long dinner much more fun. He was chatty and whimsical and full of stories about designing dresses for some of the top celebrities in the world. I knew he was trying to make me feel better so I tried harder to enjoy myself. I smiled and laughed and clinked my glass to get Marta and Raymond to kiss and fully got into the festivity of the evening, reminding myself constantly that it was not about me. My Liam thoughts were pushed to the side, at least for the evening.

After a final toast and a dessert to die for—hot chocolate flambés—Bruno Mars song *Just The Way You Are* rang out and Marta and Raymond got up to dance.

I watched them, once again thrilled at how happy they looked. Hopefully, it was a match made in heaven and would last forever.

When they were halfway through, the DJ invited the rest of the wedding party to join them. Traditionally, the best man and maid of honor danced together, but I wasn't sure what would happen. Would Liam continue to ignore me and pretend he hadn't heard the DJ?

Minutes passed before I heard someone say, "May I have this dance?"

I turned to see Liam standing behind me. Figured he was too honor-bound to mess things up for Marta and Raymond. They could count on him to do the right thing.

"Sure."

Once again, the walk to the dance floor seemed to take forever and my legs were shaking so hard, I wasn't even sure I could stand up. How would I feel in his arms? No problem. I was good at blocking out all feelings, so I figured I'd be okay. I could fake it with the best of them and I might just pull off an academy performance.

Okay, this wasn't going to be easy.

Especially, since I melted as soon as he touched me and felt my heart pounding and oh no—I started to sweat. Glad he knew a lot about arrhythmias—I might be having one. Was there a defibrillator around?

"You okay?" whispered Liam.

"Yeah."

Somehow I made it through the song. It helped that Liam held me at a distance, as if we were young kids just learning to dance and not too thrilled to have to touch someone of the opposite sex.

When the song was over, I quickly excused myself, afraid I'd burst into tears if I didn't. I knew Liam didn't want to be with me, he'd made that obvious, so I went back to the table and successfully managed to avoid him the rest of the night. It was easy—he never came within two feet of me. So I continued to fake having a good time for Marta's sake but that didn't mean I wasn't watching Liam, because I was, every single second—drinking him in, knowing I might not ever see him again.

"C'mon, everyone. Time to throw the garter and bouquet," screamed out Marta at the end of the night.

Good. At least when that tradition was over, I could justify taking off.

Reluctantly, I walked out on the floor to join the other ladies, once again planting a smile on my face.

"Here goes," she yelled out. "One, two, three."

I didn't even bother to reach out my arms for it, but wouldn't you just know it? The bouquet hit me square on the head. Guess Marta was aiming right at me.

"Ouch." I instinctively raised my hands to pull it off, not realizing that by doing so, I claimed it. If I'd just left it to hit the ground, someone else could have grabbed it.

Damn. I didn't need the attention.

"Zoey's got it!" yelled Marta. "You're next, Raymond."

He carefully pulled off her garter and whipped it out into the crowd of men, but he was definitely aiming for Liam for it practically sailed into his hand.

"Looks like the next couple to get married will be the best man and maid of honor," roared out the DJ. "Zoey and Liam."

To my horror, everyone started clapping and then someone started yelling, "Kiss, kiss, kiss."

Knowing we'd have to go through with it to get the crowd to be quiet, Liam and I slowly moved towards each other. Okay, I had to admit, I was actually looking forward to it until Liam leaned down and planted one… *on my cheek.* Like he would with a dear aunt or something.

Double-damn.

Glancing at my watch, I saw that I could actually leave now. Marta was off changing into her going away outfit and when she arrived back, I gave her a huge hug, wished her well on her flight to Hawaii. I then took one last long look at Liam and fled out the door. To hell with changing, I was getting out of here.

No doubt about it—seeing him had messed with my head. Big-time.

It sure hurt like hell… *knowing I'd lost him.*

Nineteen

Slowly opening my eyes, as if by rote, my whole body tensed and my hands clenched into fists, waiting for all my worries to swirl around me like they did almost every single morning. Now even worse, since that dreadful meeting with Liam at the wedding.

Silence.

Nope. Nothing.

Confused, I sat up in bed and looked around, feeling clear-headed for the first time in months. I'd left the curtains opened and the sun poured in, lighting up every inch of the room and painting it a soft butterscotch color—warm, rich and syrupy—a hue that soothed my soul.

Taking a deep, relaxing breath, I registered that I felt great for a change—content—the happiest I'd been in months. My mind was not running its usual ninety miles an hour marathon in several directions all at once.

Enthusiastically clapping my hands like a small child, I started to laugh out loud in pure joy until it hit me—*what was going on?*

A thread of fear began to weave itself through my

thoughts, like a snake about to strike. I had gotten so used to gray spidery cobwebs encasing me, making me feel trapped, a victim, plotting how to escape. I was sure something bad would happen any minute.

As if sensing the change in my mood, Moxie stirred beside me, crawled into my arms and leaned up for a little lick. Deciding to kick my fear to the curb, I smiled, stretched and reveled in the happiness I was experiencing—a delight that bubbled up from my toes to the top of my head. No way was I going to let anything stop me from enjoying this moment. It'd been a long time coming. A few times in the past I'd felt better but it turned out it was only a brief respite. Today, it seemed different—deeper—more real somehow. I hoped it would last.

Several days had passed since the wedding and I'd been lying about just thinking about my life, spending hours lounging on the deck or the swing in the backyard. I'd tried hard to block out Liam's coolness towards me, still focusing on sorting out my parents and Travis. I felt I needed to get a handle on my feelings toward them before I finally dealt with what was going on with me and Liam. I'd even started dreading the fact that summer was ending and soon I'd be back at work. I never wanted this magical couple of months to end and in many ways I wished I could live here forever.

Closing my eyes, pictures flashed before me. This had been a common occurrence all summer but what the… ?

This time it was different.

The order was new.

My heart started to pound as I sucked in my breath, and then let it out with a loud whoosh. I felt I was watching a complex movie mystery and finally adding up the clues and figuring out the plot.

Excited, I opened my eyes, picked up Moxie, scrambled out of bed and started dancing around the cottage with her. She looked confused but held on tight as I even managed to dip her a few times and I laughed as she leaned up to lick my face again, as if smothering me with kisses.

"Moxie, Charlie was right." I stared into her earnest little face. "In time, answers really do come."

She cocked her ear as I put her down, then led her to the deck to stare out at the lake, whose calmness never failed to soothe me.

I pictured a huge jigsaw puzzle hovering in the sky, comprised of various pieces of my life. To my delight, slowly, as if by magic, they began to click together. Now only a few pieces remained on their own but hey, most of it was in place. Oh, sure I still needed to sort a lot of stuff out but somehow in the last couple of days, things were gelling and making sense. The walls I'd built up over the years were crumbling and I could see and feel the truth staring me in the eyes—not about everything but about most things—especially about Travis and my parents.

I was finally beginning to understand why I had been feeling the way I did these past months.

It all kind of made sense now.

"C'mon, Moxie." She dropped her ball to look up at

me. "Let's go find Charlie. I can't wait to tell him the good news. He was right all along and he'll be thrilled that I'm not so messed up anymore."

I let Moxie out in the backyard for a potty break, then put some food down for her and raced to get ready. That took about two seconds flat since I didn't want to waste time.

So excited, I skipped and ran like a little kid over to the bakery, Moxie in tow. I couldn't wait to see Charlie's face when I told him what had happened this morning. I could just picture his eyebrows raising, his huge smile and the twinkle in his eye. He would be just as excited as I was because that was the kind of person he was—genuinely concerned for others. One I could only aspire to be like.

Oh no...

Was that a siren? And it was getting louder? Coming here? I glanced around the beach at the joggers and walkers. Nope—no one looked in any kind of trouble.

I now ran full tilt, then skidded to a stop when I saw the white ambulance, lights flashing, pulling in beside Charlie's cottage.

"What happened?" I screamed to Izzy who was standing with the twins on the steps leading to the bakery.

She turned and I noticed that she was crying. This was not going to be good news, I was sure of it.

"Charlie's sick," said Timmy.

"He's going to the hospital," added Jimmy.

Wiping her tears away, Izzy said, "Boys, why don't you take Moxie into the backyard and play ball with her. I think she'd love that."

"Okay," they said together, looking concerned but glad to have a job. I handed over the leash.

I looked at Izzy again, seeking answers. She moved closer and whispered, "Louise found Charlie collapsed in the kitchen." More tears spilled down her cheeks. "Oh, Zoey. She thinks he had a heart attack."

"Ohhhh, no." I'd been so happy this morning, anticipating seeing him that I couldn't even comprehend this turn of events. "Is he still alive?"

"Yes, but just barely."

My heart sunk as we watched the paramedics carry Charlie out on a stretcher, white sheet wrapped around him, tubes attached, oxygen mask on. I wanted to scream and run away, block this whole scenario out of my mind. Instead, I forced myself to stay put and my eyes were glued to his face or what I could see of it. He looked pale and his eyes were shut.

Please, God, I pleaded, raising my eyes to the heavens. Please let him live.

A sober looking Louise followed and got into the ambulance with him. She looked scared and I noticed she was clutching beads and her lips were moving in what I was sure were prayers. My heart broke for her. After all, they'd been together for forty-five years. I couldn't even begin to imagine how she must feel at the possibility of losing her best friend.

"Come on, let's go to the hospital," I said to Izzy.

"You go. I'll come later. Roger is actually picking up the boys for the day so I'll drive over after he leaves."

I raised my eyebrows.

"Yeah, weird, huh? Guess the judge really got to him or it made him look bad so he figures he should fake it. I still don't trust him one bit."

"Well, it's good timing anyway. It'll be great having you there. I'll leave now."

The boys helped me tie Moxie up in the yard and after making sure she had a bowl of water at her disposal, I ran back to my cottage and climbed into my car.

Oh no! He just couldn't die, was all I could think about. He just couldn't. For purely selfish reasons, I knew I wouldn't be able to live without this wonderful man who had come into my life when I was so messed up. I just couldn't bear to lose another person in my life.

And poor Louise.

What would she do? I started to cry so hard, I could barely see the road. I certainly had no trouble with tears now. I bet I let them rip every single day over one thing or another.

Stop it!

Charlie would want me to be strong and not blubber all over the place, especially when driving a car. After all, he wasn't dead yet. So first things first—to get there in one piece so that I could be a support for Louise. I yanked on the knob and blared the radio full blast, my usual escape whenever I was upset. At least it'd get me safely to the hospital by preventing me from thinking of anything else but singing along to some tunes. Fortunately, I'd found an oldie station that played the Beatles' hits and I knew all the words, so I was in luck. I sang so loud, I was sure I'd be pulled over for disturbing the peace.

It seemed to take forever, but I soon pulled into the parking lot of the hospital, shut down the car and turned off the radio. Only one problem—I was so petrified, I couldn't move. I was frozen, scared to go in, afraid of what I might hear or see—once again thinking that I couldn't bear it if Charlie was gone. After taking a few deep breaths in a feeble attempt to calm down, I finally gathered together enough courage to leave the car and high-tail it into the emergency room. I was concentrating hard not to focus on my own pain and think of Louise. She was the one who needed friends around at a time like this. *Enough of my own concerns.*

"Please, could you tell me where Charlie Donnelly is?" I asked the nurse at the front desk.

She looked at a chart, then pointed down the hall.

"Room six."

"Thank you."

I walked quickly, navigating in and out of the crowd of patients, medical staff and paramedics, until I found Louise, looking exhausted, drooped in a chair while a host of doctors and nurses crowded around Charlie. Heart sinking, I watched as a nurse wheeled in the crash cart with paddles ready to go. Damn. This didn't look good.

"Nice of you to come," Louise said, through her tears.

"How's he doing?" I plunked down beside her and wrapped my arm around her shoulders.

"Not good." She wiped her eyes with the back of her hand. "They had to use the paddles twice to start his heart on the way over."

Feeling helpless, I reached out with my other hand and grabbed on to hers. She clasped it tightly and I could sense her pain oozing out. No words seemed appropriate, so I stayed quiet. It was a waiting game, a horrid time of just hanging around hoping to hear good news but knowing that I might not get my wish. As the minutes ticked by, I realized that there was no greater hell than waiting for results at a hospital, while a team of doctors and nurses worked on your loved one.

"Mrs. Donnelly?" said a man in a white coat, who'd been with Charlie from the beginning. He looked dead serious.

"Yes?" Louise stood up.

"I'm Doctor Mulligan."

"Will he be okay?" she asked, repeatedly wringing her hands.

"Please, sit down."

I moved, so he could sit down beside her.

"His ECG shows that he had a heart attack. We're in the process of stabilizing him and then we're planning on sending him by helicopter to the London hospital. He'll be in good hands there."

"By helicopter?" Louise's face whitened.

"Yes. As you know we're a small country hospital. We don't have the facilities to do heart surgery. We need to get him there as fast as we can."

"Heart surgery?"

"Yes. He may needs stents or as a last resort, open heart surgery."

I held onto Louise's hand even tighter.

"Anything," said Louise, in a much quieter voice. "Anything that might bring him back to me."

"Okay." He stood up. "We're hoping to move him within the next hour."

"Can I stay here with him?"

"Yes, of course. You can wait right here."

"How's he doing?" asked Izzy, arriving just as the doctor left.

"They're trying to stabilize him," I said. "Then they're sending him to London."

"Is that safe? Can he handle the drive?"

"By helicopter," I added.

Her eyes grew round and her mouth opened in shock.

"Will he be all right?" Her eyes bounced between the two of us.

"We don't know, dear," said Louise. "But it's the only alternative at the moment."

I stared at Charlie. He looked so small in the midst of an array of machines spitting out his blood pressure, heart rate and oxygen statistics. A needle had been inserted in his hand where tubing connected it to an intravenous bag pumping fluids into him. Several nurses were recording his numbers and keeping a watchful eye on things. At least that, was reassuring.

Suddenly Louise let go of my hand, stood up and walked to the head of the bed.

"Come back to me, Charlie," she begged. "We still have a lot of living to do."

Her pain echoed exactly what I was thinking.

Please come back to us, Charlie.

"Excuse me," said one of the nurses. "Would you mind sitting back there?" She smiled. "I know you want to be by his side, but we need access to everything, just in case."

Like the crash cart, I thought, as a tremor of fear rocked me.

"Sorry," said Louise, as she came back to sit with us.

This was not looking good. The increasingly worried looks on the nurses' faces spoke volumes.

My usual pattern was to eat when stressed, but this was the first time ever that the thought of any type of food made my stomach roil. However, after about twenty minutes, desperate for some kind of normalcy and having a hard time sitting still, I asked Louise, "Would you like some coffee?"

"Well, okay," said Louise. "That might be good."

"I'll stay," said Izzy.

I hurried off to the elevator, still feeling sick to my stomach. All the way down to the cafeteria, I kept repeating over and over like a mantra, "Come on, Charlie. You can do it." At least I hoped he could. He hadn't been looking that well all summer and I'd even been shortening our walks and trying to get him to rest more on the bench. Many times I'd checked in with Louise to see if he'd relented and agreed to go to the doctor but she was having no luck. He'd simply refused to go. *Damn him. He should have taken better care of himself.* I sighed. But that was Charlie—always looking out for others and putting his own needs last, never wanting to bother anyone with his own issues.

When I reached the cafeteria, I loaded up a tray full of coffees and muffins. I wasn't sure anyone could eat or drink but then again, it might be best if all of us, especially Louise, kept up our strength. Doubt it though. The sight of food still made me queasy.

After paying, I got back on the elevator and headed to the waiting room.

"Thank you," said Louise, when I put the tray down. She latched onto one of the coffees but I saw she wasn't drinking it but clinging to the cup for its warmth. I also noticed how cold it was in the waiting room and how thin her blouse was, so I took off my sweater and wrapped it around her. I really wished I could take this pain away from her and make Charlie all better but I knew he was in the hands of God, fate, or whatever you wanted to call it. We just had to keep waiting.

"Thanks," she whispered.

Izzy picked up a muffin and nibbled on it for a bit then set it down. I couldn't bring myself to eat or drink, so we all sat in silence, counting down the minutes. Every so often I looked at the clock. One hour finally passed. It seemed like a lifetime. Guess he'd be going to London, really soon.

And then it happened...

Alarms start ringing and a voice jumped out of the intercom—*Code Blue, Code Blue.* About ten people came running, cramming into the room.

I heard words like "ventricular fibrillation, can't get a pulse, we're losing him."

Then… quiet.

One by one, medical personnel left Charlie's side.

Dr. Mulligan slowly walked towards us and the grief in his eyes said it all. Louise stood up.

"I'm sorry," he said.

"He's gone?" she whispered.

"Yes."

She rushed up to Charlie's side and took his hand. She didn't say a word, just gazed at him and the love pouring out of her was touching to see. They definitely had one of the great loves—that was for sure.

Izzy and I stayed at the base of the bed, giving her all the time and space she needed.

"The last thing he said to me this morning was 'I love you'," said Louise, turning to look at us.

"How beautiful," I said.

"That's how we started each day, saying I love you to each other. I couldn't have wished for a better husband."

"Or a better friend," I added.

"Or confidante," said Izzy.

We all stood in silence, each of us alone with our thoughts, but when Louise's sister arrived, along with her husband and children, Izzy and I quietly left. She needed to be with family now.

"So sad," said Izzy as we headed down the elevator. "Now I'll have to go home and explain it to my kids. Not looking forward to that."

"It'll be tough." I agreed. "Your boys adore him." I'd had lots of experience telling bad news to students, but somehow I wasn't sure I'd be able to hold it together talking about Charlie. Especially with my penchant for crying lately. I didn't envy what Izzy had to do.

I waved goodbye, as she headed down the opposite hallway to get to her car. Guess she'd found a parking spot nearby while I was in the hospital one. Feeling like I'd aged a million years, I slowly made my way to my car, drove home, rounded up Moxie and walked along the beach, just like we always did.

I just couldn't believe Charlie was gone.

He also died before I could tell him my good news and I'd never have the chance to see that glow of excitement he'd get whenever things went well. After all, he was the one who'd helped me the most.

The more I walked, the more depressed I got. The day had started with such promise, now it was a bust. At one point, I tried to block him out of my mind but then remembered that he'd felt I'd never mourned my parents and I didn't want to do the same thing—put him away and try to forget about him until his memory popped up somewhere down the line in a totally messed up fashion.

"I have to make sure I mourn him," I said out loud.

Moxie looked up at me, as if wondering what I was saying.

"C'mon, old girl."

I led her to the bench where we used to sit all the time, gabbing away. Or at least I was the one talking, Charlie usually just listened. Moxie jumped up and sat on my lap, while the sun encased me in its warmth, soothing my skin, melting my frozen heart. I took my shoes off and dug my feet into the hot sand, craving even more comfort.

Charlie was so full of life that it seemed surreal that he was gone. I pictured his face—his kind eyes, sweet smile and gentle spirit. Wrapping my arms around Moxie, holding on tight, I cried my eyes out, totally allowing myself to feel all the grief that encompassed my heart.

Moxie moved even closer and began licking my tears as if mopping them all up.

"You miss him too, don't you?" I whispered. She burrowed deeper into my arms.

Finally, when I was all cried out, I felt a bit better. I had always thought it was a weakness to let loose but not anymore, realizing it was a natural response to losing someone you love. It'd be unnatural not to shed tears. I'd learned that the hard way.

Oddly enough, as the minutes ticked by, I began to sense that Charlie was sitting beside me. So much so, that I turned to look. Of course no one was there, but I still felt he was.

I'd read about people who immediately sensed a loved one's comforting presence the minute they passed away, but I had never experienced such a thing with my parents. So it was strange to feel it with Charlie but then again, my parents' death had been so tragic and I'd blocked it all out. This time, I wasn't doing that and somehow I began to feel closer than ever to Charlie.

I shut my eyes, summoning up his face.

"Oh, Charlie," I whispered into Moxie's fur. "I'm going to miss you sooooo much. And I had so much to tell you today."

My eyes popped open and I felt a smile curve my lips.

"I'm going to tell you anyway," I said out loud.

I looked up at the deep blue sky.

"Charlie, I know you're up there, for if anyone deserves to be in heaven, you do."

I smiled, picturing him sitting up on one of the fluffy white clouds above, watching me, probably eating cookies. Sure that was a pretty crazy thought, might even be certifiably insane, but it helped me focus.

"You were right, you know. My walls are down and things are starting to make much more sense. And with all my heart, I thank you for that."

I then went on to tell him some of the stuff I'd sorted out, ignoring the strange looks I got from a few people walking by. I knew it seemed like I was staring off into space, talking to myself but tough, I wasn't.

Didn't they understand that Charlie was still here and always would be ... at least, in my heart?

Twenty

Obscured by sheets of rain pouring down, the lake looked cold and uninviting. Everything was gray and gloomy, which matched my mood perfectly.

I didn't want to go.

I knew I sounded like a little kid, even to my own ears, but attending a memorial service for Charlie was not something I looked forward to. Okay, that was selfish of me—I was only thinking of myself—but I still couldn't help the way I felt. Sigh. I continued staring out the window at the lake, caught up in swirls of depression, much like the whitecaps I witnessed, that seemed to grow larger and more menacing as the minutes ticked by.

I figured Louise would appreciate the support and also knew from my own experience with my parents' visitation, that having friends and family around to comfort you was sometimes a lifesaver. I needed to and yes, I would go, but it wouldn't be easy. I never thought I'd be attending a service for Charlie. Instead, I thought we'd be celebrating my breakthroughs.

I plunked myself down on the couch. Moxie jumped up on my lap and I hugged her tightly.

Even though three days had passed and I was determined not to push my pain away, I still found myself wanting to retreat into my old, safe ways. Sometimes I felt like it was a losing battle, so much so, that I'd even taken Moxie back to Louise, wanting to drop her off and just hide away in my cottage and keep at bay the world outside my door. Louise intercepted my running scared by asking if I could still keep Moxie with me, for she had too many errands to run and wasn't home long enough to take care of her.

Damn.

How could I say no?

Oh sure I loved the little dog, but she forced me to go outside and keep up those walks. It was probably the best thing for me in terms of facing my sadness but not something I looked forward to since I then couldn't ignore how I felt, not with Charlie's ghost walking beside me all the time. At least that was how I felt—that everywhere I turned, I saw his face and my heart ached and my feelings were bittersweet—excited to have sorted out a lot of things but reeling from the loss of a person I greatly respected.

At least it wasn't a real funeral for apparently Charlie hadn't wanted one. Instead, it was a 'celebration of his life' brunch at the bakery, but I wondered how I could possibly celebrate with a hole in my heart the size of a grapefruit.

Charlie!

I still couldn't believe he was gone. I buried my face in Moxie's fur but this time she scrambled away, jumped off my knee and ran to retrieve her leash from a hook by the front door.

Wish I hadn't taught her that trick.

"You really want a walk? Now? But it's raining."

Moxie wagged her tail, dancing around me, effectively tugging me out of my down mood. I even managed a smile.

"All right. You win."

Pulling on my raincoat and grabbing an umbrella, I hitched Moxie up to her leash and headed out into the rain. Moxie didn't seem the least bit concerned about getting wet, so I let her run free and she even insisted I throw the ball again and again while she chased it, slowly turning into a muddy swamp creature after rolling in the sand and running through at least a million puddles. She got me laughing, though, which I was sure was her objective. She knew me too well.

Finally, she showed signs of slowing down and we headed back to the cottage where it seemed to take forever to dry her off. I then rifled through my closet, trying to decide what to wear. Louise's invitations clearly stated that we were not to wear black so I pulled on some white pants and a red sweater. I then wrapped a bright red bow around Moxie's neck. Now she looked like steel wool with a bow but in my eyes, she was the cutest thing ever.

I held up her leash. "Guess it's time." I couldn't think of any more reasons to stall.

Moxie bounded to the door probably thinking that a second walk was a huge bonus, and sat patiently while I attached her leash, then reached her paws up as if trying to grab hold of the doorknob.

"Well, you're sure eager," I said, as I opened the door and we piled out. "Wish I could say the same."

I slowly walked toward the bakery, glad the rain had finally stopped. It felt like a walk of doom, while Moxie pranced and danced around me. She seemed so proud of her red ribbon that I decided I should dress her up more often. Maybe she was a clothes-kinda-dog. Who knew?

Arriving at the bakery, I took my place in the long line-up stretched almost to the lake. People seemed anxious to pay their respects, for I was sure Charlie had touched everyone's hearts in so many ways.

Louise was standing at the door, teary-eyed but with a smile on her face. As I drew nearer to the front of the line, I studied her, hoping she wasn't doing what I did at my parents' visitation—faking being happy to put everyone else at ease and leaving no room to mourn for myself. I was counting on her being smarter than that, but thought I'd keep an eye on her, just in case.

"So glad you could make it," she said, giving me a hug. "And, Moxie, my goodness. Don't you look beautiful." Moxie reached up her paw for a shake which made Louise laugh.

"How are you doing?" I whispered.

"I'm okay," she said, straightening up. "I have good moments and bad. But I always knew I wouldn't have him forever, especially these past few weeks when he looked so sick." A tear dripped down her face. "And of course I'm happy he didn't suffer. The doctor said it would have hit him fast and he wouldn't have known what was going on."

"That's good to know. Please tell me if there is ever anything I can do."

"I will, sweetie. Now go on in and have some food. You must be starving. Charlie mentioned how few groceries you keep in your cottage."

"That's because I keep eating at your bakery." I smiled. "Hmmmm…" I sniffed the air. "I can already smell your cinnamon buns and they're calling my name."

That got her laughing again. "They're over on the table in the dining room. Help yourself, dear."

Louise turned to greet the next onslaught of visitors, while I followed my nose to the dessert table and grabbed a rich, gooey bun. Raiding the cupboard to find some treats for Moxie, I handed over a few which she gobbled down and then searched out her doggy bed in the corner of the room. I watched her yawn as she curled up, and in seconds her eyes were shut. Guess she'd finally tired herself out.

Making my way into the living room, I joined the crowds of people walking around enjoying the various displays Louise had put together and scattered about the room. It was very impressive. Every single available space was packed full of pictures of Charlie, as well as his favorite things—his fishing rods, books, pipe, even his police chief's hat, badge and uniform. I grinned when I noticed several packets of cookies wrapped in cellophane lying around—a sure sign that Louise knew he sneaked sweets to take on his walks. He hadn't fooled her one bit.

Picking up a photo album, I leafed through it and was especially mesmerized by a gorgeous picture of their wedding. They both looked lovely and so happy I felt envious. Once again I was struck at how much he looked like my dad, even when he was younger.

The next group of photos depicted Louise sitting beside Charlie, on a pale green couch. He was holding a tiny baby wrapped in a blue blanket and gazing at the child with such love, it was touching to witness. I didn't know they had children. Maybe it was a neighborhood child they were babysitting? Whoever it was, he or she certainly meant a lot to Charlie, for his hands were wrapped around the child with obvious tenderness, making sure the little guy's head was safely supported. As a matter of fact, there were several of Charlie and the baby and in every one of them, it was clear that he was enthralled by the tiny child.

"That's Jeremy," said Louise, coming up behind me. "Our son."

Surprised, I turned to look at her. "Oh, didn't realize you have a son."

"Yes. Unfortunately, he didn't live long." Her eyes expressed intense longing, as she stared at the photo. "He passed away shortly after that. He was born with a congenital heart disease."

"I'm so sorry to hear that."

"It was the hardest thing I had to go through and it took forever for Charlie to get over it." She shook her head. "He'd been looking so forward to having children and to make things worse, Jeremy passed away during a particularly hard case Charlie was working on. He completely closed down after we buried the wee child. Wouldn't talk about Jeremy and didn't want anyone to even mention his name in his presence. It took years before he was finally able to accept and cope with what happened." A tear drifted down her cheek. "Almost thought our marriage was over, too. He practically lived at his office during that time."

So his words to me about grieving were from actual experience. He'd lost a child. Someone so precious to him. And... almost lost his marriage, too.

"How did he finally sort it all out?"

"Not completely sure. I often wondered if he saw a counselor and just didn't tell me. But one day he woke up and came into the kitchen holding a picture of Jeremy. I made us some coffee and we sat down at the kitchen table and he let loose with all the feelings he'd bottled up. From then on he was fine." She smiled. "I was just glad I happened to be there when he was ready to talk. It'd been a long time coming."

So Charlie knew all about burying emotions and running and hiding from them. He knew about trying to sort out his feelings so they didn't destroy his whole life, then waking up one day to finally feel clear-headed. No wonder he was pushing me to mourn past events, knowing that only by doing so, could I celebrate the present and move on into my future. He'd experienced the same thing.

Noticing the sad look on Louise's face, I said softly, "I bet you were a great mother."

"I wanted to be." Her eyes were lost in sentiment. "But then again, I was lucky to have the gift of my son for however long he was with me. Some people never ever get to experience such a blessing."

That was true and an inspirational way of looking at life for I, too, had wonderful parents albeit only for a short while. But Louise was right—some people never even had that. I leaned over and gave her a hug. She was quite a person and one I'd love to get to know more. Charlie had always been my sole focus but with him gone, hopefully Louise and I could become good friends. I was learning that she was a wise, kind woman and someone I could only aspire to be like—just like Charlie was.

Several people came up to offer their condolences to Louise, so I moved over to where a few more albums were laid out on a small table by the door. I was mesmerized by the pictures, thoroughly enjoying seeing Charlie in all stages from childhood to adulthood. It sure looked like he had led a rich, full and satisfying life—just too short for my liking.

"Can I have everyone's attention, please?"

I looked up to see Louise now standing in the middle of the room. Everyone stopped in their tracks.

"Charlie always said that talking and discussing was always better over food," continued Louise. "So I ask everyone to take a plate, fill it with goodies, then grab a chair and let's all huddle together and share some memories."

I saw Izzy walking in with the twins, and made a beeline to her.

"Hi there."

"Hi," she smiled, looking the best I'd ever seen her. Now that the court case was over, she was flourishing. She'd even applied back to law school.

"Things going well?" I asked, as the boys took off to play with Moxie in the backyard after I explained what was happening.

"Couldn't be better." She smiled, as she grabbed a plate and popped some sandwiches on it. "I can't thank you enough."

"Me? What did I do?"

"Well, I've talked to Ann-Marie since that meeting. She said that it really was your glowing recommendation of me that did it. She knew she could trust you one hundred percent."

Guess I never knew how helping a student could really make a difference, especially years later.

"But it's you, you know. You should be patting yourself on the back. You're a wonderful mother."

"Thanks. Your opinion means a lot." Sigh. "If only Charlie were here."

"Couldn't agree with you more."

We filled our plates and took a seat, as per Louise's instructions. Louise then led the discussion, sharing how she fell in love with Charlie the first time she met him and then opened it up for all of us to share stories. Everything I heard showed how wonderful he was—a real miracle worker around Port Dover, he had touched the hearts of so many people. I even talked about how much he looked like my dad and how I ended up confiding in him when I was hell bent not to. Everyone nodded. Guess he had the same effect on most people.

After the tributes were over, I walked out to the back yard to bring Moxie her dinner. The boys were now eating inside with their mom and I had the place to myself.

"Here, girl." I put down the bowl of goodies beside the pail of water and sat down on the stoop, enjoying the peace and quiet, thinking of Charlie and how much he meant to me. Guess sometimes it only takes a short while to cement a good relationship.

"So here you are."

I looked around to see Louise coming out the door. She sat down beside me.

"We keep being interrupted and I had a few things I wanted to talk to you about," she said, a serious tone to her voice.

"You do?"

"Yes. You know how you talk about how much Charlie reminded you of your dad?"

"I sure do."

"Well, you had that same effect on him." She took hold of my hand. "Turned out we couldn't have any more children but from the moment Charlie met you, he loved you like a daughter. He really took to you, saying he saw the same pain in you that was once in him. That's why he was always encouraging you to face your past, so that you could get on with your life."

"I'm honored that he thought of me as his daughter." A tear drifted down my cheek. "He helped me so much."

"That's because he went through similar things that you did." She squeezed my hand. "You know, he must have known things weren't that great with his health, for he said a few days ago that if anything happened to him, he wanted Moxie to live with you." She glanced down at the dog. "I told him I was surprised at that, for I would always take good care of her but his response was that you needed her more."

My eyes lit up and I turned to stare at her. "You mean I can keep her? You don't mind?"

"Yes. It would be honoring Charlie's wishes. That is, of course, if you want her."

"You bet I do." I felt a twinge of guilt for wanting to ditch Moxie a few days ago, but the fact that Charlie wanted me to have her was like a dream come true. Besides, she'd really grown on me and I'd hate to say good-bye.

"Will I at least have visitation rights?" She grinned.

"Count on it." I grinned back. "Anytime at all." I leaned over and hugged her.

Louise went back into the house to say goodbye to the people who were leaving and I was left alone with my very own dog.

"Well, Moxie. Guess you're living with me now."

She wagged her tail. Hopefully that was a good sign.

When I finally got up to leave, I decided to do one last walk through the house. There were so many beautiful pictures of Charlie, I wasn't sure I'd seen them all. I especially wanted to see what a group of people had been looking at earlier on. I hadn't been able to get near enough to check it out. Winding my way through lingering groupings of people to the wall nearest the kitchen, I stopped in my tracks, mesmerized by a large framed photo of Charlie standing on the beach, arms outstretched towards the sunrise as if embracing it. I couldn't see his face but I bet he had that twinkle in his eye, ready to take on the world.

I stared at it for a good ten minutes.

According to Louise, Charlie had suffered greatly in life, got it together and forged ahead with this business called life. That was what I needed to do—to sort out the past then put it neatly away, embrace the sunrises in my own life and reach out for what I wanted—in short, to follow my dreams or my heart, as Dad would say.

Staring at Charlie, I felt like someone pushed me. I even looked around to see if anyone was behind me. Nope, no one. *But the minute I looked back at the picture, I knew exactly what my next course of action was to be—clear as anything.*

Twenty-one

Inspired by Charlie's own self-searching and… to quote him—"You gotta grab life with both hands and hang onto it," I decided there were three urgent things I needed to do. Today—before I chickened out. Quite possibly, I could then slide a few more puzzle pieces into their rightful spot and eventually close up the cracks in my psyche. Or at least I hoped so.

I stared down at my new pet. "Want to go on a road trip?"

Moxie barked her approval and after saying goodbye to Louise, I headed back to my cottage to change into more casual clothes and make a few phone calls. Grabbing some snacks for the road, in particular some treats for Moxie, I was ready.

"C'mon, old girl. Time to go." She wagged her tail, jumped in the car and settled on the passenger seat where she could alternately look out the front and side windows, nosy girl that she was. A dog after my own heart.

My first stop was *TT's*.

I'd done a lot of thinking about Travis. As a matter of fact, my relationship with him was definitely one I'd sorted out. I was glad we'd cleared the air about what happened years ago, but I didn't feel comfortable leaving him the way I did the last time I saw him. There were also a few things I still wanted to say to him. I was considering letting the whole thing just drift away but in light of Charlie's death, I knew that wasn't the right thing to do. It also wasn't what I really wanted.

Equally excited and anxious, I had a hard time keeping to the posted speed limit, but finally pulled up to the store in one piece. Not sure if a dog could go inside, but since it was too hot to leave her in the car, I picked up Moxie and, holding her in my arms, took a deep breath, summoning up some courage and entered.

"Zoey."

Travis came towards me, smiling widely, wearing a light green shirt making his eyes seem even more brilliant.

"Is this a bad time?" I asked, trying to sound strong and firm and in control, even though I was nervous as anything, now that I saw him face to face.

"Not at all. Who is this?" He glanced down at my dog.

"Moxie, I'd like you to meet Travis. Travis, Moxie."

Moxie, still in my arms, wagged her tail and stuck her paw out for a shake.

Travis laughed and after obliging, said, "I'm honored to meet you."

"Is it okay that she's here?"

"No problem. Come on back to my office. It'll be quiet there." As we walked through the store, he motioned to one of his salesclerks and explained that he'd be tied up for a while.

Did he sense that I had something important to tell him?

He ushered me into a small room that held a desk and several chairs. After we were all settled, including Moxie who looked quite regal perched on a small wicker footstool, I smiled, took another deep breath and blurted out, “First of all, I’d like to apologize.”

“For what?” He looked surprised. “You already apologized for not speaking to me after prom. And you didn’t have to. I really didn’t blame you.”

“But I was doing it again.”

“What?” He looked confused.

“The other night after dinner, you said you wanted to be friends again.”

“Yes, I do.”

“Well, I wanted to run away, ignore you, pretend we’d never re-connected. But today… I’ve stopped running and I hope your offer is still there.”

“Of course it is.” His smile was genuine.

Staring into his eyes, all warm and shiny, my pain, miscommunications and hurt just drizzled away. Another puzzle piece clicked in. By facing all my past issues concerning Travis, I was left with his essence—or rather the essence of our relationship—we were best friends once and could be again. I’d like that. A lot.

I jumped up to hug him.

“And since I’m in true confession mode,” I grinned, pulling back. “I also really want to thank you.”

“For what?”

“For all the good times we had together. For opening

up all sorts of exciting worlds back when I was fifteen. Worlds of art and music, creativity and fun. I had such a good time with you and I can never thank you enough for that. It was a wonderful period in my life. So joyful and happy."

Now he looked stunned, as we both sat back down. "I always felt I'd ruined your life," he said softly.

"Of course, you didn't. And I totally understand your reluctance to tell me when I first met you, while you sorted out what was going on inside. It must have been so difficult. Hell, I couldn't even tell my boyfriend why I needed to be alone this summer. Sometimes, we're so mixed up inside that words fail us." I leaned forward. "And I want you to know something else. By knowing you, I was a lot more compassionate to students and staff members who were coping with their sexuality. I was and am able to help them as much as I can, all because of you. You gave me an awareness I'd never had before."

His eyes lit up. "Well, that's good news. Although people are more open about being gay these days, it's still hellish for many trying to cope with it and come to terms with it."

I reached over and squeezed his hand. "We were just young kids back then, trying to grow up in the best possible way. We never meant to hurt each other." My mind knew that but now my heart did as well.

Inspired by Charlie, my goal today was to build a bridge from my past to my present. That was why I was here. No longer was I going to hide from things or push them away and I also realized that having Travis as a friend filled in a hole I'd had since a teen. I'd really missed him. A whole lot.

"No, I never meant to hurt you," he said, shaking his head.

"Me, neither. And hey, I was wondering if you could drop by for coffee next week? I'd love you to see the cottage I rented."

"I'd like that. Port Dover is also one of my favorite places to visit."

"Oh, and please bring Bob, too. If you love him, he must be pretty wonderful and I'd like to get to know him too."

He beamed and as I said goodbye and walked out the door, I knew that I would always love him but more like a brother, a best friend, someone I admired. A buddy from my past who had left an imprint on my heart forever. I felt a supreme contentment over that part of my life—I had a good friend back. And as that old saying goes—good friends are hard to find. I was lucky, I'd found the same one twice.

My next stop was a Tim Hortons in Hamilton on Upper James Street. The second thing I needed to do—another step in my healing. One I was more nervous about.

I walked into the coffee shop and looked around. Ned Allen said he'd be wearing a Toronto Maple Leaf baseball cap and that he had red hair. I spotted him at a booth in the back and slowly walked to meet him, wanting yet dreading this meeting. I'd gotten his phone number from Carm and lucked out when I called for he was in and eager to meet with me. I couldn't say I was eager, but felt it was necessary.

He took his cap off as I approached and reached out to shake my hand.

"I'm glad you finally agreed to talk to me," he said.

"Me, too." Or at least I was hoping it would be good.

"I took the liberty and bought you a cup of coffee. Not sure what you take in it so I brought over cream, milk, sugar and sweetener. Would you like anything to eat?"

"No, thanks."

I kept my head down, as I doctored my coffee, not sure of what I wanted to say or what I really wanted out of this meeting. Another bridge, I suppose.

Silence.

"I'm so sorry about your parents," Ned said softly. "So very sorry. I was drinking that day and ran that red light. Never even noticed it. I'm really hoping you can finally forgive me."

I raised my head, staring dead on *at the face of the boy who killed my mother and father.* Actually, he was no boy now, but a man a few years older than I was. Years ago, he had reached out to apologize to us and Carm had met with him several times back then and still kept in touch. I never had—never wanted to either, and he was buried away with all the other stuff I didn't want to face. But the depth of my fury had shocked me when I visited my parents' gravesite. Thirteen years of anger weighed me down, made me bitter and ate away at my heart. I figured finally facing him might be another of the answers I sought. At least, I hoped so.

But once again, I was unprepared for the waves of anger that rolled through me.

Really, why should I forgive him? Just because he asked? No way. He didn't deserve it.

"Why were you driving?" I burst out, knowing my voice sounded harsh, but just didn't care. "Why not take a taxi, or get a ride from someone else?"

His head went down but not before I saw that I'd crushed him. Too bad. He was a murderer and I had no sympathy for him.

"I know, I know," he whispered. "It was a foolish, foolish decision and of course when you're young, you think you'll live forever and nothing bad will ever happen. I made a huge mistake that day, one I've regretted every day of my life." He raised his head and I was struck by how sincere he looked. "I want you to know that I've never taken a drink since. Not even a sip."

I stared at him.

I thought this would be easy.

That I could meet with him, say 'I forgive you' and everything would feel right again—that I could move on. Instead, I was battling my anger, as well as my compassion, not even sure which emotion would rule in the end.

"I don't blame you one bit if you never forgive me," he added. "It's what I deserve. And I can never bring them back to you. But I want you to know that I've learned from what happened and faithfully tour schools talking to teenagers about what I did. Hopefully, I can spare other horrible accidents from happening."

While he was talking, once again—at a time of great need—my father's words came to mind.

"It was an accident, honey. You need to forgive him."

"But, Dad. Josh spilt his chocolate milk all over my science project. It's ruined."

"Accidents happen and Josh didn't meant to do that."

"But..."

"No buts. We'll explain to your teacher what happened. In the meantime, I want you to make peace with him. Look at him. He's crying his eyes out."

I stared at two-year-old Josh. He was our next door neighbor and he'd been visiting us with his mom. Curious about the large volcano I'd sculpted out of clay for my fifth grade science class, he'd come over to take a look..

"'Cano," he'd said and he'd started to run, fell, and his milk tumbled down my volcano like white lava.

I was devastated but spurred on by my dad, whom I adored, I went over to the little boy and murmured, "It's okay, Josh."

I'd never forgotten the smile he gave me when he realized I wasn't going to yell at him. It was like his world was all better now—like I had kissed his 'boo-boo' and he could live again. He'd hugged me so tightly and when I'd looked over at my dad, he had tears in his eyes. He'd winked and mouthed, "I'm so proud of you."

Dad was right—accidents do happen, and the more I stared, the more Ned's face resembled Josh's—scared, sad, remorseful, panicky.

He was not the demon I'd painted and hid inside my box—nor a big black blob that hovered over me. He was just a grown man still trying to recover from a mistake he'd made as a teen. And that was what it was—just a mistake. He'd made poor choices like all of us do at one time or another.

I really did need to forgive him.

I'd be honoring my dad's memory if I did, and also honoring all the life's truths and lessons he'd taught me over the years.

Compassion flowed through me wiping out my anger and taking a deep breath, I reached out and put my hand over his. "Thank you for sharing your story with young people." I smiled. "And I do forgive you. After all, it was an accident."

He smiled. "That's all I can ask for."

Another tiny part of my heart thawed. This was the right thing to do and I even hoped I'd see Ned more often, like my sister did. Who knew? We might become friends. At least I was open to that now.

Once again, I could see my dad smiling at me and saying that he was proud of me and hey—*I was proud of myself.*

We spent a good hour talking about our lives. I discovered he had three little girls and a wife he adored.

"I don't deserve such happiness," he said, shaking his head, showing me photos of his family.

"Yes, you do." And I found, I really did mean it.

Our next stop, and the hardest one by far, was to see Liam. I figured after the way he'd reacted to me at the wedding, our relationship was over. Or at least he wanted it that way. I still wasn't sure what I wanted, but I felt it was time to at least tell him why I left. I didn't think it would make any difference to him, for I was positive he'd be angry that I hadn't confided in him in the first place, but just like I said to Travis, sometimes it's hard to do that. Sometimes we just have no clue over what was going on, so we choose to say nothing and then have to sort through a lot of junk to get to the treasures. I was still hoping to reach the 'treasure stage' someday.

I didn't call and arrange a meeting, afraid Liam would refuse to see me, washing his hands of me forever. Sure, I was ambushing him but figured it was better late than never. Hopefully, we could at least remain friends. *Yeah, right. Dream on.* It didn't seem like he was interested in doing that, in the least.

Tires squealing with urgency, I pulled into the hospital. I'd never bothered him at work before, but today I would. This was important and I was hoping I'd luck out and he'd be able to give me some time to listen to my explanations. I wouldn't take long for I had it all planned out. Short and to the point, was my strategy.

"You stay here, okay?" I tied Moxie up under a tree for shade and also where I could see her from inside the front doors. I improvised with an old coffee cup, rinsed it and filled it with water in case she was thirsty. Giving her a treat made her a happy camper and she wagged her tail as I hurried into the hospital saying, "I'll just be a few minutes." I was pretty sure Moxie would be safe because with her cranky disposition, she'd growl away any unwanted attention.

Projecting a confidence I didn't really feel, I marched up to the receptionist. "Excuse me. I need to see Dr. O'Reilly, please." I decided to be firm, brooking no argument—in other words—I used my vice principal voice.

"He's busy."

This could be harder than I thought.

"Would you mind paging him and please tell him it's Zoey Avery?"

She eyed me up and down but still did nothing.

"Please? It's very important."

"Well… okay."

"Thank you."

Guess she saw the desperation in my eyes.

I sat down and waited patiently, every few seconds glancing out the door to make sure Moxie was okay. I tried to be brave, to keep a smile plastered on my face, but the minute Liam walked in the room, I stood up and burst into tears.

Damn.

"Zoey." He rushed over. "Here, come on into this other room. We'll have more privacy." He pointed down the hall.

"I can't," I sobbed. "I need to keep my eyes on Moxie."

"Moxie?"

"Yeah." I pointed out the window.

Liam followed my finger and stared. Silence. Then, "Is that a dog?"

Through my tears, I started to laugh. I'd gotten so used to the way she looked but viewing her from Liam's eyes, she once again resembled a bunch of twisted steel wool on skinny legs with a tuft of hair on top of her head. Not to mention, she still had on that garish red bow from Charlie's gathering.

"Yeah, she used to belong to Charlie."

"Who's Charlie?"

Fresh tears poured down my cheeks.

He looked stunned. Guess so. This was the first time he'd ever seen me cry.

"Wait, I'll be right back."

To my surprise, he went out, untied Moxie, cradled her in his arms and brought her in. What I was most shocked at was that the little dog hadn't growled or bit him or anything. *Wow. Could she read my mind and know that Liam was safe?* Nevertheless, I was grateful to see her.

"Let's go in here." He led me to a small room, ignored strange looks from hospital staff, and shut the door after us. He beckoned me to sit down, releasing Moxie who made a bee-line for my lap. Sitting across from me, he asked, "Now, who is Charlie?"

"My eighty-five year old neighbor. He died."

"Oh, Zoey, I'm so sorry." He moved his chair so that he sat beside me, putting his arm around me.

That was my undoing, setting me off on another crying jag. When I finally calmed down enough to talk, I poured my heart out about Travis, my parents and the fact I'd never mourned them. I kept the wedding thoughts to myself, still not sure what they were all about.

Silence.

I snuck a peek at him and saw that he looked stunned and at that precise moment, his buzzer went off.

Damn.

He tried to ignore it but I said, "Please go ahead and see what they want. It might be urgent."

He glanced down at the message and whispered. "So sorry, but I have to go. I have two long shifts over the next couple of days. How about I pick you up on Saturday for an evening out? We can talk more then."

"You'll come to Port Dover?"

"Sure, why not."

"How about I cook you supper?"

He grinned. "You? Cook? I'll be there for sure."

I smiled. "It'll be definitely something simple. I'll email you directions."

"It's a deal. I'll see you then." He leaned down to kiss me on the cheek just like the last time. A kiss a friend would get.

Sigh.

But hey, really? As I'd said before—*what did I expect?*

Twenty-two

"I miss you, Charlie."

I leaned down to lay a red rose across his gravesite, thinking it was the perfect gift. It represented my journey with him, for often I'd felt he had plucked me out of a garden and I became like the stem travelling up through the thorns, longing to blossom. I was almost there. I felt it in my heart.

This was the first time I'd been back since he'd been laid to rest. I wasn't keen on coming, for I found it still too depressing, but somehow, I'd felt a strong sense of urgency to see him today. Weird as anything, but it was like he'd reached his hand down from the heavens and directed me here. Like he had something to tell me. Okay, that did sound odd but who was I to argue with a strong gut feeling? I drove here immediately, Moxie in tow.

"Just want you to know that I'm doing okay. Lots of things are making sense now. I've been building bridges like you suggested and the puzzle is almost complete."

Hmmmmm… speaking of puzzles—I'd always thought that when putting together a puzzle, the last piece would be the easiest. I mean, where else could the piece go?

There was only one space left.

Not in my case.

The last puzzle piece lingered just outside my consciousness, as if floating around, taunting me. Somehow, I just wasn't able to pluck it out of the air and work it into the right spot, no matter how hard I tried. It was frustrating as hell.

But enough about that.

I was here to visit Charlie, not moan on about my problems.

I'd brought a lawn chair, anticipating spending a decent amount of time here, so I sat down, Moxie curled up on my lap, thinking of Charlie's laughter, his mischievous ways and his caring heart. Once again, I considered myself lucky to have gotten to know him, even for a short while. He had taught me so much.

Feeling peaceful, the way I always did when I was with him, I closed my eyes, allowing my thoughts to fly off wherever they wanted to go. Once again, I felt I was watching a slide show of my life. Most of the time, especially lately, it had gotten stuck on a few pictures, but much to my surprise, today it just kept on clicking away—*right until the end.* That was a first.

Wait a sec…?

What?

My eyes popped open and I was so excited, I stood up, holding tight to Moxie as a surge of joy rippled through me.

Unbelievable but… *the last piece of my puzzle had slid into place.*

My heart started to pound.

Was that why I felt compelled to come here today? Was Charlie anxious to show me the total picture?

I smiled, wanting to whoop and holler and scream out my happiness. Looking around, I saw that there were other people at the cemetery and figured my screeching would disturb them, especially, since this was more a solemn place to be. I'd best keep that behavior until I was alone in my cottage where I could shout all I wanted.

Instead, I cuddled Moxie even tighter and whispered in her ear, "I understand everything now." As if agreeing, she raised her head to lick my cheek and wow—was that a smile I saw on her sweet doggy face? Really? Nah, probably my imagination, but it sure looked like one to me.

Although I'd expected fireworks, drumbeats or at least some kind of wild force of nature like lightning or a hailstorm response to my figuring it all out, it seemed only fitting that everything came together when I was with Charlie. The way it had all summer—quietly and peacefully. So it probably wasn't my imagination. He really did push me to visit him today and I was so glad I'd followed through, for it lead me to this gentle resolution.

"Thank you," I whispered, looking up to the heavens. Once again, I was sure Charlie was up there, swinging on a cloud, smiling his big, wide grin, granting me this last special gift—a wish come true.

Feeling clearheaded, I sat back down for a few minutes, thinking hard of what I wanted to do next.

A plan formed. An intricate, gutsy plan.

A surprise for Liam.

Should I? Could I? Did I have the courage?

Nah. I might get hurt, just when I'd finally figured it all out. No way did I want to risk going back into my shell again, licking my wounds, trying to stop the pain.

Once again, I felt like someone pushed me. I glanced behind. Nope, no one around.

Was that Charlie again? My dad? Mom? Urging me on?

Well… whoever or whatever it was, I was taking it as a sign to just go for it. To take the risk.

Glancing at my watch, I realized I had five hours until Liam arrived. Five hours to do what I needed to do. I was sure Izzy and the twins would help. Maybe even Louise. Because no way could I get it all done by myself.

Excited, I hurried back to my car. I dropped Moxie off at the cottage, figuring I couldn't really bring her along on my errands and raced around putting my plans into place. Just as I expected, Louise, Izzy and the boys helped me. Thank goodness I had developed great friends here, for I'd never have been able to pull this off without them. I then headed back to my cottage to get ready, knowing Liam would be here any minute.

"Hope it goes well," I said to Moxie, who cocked her head as if struggling to understand what was going on, especially when I started pacing back and forth throughout the whole cottage—through the bedroom to the living room, kitchen and hallway.

I was scared.

My legs even began to shake which was such an annoying habit of mine when nervous.

How would tonight go?

Would the evening end in joy or heartbreak? Hard to tell at this point. Especially, since it appeared that Liam had written me off. I just hoped I didn't chicken out and not stick to the plan.

The doorbell rang.

Damn. Here he was.

I rushed to the mirror to have one last glimpse at how I looked. After patting my hair down, adding another coat of lip gloss and straightening my shirt, I hurried to open the door to a grinning Liam. He looked good in faded jeans and a red plaid shirt, one I'd given him last Christmas and loved when he wore it. *Was that why he had it on? Could I at least hope so?*

"Guess we're twins tonight," I said, feeling incredibly shy, realizing I was wearing similar jeans and a pink plaid shirt.

"Sure are. You have good taste." He kept on smiling, which I hoped was a good sign.

"Great cottage," he said, looking around.

"I love it here. I'll give you the grand tour."

After showing him all the rooms, as well as the deck, I walked past him to the door. Time for his surprise.

"So are you ready?" I asked.

"For what?"

"A walk. I thought I'd show you around, especially along the lake. You've never been to Port Dover before, have you?"

"No. This is my first time. I'd love to see the local sights."

"Is it okay if Moxie comes?"

"Sure."

Hearing her name, she ran over to a hook by the door, pulled down her leash and ran straight to Liam. Hmmmm… instant love, but then again, Liam was a gentle, kind soul and I truly believed that dogs sensed that.

Liam hooked the leash to Moxie's collar and we began walking along the beach. I was so nervous that I just kept quiet, afraid I'd blurt out something silly. I waited to hear what he had to say, but surprisingly, he didn't say anything either. We just walked along in silence, taking turns throwing Moxie her ball, until it started to get dark out. Perfect timing. We were exactly where I'd hoped we'd be right about now. Time to get my plans started. I snuck a peek at Liam, hoping he'd like what I'd put together. I crossed my fingers.

I led him around a clump of trees, where he would see the whole effect.

Just like I'd envisioned it in my mind, there stood the bright white canopy that Louise, Izzy and I had staked into the ground. It was all lit up with tiny white lights encircling it, mimicking stars, giving off an ethereal effect, especially against the orangey-red glow of the sunset. Or at least that was what I was aiming for. A line of torches created a path to the entrance and a fire was glowing out front.

"Looks like someone is having a romantic evening," Liam said. "Guess we should go back and leave them alone."

He started to turn around, but I grabbed his hand.

"I told you I'd provide supper. Won't you join me?" I nodded towards the canopy.

"What?" Then it dawned on him. "You did all this?"

"Yes." I waved at Izzy and Louise who had come out to watch us approach, to let them know that I could take it from here. Izzy gave me the thumbs up and they took off.

Liam looked adorable but confused as I directed him over to a canvas chair. He sat down with Moxie snuggled in his lap and watched while I roasted hotdogs over the fire, plopped them into buns and put a couple on plates, already piled high with potato chips. I handed one to him and then poured kibble in a bowl for Moxie. I then joined him.

Honestly, it was the best meal I'd had in ages, for eventually we both relaxed, started chatting and got all caught up on our summer experiences. Oh how'd I'd missed these times when we'd share our lives, enthralled by what each one of us had to say.

Then the s'mores came out. After feasting on gooey marshmallows and chocolate, I turned on my iPod and John Legend's song *All of Me* filled the air.

"May I have this dance?" I asked.

He looked surprised but nodded. "Okay."

Dancing with Liam even beat out s'mores in terms of blissful experiences. I savored every moment, realizing it could be our last, depending on the outcome of tonight.

The next song that came on the tails of the first one was—'our' song—*You're My Best Friend* by Queen—an oldie but timeless as far as I was concerned. We'd heard it one night at a party and loved it, feeling it summed up our relationship—we were the *bestest* friends, forever. I snuggled closer to Liam, wondering how he'd handle that and to my surprise, he held me tighter. When the song finished I took a deep breath, gathered up my courage, pulled away, then dropped to one knee.

"Liam," I said, calmly but firmly. "I love you. Will you marry me?"

I stared into his eyes, willing him to see into my heart, which was wide open for the first time in my life.

Although I'd sorted out lots of stuff, I still couldn't figure out all my initial wedding thoughts. That was where I'd been stuck.

Now I knew.

I had fallen deeply in love with Liam.

Only one problem—I hadn't known it.

How coincidental that Liam and I had met on ice, for that was what my heart used to be like—frozen solid. Little did I know that Liam's love, pure goodness and kindness, had slowly unthawed me. Oh, I knew we got along and that I adored him, but I didn't realize how deep my feelings had grown. That was how out of touch I was with my heart—my dad would be appalled.

I always figured it was Marta who started the whole thing off by getting engaged and choosing me to be her maid of honor. Immersed in her plans, championing her on, I began thinking of my own wedding. That was surprising but not too weird, for I was in what I thought was a pretty good relationship. But then Travis' face showed up as the groom, which set me off into a world of panic. It made sense now because it was with him, I'd first dreamed of getting married, but somehow I couldn't seem to connect the dots. Of course, thinking of him led to memories of my parents for they died around the same time. So there it was in a nutshell—all that pain and horror I buried, finally caught up with me and erupted into a huge mess.

Everything made so much sense now.

So here I was—full circle—with the man I wanted to spend the rest of my life with. The piece that pulled it all together into a masterpiece—the fact that *I loved Liam with all my heart.* Armed with recent revelations, I decided to make the first move. After all, I was the one who had rejected his proposal so I felt I was the one who needed to take the initiative now.

Oops! Forgot something.

I dug into my jean pocket and pulled out a velvet box. Figured if I was going to do this whole proposal thing right, I wanted a ring, so I bought him an Irish Claddagh one, remembering that Liam had once said he liked the symbolism of the ring—for it depicted hands representing friendship, holding a heart of love, below a crown symbolizing loyalty.

I opened up the box as I got back into position.

Liam continued to just stare at me and my heart sunk.

Why didn't he say something? Anything?

Was this it? The moment he told me goodbye? That he'd moved on? That he loved living on his own? That he was with Jackie?

I waited it out until a smile tugged at his mouth, which

led to a laugh as he pulled a ring box out of his own pocket. He flipped it open to show me once again, the gorgeous emerald ring he'd designed. My heart raced. Was he planning on proposing as well?

Could I possibly be that lucky?

Or was he just giving it to me, figuring he wouldn't be able to use it again for he had designed it especially for me.

Silence… then… he got down on one knee, as well.

"Will *you* marry *me*?" he asked, and the love that poured from his eyes hit me square on.

That was my undoing. Tears welled up, then started to trickle down my face.

"Really?" I asked.

"Yes, really. I never stopped loving you."

"But you ignored me at the wedding," I blubbered.

"Just giving you space, Veep. You went away with little explanation and asked me not to contact you, so I didn't want to force myself on you. I was waiting for you to come to me."

So Andrew was right. Thank goodness, I'd been counting on it.

Wiping away my tears, I grinned.

"Hey, you never answered my question and I asked first," I said, teasingly.

He grinned back. "Well, in actual fact, I was the one who asked you to marry me first. So how about this—we both answer at the count of three—one, two, three."

"Yes," we both yelled out.

Sliding our rings into place, Liam reached over, grabbed my hand and pulled me up, just like he'd done the first time I'd met him. Clinging to each other, we were interrupted by Moxie jumping up on us, a paw on each of our legs.

"Woof," she barked out, obviously wanting to join in our celebration.

"Er, you do like dogs, right?" I asked, as we both looked down at her.

Once again, Moxie looked like she was smiling until she opened her mouth and let out a loud belch. I was mortified. It was like having a child and wanting them to be on their best behavior and then they go and make a fool of themselves.

Liam started to laugh.

"Of course. From the moment I saw that crazy looking animal, I figured she was going to end up in my life somehow."

He reached down to pick up Moxie.

"Thank you," I whispered.

"Oh, and I'd love to meet Travis, too. Sounds like he was a big part of your life years ago."

"That can be arranged."

So just like the endings in all the fairy tales that graced the wall on that fateful prom night so long ago, this was when the handsome prince kissed the glad-to-have-him-in-my-life princess and they lived happily ever after.

Good.

I sucked at being a villain.

The End

Meet

Suzanne Hurley

Happiness to this author is curled up with her laptop creating imaginary worlds that come from her heart. Writing is her passion and dreaming up story lines is her love. Suzanne was born in Peterborough, Ontario and currently resides in Caledonia, Haldimand County, where on morning walks with Mike and Rico, she tries out her new plots on the cows, sheep and numerous wild animals she greets along the way. Please visit Suzanne at her website –
www.suzannemhurley.com